DEAD LANDS

The Agency
Men In Black Dusters

By: John Goff

THE WEIRD WEST™

The Agency: Men in Black Dusters

Written & Designed by: John Goff
Editing & Layout: Joyce Goff & John Goff
Cover Art: Pete Venters
Interior Art: Jeff Rebner
Cover Design: Zeke Sparkes
Additional Interior Graphics: Chuck Croft

Logos: Zeke Sparkes, Charles Ryan & Ron Spencer
Special Thanks to: Lee Banson, Paul Duke, Stephen Joseph Ellis, Shane, Michelle & Caden Hensley, John & Christy
    Hopler, the Listserv Rowdies, Pat Kapera, Jay Kyle, Chris Libey, Jason Nichols, Lucien Soulban, Rob Vaux, and Dave
    Wilson
Deadlands created by Shane Lacy Hensley.
Dedicated to: Ellis and Birchie for putting up with me in the first place.

Pinnacle Entertainment Group, Inc.
P.O. Box 10908
Blacksburg, VA 24062-0908
www.peginc.com or deadlands@aol.com
(800) 214-5645 (orders only)

Visit our web site for free updates!

TABLE O' CONTENTS

Introduction 4
Posse Territory......5

Chapter One:
U.S. Special
Services Agency ... 5
Executive Order 347 6
Humble Beginnings 8
Executive Order 347 17
Agency Organization 18

Chapter Two:
Agency Field
Operations 27
Introduction and Mission . 28
Starting the Assignment . 33
The Investigation 39
Classification and
    Elimination 53
Field Communications 59
Recruitment 62
Case Study 63

Chapter Three:
So You Want to Be
an Agent? 65
Basic Training 67
Advancement 69
New Edge & Aptitude 72

Archetypes 73

Chapter Four: Tools
o' the Trade 77
Requisition Points 77
Equipment 78
Communications 78
Concealed Compartments 80
Covert Operations 82
Dead Drops 84
Demolitions 85
Observation 87
Weapons & Armor 91
Combination Devices 97
What About a
    Flamethrower? 99

The Marshal's
Handbook 101

Chapter Four:
The Truth Is In
Here 103
Updates 103
Running an Agency
    Campaign 105
Secrets of the Secret 107
We Don't Need No Stinkin'
    Gadgets! 119

Index 127

SALUTATIONS!

Welcome to *The Agency: Men in Black Dusters*. The Agency is the Union's first, best, and only defense against those things that go bump in the night—or worse!

Within the pages of this sourcebook you're going to find all the information you'll ever need on the Union's *most* secret service. Whether you're a Marshal running a *Deadlands* campaign or a player with an Agency character, this book is an invaluable tool for your game.

I.D. PLEASE...

Before you go any further you should be warned that there is some sensitive information revealed in this book. If your character isn't a member of the Agency, chances are he isn't going to have access to a lot of what's in this book. Of course, after reading it, you may find the life of an Agency operative a whole lot more interesting!

Also, a few Marshals may feel that some of this information falls into the Secrets Players Were Not Meant to Know. If you're a player, you might want to check with your Marshal to make sure reading this book won't spoil any surprises she has up her sleeve.

Why are we spilling the beans?

Agency operatives are the mysterious men in black responsible from hiding truths too horrible for the public to know. The Agency is one of the best informed groups on what's really going on in the Weird West and it doesn't send its operatives out without at least a warning.

But, rest assured, we're not spilling the whole can of beans—just a few off the top!

The Agency knows a lot, but it doesn't know everything. And even what it does know, it doesn't share

with all its operatives. After all, if many of its operatives knew what they were up against, they might turn tail and run the opposite direction as fast as they could!

USING THIS BOOK

There is no **No Man's Land** in this book; either operatives know it or they don't! The two sections are:

Posse Territory contains all the information you'll ever need to make an Agency operative character or freelancer.

The section begins with two government pamphlets on the Agency and Agency field operations. Within these two pamphlets is the history of the Agency, its mission, authority, and standard operating procedures when investigating the unknown terrors plaguing the Union. If you're interested in just how much a starting operative knows about the Reckoning, this is the place to look.

Following these pamphlets, we've included guidelines for making operatives and advancing their careers in the Agency—along with exactly what priviledges rank doth have. Finally, the section ends with a catalog of common equipment available to operatives beyond the trademark Gatling pistol.

The Marshal's Handbook exposes the secrets of the secret organization. We've provided profiles of some of the more "famous" members of the organiztion and the lowdown on a few facts the Agency doesn't share with the rank-and-file. This section also contains the details on exactly what happens when the Agency's vaunted equipment fails to work as expected!

GHOST BUSTIN'

Big things have happened since the last time we checked in on Gomorra, the setting for the *Deadlands: Doomtown* CCG—things so big, in fact, we've dedicated an entire full-size adventure to resolving them.

That adventure, *Ghost Busters*, should be hitting the shelves by the time you read this. If you're interested in having your posse help shape the course of the Weird West, you won't want to miss this shindig!

United States

Special Services Agency

Organization and Activities

RESTRICTED

Executive Order 347

In accordance with the realization of certain threats of an unexplained and potentially even supernatural origin, the creation of the United States Special Services Agency is hereby ordered. This Agency is heretofore responsible for the duties and tasks as detailed below.

1.) The Special Services Agency shall draw its initial recruitment from those operatives in the ranks of the Pinkerton Detective Agency who have already been exposed to said phenomena. Following the initial formation of the Special Services Agency, the organization shall be responsible for recruiting trustworthy and discreet individuals to fill its ranks.

2.) Furthermore, the office of Director of the Special Services Agency shall be a lifetime appointment or until such time as the appointee determines that due to physical or mental conditions he is unable to continue his duties.

3.) The Special Services Agency shall be responsible for investigation of all incidents of an unexplained nature, including, but not limited to, those occurences with an apparent occult and/or supernatural foundation.

4.) The Special Services Agency shall be responsible for eliminating the source, cause, or catalyst of all incidents falling under the blanket description in paragraph 3, above, if said incident is determined to be detrimental to the lives, liberty, or well-being of the citizens of the United States of America.

5.) In recognition of the fact that the members of the general citizenry of the United States of America may not fully understand or rationally accept the nature of the threat described in the preamble of this Order, members of the Special Services Agency are to place the highest priority on ensuring that the citizenship remains unaware of said threat and the implications thereof.

6.) Due to the nature of the undefined threat now faced by our great nation, all operations conducted by the Special Services Agency, as defined in paragraphs 3, 4, and 5, shall be treated as matters of national security. In accordance with this directive, said operations are to be considered secret in nature and the details and facts of such are not to be disclosed to members of the general public, the press, the military, law enforcement agencies and their representatives, nor any other member of the United States government, its allies, or enemies outside the ranks of the Special Services Agency and designated members of the Executive Office, even under pain of imprisonment or death.

7.) To assist in the pursuit of these duties as outlined above, members of the United States Special Services Agency are to be afforded the wherewithal to draw upon the services of law enforcement agencies and military assets as necessary to accomplish their assigned task. This authority is limited by the stipulations in paragraphs 5 and 6 above. Documents are to be provided by the Executive Office to assist in the securing of said assistance in the most discreet manner possible.

To preserve the security of the mission and responsibilities detailed to the Special Services Agency, the Executive Office heretofore shall forswear knowledge of the existence of Presidential Order 347 to all but those members of the government deemed authorized to share and protect the implications thereof.

Given this day, February 11, 1877, by my hand,

Ulysses S. Grant

GM 28-51

U.S. Special Services Agency

Presumably, if you're reading this manual, you're either a member of the Special Services Agency—most often referred to as simply "the Agency." Or it's remotely possible you're one of the select few deemed trustworthy enough by the country's highest office to view the contents without belonging to that organization. However, since those individuals are few and *very* far between the rest of this manual, and its companion pamphlet, *GP 28-51A Field Operations*, are written with the field operative in mind.

So excuse us if we occasionally seem more "familiar" in this publication than many other government documents. These documents are a survival guide for members of the Agency, not primers on grammar and formal writing procedures.

On the Other Hand...

If you belong to neither section of the population listed above, do yourself a favor. Immediately stop reading. Forget what little you've seen thus far and wipe the words "Executive Order 347" from your mind. Next, build a big fire and toss this publication right on top of it. The consequences of not doing so are severe, to say the least.

Rest assured, when the transgression is discovered—and it will be—you can expect to be prosecuted for treason, reckless endangerment of Agency personnel, and a number of other crimes. According to the rights granted all citizens by the Constitution, a fair trial will ensue—quickly followed by a verdict of guilty, and immediate sentencing of the maximum punishment by law.

If that warning is too unclear, let us be more direct: If you are not authorized to be in possession of this document, at best you're facing a *very* long prison sentence. At best.

So get rid of it. Now.

Welcome to the Agency

First, let us congratulate you on your acceptance into the ranks of the Special Services Agency! Although the Agency practices voluntary recruitment, very few of those applying are actually admitted to the organization.

The importance of our mission requires we select only the best qualified for Agency positions. We subject all potential operatives to a strict screening process. You may not even be aware that you were screened, but trust us, you were.

Now that you're in, know one thing: Although you are going to be assigned tasks requiring great sacrifice and heroism in defense of your nation, no one outside of the Agency and the President will ever know of the importance of your contributions. This may be the heaviest burden you'll bear.

The first rule of the Agency is: No one talks about the Agency.

An Introduction To This Manual

The book you hold in front of you contains the basic information on the goals and structure of the Special Services Agency. Within, you'll find an explanation of the organization's mission, as defined by Executive Order 347, and a brief outline of the Agency's structure and how it functions to fulfill that directive. It also explains, as much as we understand, what precipitated EO 347 and why its secrecy is of utmost importance.

This manual is *not* a guide to conducting a successful mission or investigation! See *GP-28-51A*, for that information.

Humble Beginnings

It would appear, to an uniformed observer, that the Agency is a new government organization. After all, the executive order responsible for its creation is dated February 11, 1877. And, to be completely accurate, that is true.

Before that date, the Agency did not exist—or at least not as the U.S. Special Services Agency. But for over a decade prior to the issuance of Order 347, another group, the Pinkerton Detective Agency, had been performing the duties recently assigned to this organization. In fact, most of the first operatives of the Agency were former members of the Pinkertons.

In many ways, to understand the origins of the Agency, it's necessary to understand the origins of the Pinkertons.

Allan Pinkerton

It's impossible to consider the beginnings of the Pinkerton National Detective Agency without a discussion of its founder, Allan Pinkerton.

Born in 1819, Allan Pinkerton, spent his youth in his native Scotland. When his father died, Allan had to give up formal education and become an apprentice weaver at the young age of 8 years old. He later changed apprenticeships and learned the trade of barrelmaking.

By his twenties, he had become active in politics—at least so far as to call for a change in the standing British government. So active in fact that local police issued a warrant and reward! In 1842, he married his wife, Joan, and the very next day set sail from Glasgow for the land of opportunity, the United States of America, most likely to avoid imprisonment.

The Pinkertons settled in Dundee, Illinois, near the city of Chicago. There, Pinkerton set up shop as a barrelmaker. Thanks to the tide of western expansion, his business was soon booming and his small company expanded to hire on nearly ten employees.

However, little did he know that in less than three years, his life would take an abrupt turn down a completely unexpected path. A path that would lead him away from his devil-may-care youth and to the profession of his father—a policeman.

Allan Pinkerton brings an early end to a counterfeiting gang.

Government Manual 28-51

The Fork in the Road

One afternoon in 1846, while out surveying a supposedly uninhabited island in the nearby Fox River, Allan stumbled upon the remains of a campsite. Even then, he was a canny sort and knew something was up on the island. After all, it was in the middle of a river and supposedly uninhabited—the perfect location to hide misdeeds from prying eyes. Or the law.

Allan kept an eye on the location for the next few days, but it wasn't until he returned to the island after dark one night that he discovered the source of the campfire. A group of counterfeiters had set up a small minting operation. After determining the outlaws' business, he crept unnoticed from the island.

After escaping the island, he hurried to report them to the local sheriff. On the sheriff's request, Allan agreed to guide him back to the camp and assist in capturing the outlaws. Within no time, the entire county had heard the story of how Pinkerton the cooper had foiled a counterfeiting ring.

With his name abuzz in taverns across the area, it's no surprise local merchants turned to him when a second counterfeiting operation reared its head. This time, Allan was a bit more creative. Setting up a false identity for himself, he convinced the perpetrator he was also a criminal.

Before the man realized it, he had incriminated himself and a pair of nearby policemen had carted him off to jail!

These two successes convinced Allan that his true calling lay in investigation and a short time later, he was working part-time as a Deputy Sheriff in Chicago.

The Pinkerton National Detective Agency

In the late 1840s, city police departments, a relatively new institution in the United States at that time, suffered from accusations of graft, ineptitude, and corruption. To be honest, these claims probably had more than a minimal basis in fact; city police departments were understaffed, underpaid, and received no formal training at the time.

This perception led many ambitious souls to found their own private police companies. These enterprises contracted their services to private citizens and businesses to provide the protection many felt was not available from the city departments.

In 1850, Allan abandoned his barrelmaking to form a partnership with a Chicago attorney. The men set up the North-West Police Agency, which provided both simple protection and investigation services to its clients. Within less than two years, it was obvious that Allan's reputation was the company's most valuable asset. To capitalize on that, the firm was renamed the Pinkerton National Detective Agency.

Guarding the Iron Horse

If city departments were incapable of protecting those within their jurisdiction, how could they be expected to pursue a criminal once outside it?

This question especially plagued the rapidly growing railroad companies. Most robberies committed against their holdings occurred in the trackless wilderness far from any major city or town. Worse yet, the outlaws frequently fled across several states and territories to further complicate the legal technicalities of pursuit.

Allan was quick to catch on to the opportunity the railroads presented someone in his line of work. Functioning as a private company, the Pinkerton Agency was not bounded by the strictures of jurisdiction. This fact appealed to the railroads and, in 1855, the Pinkerton Agency signed a contract with six railroad companies to protect their lines for a yearly retainer of an astounding $10,000.

The Pinkerton Agency soon gained a reputation as a dogged pursuer of criminals, more than willing to chase an outlaw across the length of the country.

Working Harder...and Smarter

While determination played no small role in the early successes of the Pinkerton Agency, its operatives also exhibited a keen eye for detail in investigations and shrewd cunning when on their quarry's trail. The detectives also kept a high work ethic; according to Allan himself a man needed only common sense, honesty, and strong morals to find a place in the Pinkerton Agency.

Surprisingly, Allan seldom hired former law enforcement personnel. Instead, he drew his detectives from all walks of life. This, he believed, gave him a blank slate with which to work. Often, he found he had to strip away years of bad habits from former police officers, before teaching them his methods of surveillance.

Nor did Allan limit his recruitment to men. When he hired Kate Warne, she not only became the first female Pinkerton detective, she became the first female detective in the United States.

You Know My Methods...

He believed undercover work was of the highest importance for a detective. His training reflected this, teaching disguise and role playing as vital skills. Allan himself kept a closet in his office filled with disguises for those cases in which he took a personal hand.

The Pinkerton Agency was quick to realize the importance of the invention of the camera. Soon, the detectives began compiling files of known criminals and including photographs whenever possible. On at least one occasion, Pinkerton detectives were able to identify a criminal based solely on eye-witness descriptions and the suspect's method of operation!

In keeping with his ethical philosophy, Pinkerton detectives were not allowed to accept tips or rewards for their services. Acceptance of a reward for a completed job made a detective's performance suspect in Allan's mind. The client could never be certain whether the detective had really solved the case or merely claimed so to gain the reward.

Neither would his detectives obtain testimony or evidence through the use of drugs or alcohol. In addition to preserving the valued Pinkerton reputation, this practice provided the detectives a stronger foundation in the courtroom. A defendant could readily claim it was the liquor talking if his confession had been plied with whiskey, but a sober one had no such option.

These strict ethical practices, combined with the company's continued successes in fulfilling its contracts, soon made the Pinkertons and their motto "We Never Sleep" known across the land.

Protecting the President

However active he and his detectives were on and behind the lines of the war, Allan Pinkerton's greatest claim to fame undoubtedly occurred during President-elect Abraham Lincoln's inaugural journey to Washington.

Early in 1861, one of the Pinkerton Agency's client railroads alerted Allan to the possibility of a treasonous plot in Maryland to cut off Washington, D. C., from the rest of the Union. While investigating this tip, his detectives uncovered evidence of a plot to assassinate Lincoln as he passed through Baltimore.

Fearing the worst, Allan ordered Harry Davies, one of his best men, to infiltrate the conspirators' circle to determine how serious the threat was. When Davies confirmed that the plan had supporters even among the Baltimore police, Allan knew he had to move quickly. Lincoln had already departed on the trip from Springfield, Illinois, for the nation's capital!

Allan presented his evidence to Lincoln in Philadelphia. At first, the President-elect was skeptical, but after a lengthy conversation with the detective, he agreed to postpone a leg of his journey. Within hours of Allan's warning, a similar message arrived from another source acting on behalf of the Union Army. Lincoln realized the danger was likely real and turned his protection over to Allan and his men.

Following the detective's instructions, Lincoln and his party maintained a low profile as they passed through Baltimore. The trip passed without incident, and the conspirators Davies uncovered fled to the Confederacy before they could be arrested.

Thanks to the Pinkerton Agency's vigilance, Lincoln arrived safely in Washington. Allan returned to his normal business, but only for a short time. In late April, he was summoned to consult with Lincoln and his Cabinet. The purpose of the consultation was to explore the possibilities of organizing a secret service to protect the Union from unseen Confederate threats.

Unfortunately, the Cabinet was unable to reach any conclusions and Allan departed once again for Chicago and his Agency.

But, he didn't get far...

War!

Prior to the outbreak of rebellion, there had been no organized intelligence-gathering units in the U.S. Army since the Mexican War. The Union was woefully unprepared for war in this respect.

For all his other shortcomings as a commander, General George McClellan realized he needed a good set of eyes and ears on the battlefield. He'd been chief engineer for one of the Pinkerton Agency's railroad clients and president of another prior to the war. As such, he'd had first hand experience with Allan Pinkerton's skill as a detective.

McClellan could think of no better man for his Chief of Intelligence than Allan Pinkerton. His message requesting the detective's assistance found Allan before the detective even reached Chicago. Allan accepted the offer.

Military Intelligence

What neither McClellan nor Allan understood at the time was that a good detective was not always a good Chief of Intelligence for an army.

Pinkerton himself held McClellan in the highest regard. And, like many other members of the Union government, he had utmost confidence in the abilities of the general who had been nicknamed the "Young Napoleon." Combined with his own military inexperience, it was almost inevitable that his reports would be colored by McClellan's own opinions.

McClellan tended to overestimate Confederate strengths. Pinkerton's lack of experience in the field led him to doubt his own agents' reports when they contradicted this. During the Peninsula campaign, in fact, he provided an estimate of 200,000 Confederate troops when in actuality only 80,000 were in the field. McClellan used these figures to explain his failure to engage the enemy.

Pinkerton the Spymaster

While Allan failed as a Chief of Intelligence in the field, in Washington, he was much more in his element managing the tasks of espionage and counter-espionage. His previous performance in protecting the President and his presence during the Cabinet discussions on security made him the logical choice for the

One of Pinkerton's operatives gathers intelligence on Confederate troop movements.

government to seek out to perform these duties. These areas were much better suited to his abilities and those of the operatives he brought along to assist him.

During his period of service, he exposed several Confederate spies and numerous seditious plots. What Confederate spy network remained after his campaign of counter-espionage was littered with such disinformation that it was rendered useless.

On the intelligence gathering side, several of Allan's operatives managed to secret themselves in the Confederate capital of Richmond. From there, they gathered a wagon-load of information on secessionist activities for the first two years of the war.

Hattie Lawton, another female detective, crept behind rebel lines to spy for the Union. Unfortunately, Confederate forces captured her and one of Pinkerton's most experienced spies, Timothy Webster, when two other agents were exposed in a freak coincidence. While the Confederacy was willing to work an exchange for Lawton and the other agents, in spite of numerous attempts to negotiate his release, Webster was eventually hung for espionage.

His loss weighed heavily on Allan's conscience for years. However, that didn't dull the detective's determination; if anything, it strengthened his conviction to do the best possible job in gathering intelligence.

Catching a Falling Star...

Unfortunately, General McClellan did not live up to his nickname and by late 1862, he'd fallen from favor in Washington. Allan Pinkerton, in spite of the fact his organization was unofficially known as the "U.S. Secret Service," was actually on the personal payroll of McClellan, and when his employer left, Allan was not too far behind. In January, 1863, he returned to his criminal investigations.

Following his departure, espionage duties were assigned to Lafayette Baker. Baker had offered his services as a spy to General Winfield Scott at the beginning of the war. Scott, well accustomed to the need for battlefield intelligence from the Mexican War, accepted—even though the young man had no experience in the line of work whatsoever.

However, Scott, unlike McClellan, was not as vulnerable to the fickle finger of politics. Baker, riding his employer's coattails persisted at the job, in spite of his failings.

That's not to say that Baker did a bad job. Far from it—he was far more successful than his Confederate counterparts. But, he was no Allan Pinkerton. And that was a shortcoming that would one day be felt by the entire nation...

Event 070363

Just about half a year after Allan Pinkerton left Washington, D.C., Confederate and Union forces met at a little town in Pennsylvania named Gettysburg on July 3, 1863. Here, General Robert E. Lee's attempt to invade the Union and threaten the capital was thwarted—a feat worthy of mention in and of itself.

Would that it was all that occurred on that day.

Survivors of the battle told of dead comrades returning to life with an unholy taste for human flesh, of monsters from nightmares roving across the battlefield at night, and madmen who became worse than monsters. Publicly, the Union government denied these reports, attributing them to battle fever and stress.

General Ulysseus S. Grant experienced similar horrors that same day as he lay siege to Vicksburg. And soon, reports began springing up from across the Union that unexplained and terrifying events were taking place.

The strange occurrences on that day marked a turning point for the world, and is now referred to by the Agency as Event 070363.

Vengeance from the Grave

Back in Chicago, while reviewing his operatives' case reports, Allan Pinkerton came upon a file that made no logical sense. A rich young widow with no heirs and no will had been murdered in her home. Although she kept a kennel of guard dogs, the animals not only did not stop the intruder from entering, neighbors reported they had not so much as barked that night.

Her husband had recently passed away under suspicious circumstances as well, leading the detective to believe a third party stood to somehow profit from the death of the couple. Digging deeper, he discovered no possible motive for the murder; all the widow's possessions passed to the state.

A methodical thinker, Allan was also capable of considering all angles on a case. He systematically eliminated the impossible and found the only explanation left was not only implausible, but nearly unbelievable. The wife had poisoned her aging husband to gain his wealth. Then, before she could realize her fortune, *he* had returned from the grave to avenge his death!

He and a few trusted employees tracked the revenant down and ended its unlife with a hail of bullets. Knowing the impact this tale would have on the public, he and his men took an oath of secrecy.

Soon, more reports of similar unexplainable events began entering his office. Allan realized the already battered Union faced a terrible threat, possibly even worse than that posed by the Southern rebellion!

Back in Washington

President Lincoln, already under tremendous strain from the war, now found himself faced with rumors of terrible creatures or the dead returning to life from all across the Union. It had been difficult enough to keep a lid on Gettysburg, but now it was progressing far beyond one or two isolated battlefields.

While the President was concerned with the effects of these unexplained horrors on the civilian populace, the newest commander of his armies, General Grant, was equally worried about the war effort.

The general was perhaps the first Union war leader to realize that the quickest way to victory was to simply overwhelm the Confederate forces. The Union far outstripped the Southern rebels in resources and manpower, and, as brutal as it seemed, could afford to fight a war of attrition.

However, when the dead on the battlefield rose up and began attacking the living, this strategy was far less effective. Worse yet, Grant had noted that Union forces seemed to be the target of these attacks more often than not.

107

A Secret Meeting.

The President knew that, for the good of the Union and its citizens, the government must investigate these occurrences, and, if possible, put a stop to them. However, he also strongly believed if the authorities acknowledged the existence of a supernatural threat, the general public would be even more terrified.

The Union needed a competent agency that could answer the call without being formally tied to the government. That immediately eliminated Lafayette Baker's new "Secret Service." Fortunately, the President remembered the Pinkerton Agency's service to both himself personally and the country as a whole.

General Grant, acting on a request form the President, sent word to Allan Pinkerton in early 1864, asking him to come to Washington for another meeting. The meeting was ostensibly to employ Pinkerton once again in an espionage role.

Presidential Commission

It was inevitable the public would eventually hear of Allan's visit and the secret meeting, so he started building his cover story from the start.

By his request, his trip to Washington was kept secret. He traveled incognito and even entered the Oval Office in the guise of a White House servant. However, the three men were careful to allow just enough information to leak out to bolster the initial cover story that he was there to aid the war effort.

When he left, Allan Pinkerton had a new, albeit secret client—the United States' Government. Initially, he was charged with determining the cause and extent of these apparently supernatural events. To keep his mission as secret as possible, he alone pursued his new assignment.

Allan spent months canvassing the battlefields and backwoods of the Union chasing down leads. Although he failed to determine any underlying cause, he did make one discovery: The Confederacy appeared to be suffering the same unexplained and frightening episodes.

Expanding Authority

Allan reported his findings back to the President. While he had no explanation, what he had found indicated that the events seemed to intensify as the local populace became more nervous.

First, a single, terrifying occurrence would cause tensions in an area to heighten, then, as the inhabitants became more fearful, more of the strange encounters would take place. The effect became a vicious cycle of terror. As people became more frightened, more horrors reared their heads. As more supernatural events happened, people became more frightened, causing more events to occur, and so on, and so on..

His theory also helped explain why the battlefields seemed to be particularly prone to these spontaneous events. The only way to stop the cycle was to break the circular effect—or never let it happen in the first place.

Executive Order 259

Unfortunately, Allan added, his agency lacked the authority to take the steps necessary to combat the threat. Lincoln agreed. The President quickly drew up Executive Order 259, granting employees of the Pinkerton National Detective Agency the authority to enjoin local law enforcement agents in the course of their investigations.

However, he added one catch: Pinkerton detectives could not reveal the true nature of their mission. While Allan understood and supported this stipulation, it did place him and his detectives in something of a quandary. How could they impress the support of lawmen without exposing their true goals?

As a result, more often than not, Pinkerton detectives tended to work without the assistance of the law. This suited the local sheriffs and marshals just fine, as most of them thought of the Pinkertons as upstart tinhorns.

When they did use their federal authority, they frequently fell back on the cover story Allan had developed with his initial visit. Soon, it became public knowledge that the Pinkertons were hunting "Confederate spies," a deceit that served them well for years.

A Disastrous Failure

Shortly after Lincoln commissioned the Pinkerton Agency to root out the source of Event 070363, or simply "the Event" as it was coming to be known, he was to fall victim to a failure of another intelligence agency. On April 14, 1865, one of Baker's operatives was assigned to guard the presidential box at Ford's Theater. The man was conspicuously absent from his post.

The assassin slips through to the President.

John Wilkes Booth entered the box during the play. Unnoticed at first, he fired a bullet into the back of President Lincoln's head. Although the wound did not kill the President outright, he died later that night of complications.

Conspiracy or Incompetence?

Booth was soon apprehended, but rumors poured through the city like a flash flood. How could Baker, chief of the "Secret Service" have allowed a lone assassin to reach the President so easily? Why wasn't Allan Pinkerton, the man who had defended Lincoln against a veritable army of traitors in Baltimore entrusted with guarding him?

It didn't take long for accusations of Baker's complicity in the assassination to surface. Baker and Lincoln had several times come at odds over the chief's pursuit of his duties. Baker was also held by many to be an unscrupulous scoundrel who abused his position for material gain. How hard would it have been, the whisperers asked, to bribe such a man to momentarily drop the defenses around the President?

It didn't help his case that he never provided a believable answer for the missing guard's whereabouts. Certainly, under his direction, Booth and his co-conspirators were rounded up quickly, but many believed Booth's "accidental" death during capture was anything but. They claimed Baker had the man killed to avoid being implicated himself.

The accusations went so far as to tie him and Vice-President Johnson together in a plot to seize control of the Union. When he later **108** assisted in the impeachment proceedings against Johnson, conspiracy theorists once answered by saying he was simply removing another rival.

Whether Baker was indeed guilty of crimes of treason is likely to never be known. He died in 1868 of meningitis with many questions unanswered.

Secret Services

Now is probably a good time to point out that the name "Secret Service" is pretty popular among U.S. agencies. Near the beginning of the Southern rebellion, at least three different organizations claimed that title simultaneously. In addition to the section of the Treasury Department, both Lafayette Baker and Allan Pinkerton referred to their espionage groups as the Secret Service. Later, Baker renamed his organization the National Detective Police, but this didn't help alleviate the confusion.

This multitude of similarly named groups has caused no end of confusion, not only amongst the groups themselves, but the government and populace as a whole. The spymasters in the Confederacy have even gone so far as to level the blame for Baker's failure to protect the President on the Treasury Department's division!

The Secret Service was created as a part of the Treasury Department prior to the onset of rebellion, but solely for the purpose of defeating counterfeiters. It didn't even have a formal head until after Lincoln's assassination. Since then, its duties have greatly expanded, but it bears no responsibility in Baker's failure.

Double Duty

Doubts in Baker's Secret Service ran rampant in the aftermath of Lincoln's assassination and the subsequent impeachment of Vice-President Johnson. Newly-elected President Grant found himself short a reliable intelligence service.

The Pinkerton Agency already had a solid network of detectives in place and the blessing of the government for its activities. It seemed the logical choice for the broader mission of espionage and counter-espionage work in support of the war effort.

For a time, the Pinkertons did double duty rooting out spies and working to dull the edge of the Event. The detectives also accepted normal cases as well, to assist in covering their tracks on the more supernaturally-oriented assignments. As one might expect, these multiple missions severely taxed the Pinkerton Detective Agency as its resources were pulled in first one direction and then another.

In response to this increased demand, the Pinkerton Agency swelled in size. By the middle of the 1870s, nearly 4,000 employees worked under the "All-Seeing Eye" of the company. In addition, even more part-time "trouble-shooters" were called upon to assist with investigations.

There's a saying that loose lips sink ships, and the Pinkertons had grown to the point that they had around 8,000 lips which could become loose. While not all of those detectives were involved in supernatural investigations, enough knew of them that it was only a matter of time before one—or more—let slip the company's most important secret, the Event..

Both Allan Pinkerton and President Grant came to realize that the very success of the organization in fulfilling its numerous roles threatened its most valuable mission.

Reorganization

In January of 1877, President Grant revoked the Pinkerton Agency's contract to investigate reports of unusual activity or espionage. Obviously, since the government had never acknowledged the first duty in the first place, it didn't mention that it had taken it away either!

The President noted that the Pinkerton Agency had performed to the highest standard. However, he cited a need for tighter government control over such espionage activities as the reason for the termination.

Behind closed doors, rumors circulated about the impropriety of putting federal enforcement powers into the hands of a private contractor also being a consideration in Grant's decision.

Both public and private explanations were merely more smoke and mirrors to distract public attention from the truth.

The Special Services Agency

At the same time the announcement was made regarding the end of the Pinkerton contract, word began to spread about a new government intelligence service. This new organization, called the Special Services Agency, was to take over the former duties of the Pinkerton Detective Agency.

To the vast majority of the people, that meant another "Secret Service" of the sort that had come and gone at least two times since the start of the war. However, fewer things could have been farther from the truth.

The more mundane espionage and counter-espionage duties previously performed by the Pinkertons were spread among other

government groups. However, President Grant was careful to make sure that the duties were so thinly dispersed that no outside observer could tell that there really was *no* espionage work left for the Special Services Agency to perform!

Nor is it common knowledge that the founding members of the Special Services Agency were pulled directly from the Pinkerton Detectives—exclusively. Allan Pinkerton turned over his day-to-day business duties to his son, Robert, and assumed the post of the Director of the Agency.

109

Presidential Smoke Screen

To further confound examiners, the President reshuffled other duties and passed some *to the* Agency. All of the duties were somehow related to the Event or brushed uncomfortably close to it.

Foremost among these was the monitoring of "new technologies" that had formally been assigned to the Secret Service. This seemingly innocuous mission had far too often brought Treasury agents into contact with events or devices that bordered on the supernatural.

By moving it to the Agency's jurisdiction, he effectively killed two birds with one stone. First, he padded the Agency's cover story with a "real" assignment. And second, he lessened the chance that an unprepared Treasury operative might inadvertently do more damage than good to the Union in the innocent pursuit of his duties.

By and large, these efforts, combined with Allan Pinkerton's own seemingly in-born knack for hiding his activities in plain sight, have been tremendously successful. No one outside of the Agency, President Grant, and a few of his most trusted confidants knows the true agenda of the organization.

Instead, the average person on the street believes the Agency to be some nebulous government entity responsible for investigating a broad and nearly undefined range of transgressions, primarily related to the war effort .

Which is pretty much exactly what its founders want people to think.

Our Authority

Now that we've given you a little background on the creation of the Agency, let's spend a little time discussing the origin and limits of its authority. The entirety of the Agency's legal powers derive from the document reproduced as the frontispiece for this manual—Executive Order 347.

This is the only official document to reference the creation, authority, or even the very entity of the Special Services Agency. Ironically, by the very wording of that document neither the Agency nor the Executive Office can acknowledge its existence. Wrapping your mind around this paradox of reasoning is the first step to mastering the fine art of being an Agency field operative.

We Have a Big Stick...

The Agency needs access to nearly blanket legal authority to pursue the President's mission. The simplest solution, of course, is for the government to simply grant the Agency and its operatives full legal powers throughout the length and breadth of the Union. That approach is similar to the one the Confederacy has taken with the Texas Rangers, who, our sources indicate, pursue many of the same goals as the Agency.

However, the Rangers existed prior to the occurrence of the Event as a paramilitary legal enforcement organization. They continue to serve in exactly that capacity even today—a fact that often serves to complicate their own endeavors.

Creation of a new organization out of the blue with the broad-ranging authority of the Rangers would be a political land-mine. The President would have to defend its power and existence to Congress, and possibly even the Supreme Court. This becomes especially difficult when one realizes the President could not explain to Congress the true purpose of the Agency without hamstringing one of its primary goals— the suppression of public knowledge about the supernatural.

Instead, President Grant chose to take a path of lesser resistance. He gave the Agency blanket authority to call upon the legal powers of already existing law enforcement groups similar to that given to the original Pinkerton Detectives.

An Agency operative exercises his authority under Executive Order 347 and enlists the aid of a U.S. Marshal.

A nod to the fact that the Union is in effect under martial law and the Agency is an authorized representative of the federal government circumvents most Constitutional restrictions on Agency operations as well.

All Agency operatives regardless of rank or specific duty carry a badge and excerpt from Order 347 to assist in "convincing" law enforcement personnel of their legal authority. Naturally, the excerpt has been thoroughly sanitized of any reference to the supernatural, or even its number!

...But We Walk Softly

In spite of the broad authority to command legal and even military entities in pursuit of their duties, the Agency strongly cautions against doing so. The ideal investigation not only does not involve the authorities, it leaves no evidence that it ever occurred in the first place.

Should field operatives become too free in exercising the authority vested in them by Order 347, it is only a matter of time before some legal eagle delves deeper into the matter than we'd like. Flash a badge too many times and people start reading the fine print.

Or, worse, the operative may find the local sheriff in Chickasaw Falls, Montana, isn't too impressed with his "fancy papers from Washington." Such independent lawmen tend to actually hinder an operative's work rather than aid it. Some have even been known to arrest Agency members for no other reason than a bruised ego! In the long run, the Agency will likely win such a battle, but if the fight can be avoided in the first place, it's best to do so.

Another reason for avoiding embroiling the authorities is that such activity creates witnesses. Not to misdeeds on the part of the operative, but to the horrors of Event 070363. When no one's around, there's nothing to explain. On the other hand, the operative who's leading a posse of deputies may have some fast-talking to do when the murder suspect turns out to be something other than human.

Finally, involving law enforcement exposes the operatives methods to unnecessary scrutiny. The Agency is *not* interested in enforcing laws nor does it follow accepted procedures. Some lawmen take exception with this.

Although the country technically remains under martial law, flaunting this fact is likely to cause a certain amount of civil unrest. Particularly if the operative is violating what the officer perceives to be a citizen's civil rights. A few get inordinately prudish about that sort of thing.

The important thing to remember is that the Agency does not conduct its investigations to bring about a legal solution. Many of the events we act against aren't even acknowledged as conceivable, much less illegal. Whenever possible, missions should be completed without the involvement of the authorities. The law is only a means to an end, not an end in and of themselves.

Agency Organization

Compared to the heyday of the Pinkerton Detectives, the Agency is a trim organization. Its total strength is right around 900 active operatives and support personnel. That's a far cry from the Pinkerton high-water mark of 4,000!

These operatives are more tightly organized than their civilian counterparts as well. Government backing has a lot of advantages over a run-for-profit company when it comes to these matters. On top of that, all the unrelated civilian and military espionage duties are now other departments' worries. This greatly reduces the amount of work crossing the Agency's desk, allowing it to focus its resources on those missions detailed in EO 347.

Altogether, the improved organization, government backing, and redefined focus allow the Agency to handle an equal, or possibly even greater, case load of supernatural investigations than the Pinkerton Detectives could—with less than one-quarter of the staff. And a smaller staff means far less threat of internal security breaches.

To best allocate its resources, the Agency has broken the country down into two Bureaus, the East and the West. Each Bureau, in turn, is divided into Regions and underneath each Region are any number of local Wards—usually based in the largest city in the area.

The Eastern Bureau

The Eastern Bureau is responsible for the portion of the Union east of the Mississippi River. Agency assets are roughly allotted by the regional population base, so it's no surprise that the Eastern Bureau is by far the largest of the two major divisions in the organization. Roughly two-thirds of all Agency personnel—or approximately 600 operatives—are assigned to the Eastern Bureau.

The Director of the Special Services Agency oversees all operations in the Eastern Bureau. This is due in part to the sheer size of resources allotted to the Bureau. More importantly, investigations in the Eastern Bureau are very high profile. Operatives must tread lightly indeed to avoid attracting undue attention.

The Bureau is divided into four Regions: Boston, Chicago, Philadelphia and Washington. In addition to three Regional subdivisions, the Eastern Bureau also houses two of the Agency's special duty stations: the Salem Training Academy and the Mount Kahtadin Institution. We'll discuss both of these in further detail a little later, as they don't fall under a specific Regional office's authority.

Boston

The Boston Office has the largest numbers of operatives of any of the Regional districts. If you consider it is responsible for most of the northeastern portion of the Union, including the heavily populated Atlantic coastal states, that's really no surprise. The Region encompasses New York, Massachusetts, Connecticut, Rhode Island, New Hampshire, Vermont, and Maine.

To cover this large population base, the office has approximately 250 operatives on hand. Following Pinkerton's original observation that fear amongst the populace tends to generate more events, it would seem that because of the larger population, this area would have a greater incidence of supernatural events.

For some as yet unknown reason, this has not proven to be the case. Perhaps there is a population threshold at which the mood of the region is not so easily affected by unexplained events. Or perhaps, as some have suggested, New Englanders are less prone to flights of fancy or just less likely to panic.

Whatever the cause, operations in this region are more low key, focused on countering esoteric cults or occult-oriented murderers. In

Eastern Bureau operations more often involve actions against organized cults and other less fantastic opponents than those in the West.

both cases, the investigations require a greater amount of planning and resources to carry out undetected and hence the greater need for manpower than the Western Bureau.

Of course, to every rule there is an exception, and the sparsely-populated areas of Vermont, northwestern Massachusetts, New Hampshire and portions of Maine do seem to follow Pinkerton's model of a fear-to-event relationship.

To manage the Region, 30 Agency operatives staff the Boston Regional Office. The Office conducts its operations behind the cover of a major accounting firm, Abercrombie & Sons. The Agency has gone to great pains to support this cover, even to the extent of "hiring" Abercrombie & Sons to manage the accounts of the cover businesses of other field offices. These reciprocal ties in turn provide the other offices with "proof" of their own cover businesses.

The major Wards within the Boston Region are Buffalo, Albany, and Providence, each of which maintains a staff of no less than five operatives in the field office. The New York City Ward employs 25 full-time personnel alone. Other prominent Wards include Providence, Montpelier, and Portland, although none of these has a staff of greater than three agents.

Chicago

The Chicago office handles all Agency operations in Indiana, Illinois, Michigan, Minnesota, and Wisconsin. Although a mere 120 operatives are assigned to Chicago, making it the smallest of the Eastern Bureau Regions, it also has the most varied assignments.

Operations in the large industrial cities of the lower Great Lakes are similar in nature to those found in Boston's coastal metropolitan areas—low visibility investigations. To the south, along the Ohio and Mississippi Rivers, field agents encounter much higher profile events, likely due to the frequent flare-ups of hostility along the border. Finally, the lightly populated northern woodlands of Wisconsin, Minnesota, and Michigan produce phenomena not unlike that encountered in the Western Bureau.

There are three major wards in the Chicago Region: Milwaukee, Detroit, and Indianapolis. Each of these has a staff of at least five operatives assigned to it—or did, in the case of Detroit.

Following the British seizure of Detroit, Agency operations there have been curtailed. At least three operatives have been detailed to remain in the city and monitor events, but investigations there are at a temporary halt until the Union regains control.

The Chicago office keeps a mere 20 personnel on site to assist with administration of Regional activities. However, the Chicago office maintains a close working relationship with the Pinkerton Detective Agency main office also located in the same city. On occasion, experienced detectives are hired as freelance operatives for low exposure missions. The Regional office takes great care to safeguard against any violations of EO 347 in these joint operations.

The Regional office operates under the cover business of the legal firm Allen, Allen, & Roberts, and purportedly practices corporate law. Among the clients claimed by the firm are Abercrombie & Sons, Pendulum Publishing, and the Union Blue Railroad. The guise even serves to legitimize its employment of Pinkerton detectives, under the auspices of preparing evidence for upcoming trials.

Philadelphia

The Philadelphia Regional Office is responsible for all investigations in the states of Ohio, Pennsylvania, New Jersey, Maryland, Delaware, and West Virginia. The Baltimore Office also oversees all EO 347 operations within the District of Columbia. To fulfill this mission, approximately 200 full-time operatives are assigned to the Region.

The majority of the Region's operations take place at or near the current line of battle with the Confederacy. As President Grant noted years ago, battlefields and their surroundings manifest an unusually high frequency of supernatural occurrences. Because of this, Philadelphia Regional operatives tend to remain busy. Ironically, the very battles themselves make low profile operations easier.

It's surprising how many folks are willing to overlook a number of strange events in the middle of a life-or-death battle!

The Region is divided into too many Wards to detail each thoroughly, but several Wards are large enough in and of themselves to

Government Manual 28-51

maintain a full-time staff of three or more operatives. Among these are: Pittsburgh, Baltimore, Columbus, Cleveland, and Newark.

Coordinating so many field operations is a complicated task. The Philadelphia Office keeps 25 operatives on staff to perform administrative tasks, such as archiving investigation reports, coordinating field efforts, and providing limited logistical support.

The Regional Office currently operates in an office building near the corner of Market and 2nd Streets under the cover of Pendulum Publishing House. Several Ward offices have established a cover for their operations as subsidiary offices for Pendulum Publishing as well.

The main office does have presses on site and occasionally the Agency uses these to produce mass printings that cannot be entrusted to civilian publishers—such as this manual. Pendulum Publishing books containing sensitive information are usually encoded with a common cipher identified by the author's pen name.

Washington, D.C.

If you're a sharp-eyed reader (and you'd better be if you're working for us!) you've already noticed that the Philadelphia office conducts all investigations within the District of Columbia. If this is true, why then does the Agency have a Regional office in Washington?

A better question is why the Agency makes its office in the capital such an obvious one. All the other Regional offices have a false business front, yet not only does the Washington office lack this, it almost seems Pinkerton went out of his way to draw attention to the construction of it.

The true reason is the Washington office is in itself a front for the entire Agency.

Pinkerton realized the best way to continue the charade the President began in EO 347 was to build a straw man. The Washington office is a complete sham. The operations undertaken by the staff of the Castle have nothing to do with the true goals of the Agency.

In fact, the Washington office is so removed from the real Agency that it is, in effect, another organization altogether.

The operatives conduct the counter-espionage that the public believes the Agency was created to perform. They maintain extensive files and keep a close eye on everyone in the city. So close that everyone in Washington is aware of their work.

The Washington office has nearly 50 operatives assigned to it, making it the largest Regional office. However, these agents—referred to somewhat derisively as Castle agents by the rest of the Agency— are completely occupied with intelligence work. With the exception of the Director, who maintains his office in the building, and one or two other assigned to the Castle, none of the staff is even aware of EO 347.

All training for these agents takes place in Washington and Castle operatives are *never* assigned duties outside of Washington, nor do they ever take part in an actual Agency investigation. On rare occasions, a Castle operative may be recruited into the Agency proper, but if so, she is never reassigned to Washington. This ensures these agents play the role of spy with complete sincerity.

While the Director does keep his "official" place of business in the Castle, all he conducts Event-related operations from the nearby Philadelphia Regional office. That office also serves as the repository for the central Agency case files.

Oh, and by the way, if you've not guessed, Castle agents do *not* receive—or even get a look at—GM 28-51 or GP 28-51A! If you should be tasked to an assignment with a Castle agent, treat him as you would an ordinary civilians with respect to EO 347.

The Western Bureau

The Western Bureau has only about one-half the manpower of its eastern counterpart, which might seem somewhat disproportionate in comparison with the population ratios of the two regions. On the other hand, the area covered by the Western Bureau is considerably larger, forcing the operatives who are assigned to be much more widely spread.

As a result, Western Bureau operatives have a reputation as a little more independent in their methods—more prone to act on their own initiative than await orders.

Government Manual 28-51

Agency personnel back East often refer to Western operatives as "mavericks" or, in extreme cases, "loose cannons" because of this. Any field agent who's spent any time in that Bureau responds that only an Eastern "tinhorn" who's never met the Ghost would think that to be the case!

110

The Ghost, as the popular press refers to Andrew Lane, is the Bureau Chief for Agency operations west of the Mississippi River. He's a stickler for details and believes that operating procedures exist for a reason. He's known for giving his operatives room to use initiative, but woe to the one who oversteps her bounds or makes a costly error in judgement.

The Western Bureau has three Regional offices—Denver, Sacramento, and Seattle—and three independent local Wards: Gomorra, Salt Lake City and Deadwood. In addition to these, the Agency Supernatural Research Center—referred to as the "Tank" by old-timers—is located in Denver and nominally under the direction of the Western Bureau.

Few and Far Between

Currently, there are only 300 full-time operatives assigned to the Western Bureau. Now that's not many folks to cover such a large area, so the Western Bureau is much more amenable to using "freelancers" or hired help on its operations. As you might expect, that means the operatives have to be slippery as eels when working with these potential security hazards. Government Pamphlet 28-51A provides suggestions and guidelines for handling these mercenary troubleshooters.

Also, unlike back East, operatives assigned to the Western Bureau tend to be more fluid in their localities. It's not uncommon for an agent to be assigned to the Seattle Region on one mission and then the Deadwood office on the next. This shuffling of personnel is one way the Bureau helps offset its manpower shortage.

As you'll see in a moment most Regions have only a few operatives permanently assigned to them. The majority of the rest are "floaters" transferred about by the Bureau office as mission requirements dictate.

Denver

The Denver office was, until recently, directly overseen by the Ghost. It's primary areas of responsibility were the Disputed Territories (Kansas and Colorado), Iowa, Nebraska, Montana, and Wyoming.

Operations in the Denver region are particularly hazardous due to the shifting political climate in the area. Field operatives not only have to worry about the potential threat from the target of an investigation, but also Confederate raiders and night-riders from both sides of the conflict. As a result, the Ghost took a very active hand in selecting agents for missions in this Region.

111

By virtue of that, while this is one of the most dangerous areas in which to operate, it's also considered to be a "choice assignment" due to the close scrutiny applied by the Ghost. Selection for Disputed Territory missions usually indicates an operative has secured a degree of trust from the Bureau Chief—always a good thing! Furthermore, succeeding at a difficult assignment in this area is often a leg up on a promotion.

Not counting the technicians assigned to the Tank, there are about 20 agents assigned to the Denver office. It operates behind the front business of the Nevada Basin Land Office.

Primary Wards for the Denver Region are Helena, Lincoln, Dodge City, Cheyenne, and Kansas City. Each of these maintains an administrative staff of four operatives.

Sacramento

A mission in the Sacramento Region is considered a "hot seat" assignment. This Region is comprised of California (more commonly known as "the Maze") and Nevada. The Maze is in such turmoil that an operative working here doesn't only have to watch her back, but her sides, the top of her head, and even the soles of her feet. There are so many groups vying for control that a threat can quite literally come from anywhere.

Not counting the powder keg boomtown Gomorra, an operative may find herself in conflict with Iron Dragon, the Church of Lost

Angels, Texas Rangers, the Mexican Army, or any number of smaller cabals and gangs. This territory is a state-sized game of king-of-the-hill—Boot Hill, that is.

And, unlike the Denver office, few operatives view the Maze as a premier assignment. The general consensus is that the Maze is in such turmoil that no one mission can begin to have a telling effect. The best an agent can hope for is to not make the situation *worse*.

Such agents would be advised to remember that nowhere does EO 347 dictate that part of the purpose of the Agency is to further the career paths of its operatives! No assignment is any less important than another.

Due to the recent drain of manpower to Gomorra, the Sacramento office is down to a skeleton crew. Most the few full-time agents assigned to staff the office find themselves tasked out to field investigations. As a result, the Sacramento Region is presently situated in private residences. Each agent in Sacramento maintains a personnel cover and daily administration rotates among them.

In the future, the Agency hopes to rectify this situation and provide a permanent duty office complete with a business front.

Seattle

The Seattle office has the least full-time operatives of any Region. Only four agents are permanently assigned to it. Part of the reason for this Seattle's area of responsibility: Idaho, Washington, and Oregon. Pockets of civilization in this area are sprinkled and sparse, keeping most operatives constantly on the move just to stay on top of *potential* investigations, much less active ones!

The other reason is that Seattle and it's nearby neighbor seem fairly sedate compared to other metropolitan areas. Not only has the area for the moment remained untouched by the conflict with British forces from Canada, but it also sees relatively few Event 070363-related occurrences.

112

For this reason, the Seattle office is often called "sleepy Seattle" by agents visiting from other Regions. A long-term assignment to this Regional office is usually considered a vacation by other members of the Bureau.

Important Wards within the Seattle Region are Boise, Portland, and Spokane, each with three agents assigned.

Andrew Lane, head of the Western Bureau, is so secretive, this *Epitaph* artist's rendition shows him as a specter—hence his nickname "the Ghost."

Deadwood

Deadwood enjoys—if "enjoys" is really the right word for it—a rather unique position in the middle of the Sioux Nations. The only access to the town is along a narrow rail corridor granted to the Iron Dragon Railroad. Even with the Deadwood Treaty, it's not really clear to whom the settlement belongs. Is it a Union settlement in the Sioux Nations, or is it an area of the Sioux Nations set aside for miners and other non-Indians?

Either way, it's a sticky situation.

Regardless of who owns the real estate, Deadwood represents an important piece of property with a fair number of Union citizens residing on it. Not only that, but the area has more than its fair share of Event 070363-related occurrences reported.

113

Needless to say, a wild-and-wooly frontier town with Deadwood's reputation also attracts more muckraking journalists than a dead horse does flies. Particularly with all the reports of strange happenings in and around the settlement. Keeping a lid on those rag reporters is cause enough to draw the Agency, but with all the other factors, it's just icing on the cake.

Even though it is only a relatively small town, Deadwood has four operatives assigned there full time due to its volatility. The current Ward Chief, Richard Speakman, operates from behind the Black Hills Miner's Supply storefront and employs one of the other operatives at that site. The other two field agents are detailed to long term deep cover assignments in and around town.

Gomorra

To look at a map, a new operative might be somewhat confused as to why the small Maze mining town of Gomorra was important enough to warrant all the attention its receiving from the Agency. Not only are nearly ten full-time operatives assigned to the boomtown—and numerous freelancers as well—but the Ghost himself considers events there important enough to temporarily oversee the operation personally!

The exact nature of the Gomorra investigation is currently restricted, even to others in the Agency. However, it is known that recently affairs there came to a violent head—thanks primarily to the Tombstone Epitaph's rogue reporting of the situation. The Gomorra detachment has suffered a high rate of attrition in the past few months, with as many as four, or even five, operatives dying in the course of the investigation.

114

Currently, the Agency's focus in the region is stabilization of the local situation and rumor control. Additionally, a number of factions retain a hold on a significant amount of influence in the region and until the situation settles out, the operatives there have their hands full countering various schemes and agendas.

Salt Lake City

When Brigham Young declared the "State of Deseret" independent of the Union until the end of the War, you can bet some feathers were ruffled back in Washington. However, since he declared an intent to rejoin the Union once hostilities were ended, the President hasn't seen fit to deploy the U.S. Army yet. Besides, the Southern rebels are keeping most of our resources tied up back East. However, as soon as the present hostilities are finished, the Union will be paying the *Utah Territory* a visit!

Until that time, while it is expedient to consider Deseret an independent entity, it remains part of the Union—regardless of the decrees of the Mormon Church. As such, the Agency has a duty to investigate all occurrences related to the Event.

And, as a corollary to those duties assigned by EO 347, it must also monitor the advance and research into areas of new technology. Since both Smith & Robards and Dr. Darious Hellstromme call Deseret their headquarters, it's of even greater importance than in other Wards or Regions.

Needless to say, as Deseret is technically an independent state (or in rebellion, depending on your view), operatives, as federal agents, must keep a very low profile. With that in mind, only two full-time operatives are assigned there. But rest assured, they are among the best the Agency has.

115

Alaska Territory

The newest Union Territory poses something of a quandary for the Agency. No set policy for its administration has yet been formulated. At present, operations there are overseen by the Eastern Bureau, even though it is inarguably *west* of the Mississippi River.

The real difficulty in dealing with Agency investigations in the Territory isn't bureaucratic, it's Alaska's geographical isolation.

It's simply impossible to maintain regular communications with operatives in Alaska. Even were the terrain between Washington and Alaska more favorable to overland travel, the current state of conflict between the Union and Canada makes routine border-crossing impossible. Nor does a single telegraph line reach even the southern most tip of the Territory.

The only way to contact field agents in Alaska is via ships departing from Seattle and the Maze. Thanks to the recent discovery of ghost rock deposits in the far north, vessels are beginning to depart for the Territory on a regular basis.

However, this method of communication is slow; often it takes an operative over a month to respond to a simple update query. Therefore, operatives in Alaska conduct their missions and investigations virtually independent of supervision.

Needless to say, this is not the Agency's preferred method! The organization's leadership hopes to resolve this situation one way or another.

Special Facilities

In addition to its administrative and field offices, the Agency also maintains three special facilities. The organization uses these locations to provide support functions to its operatives it cannot entrust to those without clearance for EO 347. These are the Agency Supernatural Research Facility (SRF) in Denver, the Salem Training Academy in Massachusetts, and the Mount Katahdin Institution in central Maine.

Agency Supernatural Research Facility

Also known as the "Tank" by former Pinkerton agents—or the "SRF" (pronounced "Surf") by new operatives—the Supernatural Research Facility is responsible for the examination and exploitation of all items of advanced technological or supernatural origin. That's quite a job when you consider all the Agency does is deal with one or the other.

The SRF is also responsible for the production of all specialized Agency equipment and gadgets, as well as the training of the rare

Technicians hard at work at the SRF.

operative who shows a talent for the alteration of reality through probability manipulation—or a "huckster" in layman's terms. The SRF combines the old Pinkerton Supernatural Research Facility and the "Library" into a single office.

The SRF is housed in a series of warehouses in the Denver railyard, and, in fact, encompasses the original Pinkerton buildings. The area is ostensibly marked as Union Blue Railroad property, thanks to the long-standing relationship between the railroad and the Pinkertons which has carried forward to the Agency in recent times.

116

A successful field test of SRF equipment.

The Mount Katahdin Institution

Due to the nature of occurrences related to Event 070363, occasionally operatives exposed to them on an extended basis come under such strain that it an extended recuperative period is necessary. Obviously, given the strictures imposed by EO 347, placing an agent no longer in full possession of her faculties into a public facility for treatment is not a viable option.

For that reason, the Agency has secured a private institution in the central Maine woodlands for just such an occasion. Located on the shores of Millinocket Lake near picturesque Mt. Katahdin, the Mount Katahdin Institute offers Agency employees the opportunity to receive the care and security they need in those unfortunate times.

117

Overseen by Dr. Geoffrey Kohms, renowned neurologist—and briefed on EO 347—the institute has a large central dormitory and administrative facility. Those visitors deemed capable of a degree of independence may take advantage of one of the many private cabins on the institute grounds.

Salem Training Academy

If you're reading this manual, you already know what this is: the initial classroom for all Agency employees. Here, new operatives—except for those assigned to the Castle, of course—receive basic instruction in investigative techniques and covert operations, as well as the nature of the Event and what obligations we hold under EO 347. All new operatives are required to attend the two-month training course on site prior to assuming field missions.

Located in the countryside near Salem, MA, the school occupies the estate that was formerly home to the "Library"—the former Pinkerton facility dedicated to occult research and training. The old English architecture of the manor and outbuildings provides an interesting counterpoint to the new Gatling weapon range located nearby. At the Salem Academy, modern technology sits side-by-side with ancient tomes of arcane lore, speaking volumes about the mission and lives of Agency operatives today.

Government Pamphlet 28-51 A

Special Services Agency

Field Operations

Introduction and Mission

This pamphlet is your textbook, your field guide, and your scripture for your new life as a member of the United States Special Services Agency.

While you're receiving your basic techniques courses at the Salem Training Facility, your instructors are going to quiz you day and night on the information within the covers of this book. If you're the least bit interested in graduating the Academy, you'd be advised to study it every waking hour—and make some time during sleep for it too!

Once you leave Salem, you're welcome to carry it with you. We designed GP 28-51A as a field manual for operatives. Two months of training is a good start, but even the best students forget things after class is over. If in doubt, just crack the spine on this little bit of literature and find some words of wisdom.

When the Agency's mission was handled by a private firm, they did a good job at it. In fact, it's likely most of your instructors at Salem were ex-Pinkertons—all the writers of this manual were. However, the one place they fell short was preparing new operatives.

There was a great deal of emphasis placed on hands-on experience and on-the-job training. However, that sort of instruction is either very time consuming or rushed.

Fortunately, the Pinkertons had the manpower to spread new detectives throughout the organization and pair them with experienced operatives for the necessary time. We don't have that luxury in the Agency. We're not even a quarter the size of our private counterpart and we've got to spend our resources carefully.

Including training time.

With that in mind, all new operatives spend a solid two months at Salem, learning the basics of investigation, disguise, legal matters, firearms, and Agency procedures. They also receive a crash course on Event 070363, how it relates to the Agency's mission, and what they can do to counter it.

However, the senior operatives in the Agency have all been around the block a few times. We're not so foolish to believe that we can prepare an operative to effective face Event-related occurrences with only two months training. Especially those assigned to the Western Bureau where they're likely to be called upon to function independent of direct supervision!

With that in mind, we've compiled GP 28-51A to assist the new operative once she departs the initial training course. It's not as good as a ten-year field veteran at her side, but it's a sure sight better than nothing.

One Caveat

There's just one thing to remember...

This pamphlet violates EO 347 just by its existence. If you don't recall the exact wording of EO 347, take a look inside the front cover of Field Manual *GM 28-51: United States Special Services Agency*; it's been thoughtfully reprinted there.

Should anyone outside of the Agency proper get a look inside your copy this booklet—or *GM 28-51*—you are in violation of Executive Order 347, Paragraph 6. And that means, if you're slow on the uptake, you've caused a violation of national security which we won't allow to go overlooked.

The Agency is not forgiving of trespasses.

Keep this book close to your heart. Better yet, memorize it—and *GM 28-51*—and burn them to be safe.

However, that does defeat the purpose of this pamphlet, so if your memory isn't perfect, just keep a *very* close eye on this book.

The Agency Mission

If you've been paying attention in class you already know what we're about to discuss, but it won't hurt to have it hammered home once or twice more. If you're just arriving in Salem, here's your chance for you to get a jump on all the other new students and score points towards being a teacher's pet.

Either way, it's in your best interests to sit up and take notice.

The Event

That's "Event" as in Event 070363—the Agency's terminology for the as-yet unexplained occurrences that first took place on July 3, 1863. First noted in Gettysburg, these phenomena in retrospect appear to have simultaneously been experienced across the Union—and Confederacy.

The government has put substantial effort into either covering up these phenomena or casting doubt on the testimony of all involved with these occurrences both on that day and every other since then.

In a nutshell, that's also your job now as well.

So What Did Happen?

Well, to be completely honest, just about everything the sensationalist newspapers claimed.

Sometime in the evening on the 3rd of July, *something* changed in the world as we know it. Exactly what that something was, we don't know yet. It's one of the things we're trying to figure out. However, we do know from eye-witness reports that the initial phenomena were observed around 7PM that evening.

The first encounters were easily dismissed. Several soldiers claimed to have seen dead comrades or enemy troops rising on the battlefield. Most veteran troops passed these early sightings off to skittish first-timers rattled by the ferocity of the day's battles. Most likely, it was assumed, the men had seen wounded or unconscious soldiers stirring awake.

Within less than an hour, it would be clear that the dead had indeed risen. Brutally so.

By 8PM, these revenants had entered Federal battle lines along Cemetery Ridge. Once there, they proved quite ferocious—seemingly intent on devouring the flesh of the living.

And, not surprisingly, the "dead" proved quite difficult to kill a second time!

A field operative gets first-hand experience with Event 070363-related phenomena.

A Downhill Ride

Those first hours on the battlefield were only a taste of what was yet to come. Over the course of the night, wholesale slaughter began. Walking dead rose in hordes from the field and assaulted the living. Panicked and in the dark, soldiers shot living compatriots as well as the reanimated dead. And worse, some of those killed by accident also arose, further confusing the situation.

Although we at first thought only the Union was affected, we have obtained evidence that the walking dead plagued the Rebel lines as well. Reports have leaked out that a crazed battlefield surgeon, perhaps driven to insanity by the Event, began butchering patients in a field hospital. Perhaps the supernatural is Blue-Gray colorblind.

Since it now appears that similar events were taking place halfway across the continent at Vicksburg at the same time, we can only conclude that the Event took place on a very large scale— possibly hemisphere or even worldwide

Furthermore, incidents of apparently supernatural origin continue even today. In fact, they are occurring with greater frequency than before. This has led many Agency researchers to believe that the Event is actually still resolving toward some unknown end.

What It Means

On a theoretical level, we have no idea what it means. One of the top-priority missions at the SRF is determining what caused—or *is* still causing—the Event. But, lucky for you as an Agency field operative, you don't have to worry about the theoretical level. You only have to concern yourself with the here-and-now.

That means flesh-eating dead, ghosts, goblins, ghouls, and just about every creature of myth, legend, and some that deny description.

What do we expect you to do about them?

Well, since you've asked, all we expect is what the President of the United States directed in Executive Order 347. Nothing more, but definitely nothing less.

Let's take a moment and look at EO 347 in detail. Understanding the foundations of your job now may aid you in performing it later.

EO 347

As you've no doubt heard by now—or at least figured out for yourself—EO 347 is the document responsible for the creation of the Agency and its source of authority. In short, it's *the* document as far as the Agency is concerned.

However, it's a complex and, at times, seemingly self-contradictory order. Let's take a quick run through it, paragraph by paragraph and iron out some of its rougher spots.

The first two lines are clear enough, merely acknowledging the existence of supernatural activity, the potential threat they pose to the Union, and ordering the creation of the Agency. The real meat of the document is in the seven numbered paragraphs immediately following.

Agency Membership

The directive in Paragraph 1 primarily applied to the creation of the Agency. You'll note that the founding members were drawn from the Pinkerton National Detective Agency. Prior to EO 347, the Pinkertons were responsible for investigating the Event and its ramifications. For reasons discussed in detail in *GM 28-51*, those duties were transferred to the Agency with EO 347.

However, since the Pinkerton detectives had been doing an admirable job of handling the assignment to date, rather than lose that experience and skill, they were tapped to form the foundations of the Agency.

Moving forward, the Agency no longer has a pre-trained, veteran group to draw upon. It is now responsible for filling its ranks with suitable operatives from outside the organization.

Paragraph 2 makes the position of Director a lifetime appointment. This prevents it from becoming a career-furthering step on a political ladder. Placing a term on the office not only requires a procedure for appointing a new Director on a regular basis, thus jeopardizing the intent of Paragraph 5. Finally, with a lifetime appointment, the Director need not concern himself with job security, and thus is less vulnerable to political blackmail.

Government Pamphlet 28-51A

Investigation of the Unexplained

The first mission EO 347 assigns to the Agency—outside of membership requirements, at any rate—is defined in Paragraph 3: the investigation of all unexplained events. The order is careful to not limit Agency investigations to only events of *apparent* supernatural or occult nature. Many times in the past an incident that appeared innocent enough on the surface after thorough investigation to be an Event 070363-related episode.

By leaving the requirement only "unexplained" this opens a wider number of incidents to Agency scrutiny. It also provides some basis for the Agency's recent acquisition of all crimes related to new technologies. Many SRF researchers are beginning to believe there is a relationship with some of the more exotic inventions of recent years and the Event.

In simplest terms, by Paragraph 3, if an event has no readily obvious explanation for its occurrence, it's the Agency's responsibility to find one.

Of course, that doesn't mean every time Widow Jones' cat goes missing, we detach an operative to find out why! We have a limited manpower base and must shepherd our resources carefully. The Regional and Ward offices are responsible for assigning priorities to investigations and detailing operatives to them accordingly.

Elimination of Threats

More often than not, supernatural or unexplained events pose a threat to the citizens of the Union. After completing an investigation, if the operative assigned deems that the source or cause of the incident poses a significant threat to public safety, it's her duty to eliminate it according to Paragraph 4 of EO 347.

Now, just like the preceding paragraph, the wording of this is decidedly vague as to what constitutes a threat. "Life," "liberty," and "well-being" are listed as those qualities which a threat to justifies elimination. The first two are obvious, but "well-being" is a more...nebulous quality.

Nor does the paragraph define *who's* judgement determines whether the threat is significant or not, allowing an agent considerable leeway in making decisions in the field.

The reasons for this become evident in the next paragraph of the Order.

Often, a operative has little more than circumstantail evidence at the beginning of an investigation.

Maintain the Status Quo

Eye-witness reports reveal that more casualties were caused on the first night of the Event by frightened soldiers than by the phenomena themselves.

Now, given the reactions of battle-hardened, veteran soldiers when faced with Event-related activity, the President has determined that a wide-scale panic is likely to ensue should the general public become aware of all the implications of Event 070363. For that reason, Paragraph 5 makes it the Agency's duty to ensure that does not happen.

This is perhaps the most important duty assigned to the Agency, one that encompasses nearly all of the other assigned missions. It's the reason for controlled recruitment and the lifetime appointment of the Director. It's also the underlying reason behind the elimination of those incidents deemed detrimental to the citizenry.

Certainly, the Agency seeks to preserve the lives of Union citizens from harm, but it is also responsible for viewing the "forest" of Event 070363 and not just the "trees." In some cases, operatives must take a pragmatic approach to their assignments. It's preferable to suffer a few casualties and keep the event under wraps than it is to sacrifice secrecy in order to save a single life—or even many, in some cases.

Remain in the Shadows

In keeping with Paragraph 5's directive to deny the reality of Event-related phenomena, the Agency itself must remain anonymous. After all, why would the government create a clandestine organization to combat a nonexistent threat?

In spite of Executive Order 347, it is inevitable that the Agency's existence will eventually be discovered. For that reason, an elaborate cover is already being developed and the seeds of deception sown. To all outside the organization's confines—including those members assigned to the Washington Office, the "Castle"—the Agency is simply an espionage bureau.

However, all effort must be made to maintain this illusion. That means, paradoxically, an operative can *never* admit openly to this cover story, anymore than he can admit to his actual duties. To remain effective, the cover must be denied nearly as fervently as the truth.

Welcome to the world of double- and triple-deceptions that is the Special Services Agency.

Total Authority

To assist in pursuit of these duties, Paragraph 7 thoughtfully provided Agency operatives with the authority to co-opt local, state, and federal law enforcement in pursuit of their mission. Furthermore, they can even draw upon military assets as well.

There is one *big* catch to this genie in a bottle, of course: Paragraph 5.

The operative must be careful not to expose the Event or any related phenomena when using the authority granted under Paragraph 7. Therein, as Shakespeare said, lies the rub.

In effect, as an Agency operative, you have been given a very big gun and all the ammunition you could possibly want to accomplish your mission—with the stipulation that if anyone ever hears it fired, you fail.

We'll let you in on a secret—most experienced agent avoid law enforcement officials like the plague. We'd advise you do the same, at least until you get a little experience under your belt.

Using This Pamphlet

We've designed this booklet to flow as easily as possible. A field guide that's too complicated to read is a waste of time, no matter how complete it might be.

With that in mind, we've started where you're likely to start, at the beginning of an investigation. We've laid out a few guidelines for the opening phase of a mission, from gathering information, choosing a cover story, and entering a locality. The pamphlet then follows through the steps of an investigation as you, the operative are likely to encounter them. Finally, it closes with procedures for communication, recruitment, and other miscellaneous tasks.

That's what's covered in this pamphlet. Now it's time you start learning it, Agent.

Starting The Assignment

The quickest way to fail an investigation is to get started on the wrong foot. Go in half-cocked and not only are you unlikely to get to the bottom of the occurrence, you're also in danger of blowing your cover, the Agency's mission, and the nature of the Event.

And that would be bad.

Fortunately, there's a system for nearly everything and starting an investigation is no different. In fact, we're going to show you an approach to solving problems that you can apply to nearly every endeavor you'll pursue under the Agency.

The Five Steps

Plain and simple, the Five Steps are little more than common sense laid out in the form of a procedure. They're adapted from methods used by a variety of professionals from private detectives to military officers to resolve difficult situations..

In order, these steps are:

Identify the problem.
Gather information.
Develop potential plans of action.
Select the best plan.
Execute the plan.

While it is a simplistic approach, it has a lot going for it as a technique for field agents to organize an operation.

First, it *is* simple, which means it's harder to mess up. There are only five steps and each of them obviously follows from the previous, making it hard to overlook one of them.

Second, while obvious, it does cover all important aspects of organization, from information gathering to final implementation. If you've covered those five activities, you've covered all the vital steps to preparing an op.

Finally, it helps an operative organize her thoughts. Often, on a mission, a field agent is going to find herself overwhelmed by unusual— *really* unusual—circumstances. During those crucial periods, it's invaluable to have a tool to help quickly structure a reasonable and measured response.

The real trick is learning to apply these steps to any given situation. In time, most operatives perform them without any conscious thought. However, spelling them out helps reinforce the procedure.

The goal is to be able to think clearly when you realize you're in a town populated entirely by cultists looking for the next sacrifice to their unholy religion. Especially when that sacrifice is you!

Let's briefly break each step down to better understand what it entails.

Identify the Problem

This is usually the simplest of all the steps. All that's necessary here is to put your finger on the problem at hand. Most of the time, your superiors are even going to do this for you when they give you an assignment.

An example of this would be: "Investigate a series of cattle mutilations near Cheyenne." The problem is something or someone is mutilating cattle. Simple enough.

The trick here is not to make any assumptions at all. For all you know the cattle may be mutilating themselves. Don't laugh— there is already a case on record of exactly that. You shouldn't eliminate any possibility until the second step of gathering information is complete. Doing so could very well hamstring you later!

Unfortunately, not every problem is going to be so clear cut. Say you've just entered a quiet little town in Nebraska. You can't put your finger on it, but something doesn't seem right. Perhaps there's no sound of children laughing, or there are no animals anywhere to be seen.

But there is no outward sign of any Event-related activities. What's behind your uneasiness, or, in other words, what's the problem?

Well, that's a good question.

The best way to address this situation is to treat identifying the problem *as* the problem and apply the five steps to it. In that case, you've identified the problem, now begin gathering information, develop a course of action, etc. Then, once you've completed the steps, you will have hopefully identified the original problem and can move on to resolving it!

Gather Information

Here you begin compiling facts pertaining to the problem. Without information, you cannot form a viable course of action to deal with the problem—at least not reliably. Sure, a simple bullet may be all it takes to put the abomination down, but what if it isn't?

Every piece of information you obtain tells you something. Even the absence of certain clues can point you in the right direction.

For example, a murdered body is found in the middle of a field, but there are no footprints in the loose dirt around it. You now know either the killer covered his tracks and those of the victim, or the body got there somehow without leaving any. Either way, you know more about the incident before you noted the absence of prints.

This step is the reason you don't rule out any possible conclusion when identifying the problem. Every piece of information related to the problem may prove of value, whether you're investigating a series of murders or trying to determine how to exorcise a vengeful spirit. If you've already reached a premature conclusion, you may overlook a vital clue or evidence.

Later in this book you'll find a variety of methods for gathering information, from investigations of the scene of a crime or other activity to interviewing eye-witnesses.

Once you've gathered sufficient information—and only you can determine when that is—you're ready to develop courses of action.

Develop Courses of Action

Analyzing the information you've put together, you should next come up with one or, preferably, more courses of action. These should be based on what you know and what your desired resolution for the situation is.

If you're beginning an investigation, that's most likely going to be for you to arrive on the scene with a solid cover story and the ability to begin your assignment. On the other hand, if you're attempting to eliminate an already identified threat, your resolution should probably be to remove it with as little traces left as possible while remaining among the living yourself!

Select the Best Course

We advised you develop more than one course of action above so that you'll have some choice in how to proceed.

No doubt one of your ideas will be better suited to the problem than the others, but all are likely to have strengths and weaknesses. By contrasting them, you may be able to combine two or more to reach an even more favorable option.

When making the final decision on which plan you're going to use, be sure to weigh in all factors. For example, does your plan risk violating Agency security? Does it endanger lives or property unnecessarily?

Finally, remember that all other factors equal, the simplest plan is probably the best.

Execute the Plan

It doesn't get any simpler than that. Not the plan—those invariably get complicated and few survive the first minute or so of their execution. No, we meant the step. Once you've settled on the plan, put it in action as soon as possible.

Once you've decided, stick by your decision. In the words of a carnival hawker, "You pays your money—you takes your chances." Changing course in mid-execution is a nearly foolproof way to ensure failure!

Now that we've gone over the basics of five step mission planning, let's narrow our focus to specific aspects of an investigation's phases.

Before You Leave Home

You don't go into a strange room blindfolded and you shouldn't enter a strange town that way either. No, we don't mean literally wearing a blindfold.

What we're talking about is knowing what's going on in your area of assignment—at least a little—before you actually arrive there.

You're going to use this information in a couple of ways, so it's very important that you start the investigation before you ever set foot on the site of the Event-related occurrence.

External Sources of Information

There are several places you can gather some preliminary information on a region without actually travelling to it.

The first source is readily available in most large cities. We highly recommend any operative have one nearby at all times. It's a simple atlas. A decent one covering all the states and territories in the Union can be picked up at a bookstore or reasonably well-stocked department store in a city for a little more than a dollar and can prove invaluable. Not only does it tell you the location of your target area, but what terrain lies around it and the relative sizes of towns nearby. Sure, the maps may not be perfect, but they're a sure sight better than none at all.

Another good place to review is local newspapers. Most counties publish at least a monthly or, more commonly, weekly newspaper. Even if it doesn't contain references to the exact incident you've been assigned, it will likely give you some indication of what else going on in the area and who's important. Never underestimate the power of social influence in an area.

A wealth of gossip and hard facts fill local circulars. If you're lucky enough to get your hands on one prior to arriving at your destination, milk it for all it's worth.

If it's a relatively isolated or small community, chances are that inhabitants have to file official paperwork in a larger municipality, like a county seat or state capital. Many of these records are easily accessible, even without a Special Services Agency badge to back your request. Property records, marriage, birth, and death certificates are routinely available if the right questions are asked. While these won't necessarily appear readily applicable to your investigation, they provide the groundwork for later information.

If you don't have the basics on the area before you arrive, odds are you're going to be playing catch-up while you should be gathering facts pertinent to your mission. At the very least, you should have some idea of the surrounding towns and terrain, the area's main

Surprises—of any type—are to be avoided!

industry, who's in charge (and who's *really* in charge), and any important historical data on the locality and its environs.

Other facts that could prove helpful are existing feuds or conflicts such as range wars or property disputes, nearby rail lines (existing or proposed), neighboring Indian tribes, and any secondary industries pursued in the area.

Building Your Cover Story

After you've gathered the basic information on your target locality, you need to lay the foundations for your cover identity. It's not as simple as merely pulling a name out of a hat, either.

Why a False Identity?

As we mentioned in passing earlier, a cover identity is a necessity for an Agency operative. Not only does it serve to protect the Agency's mission from scrutiny, it also helps lend credence to the Agency's own blanket cover. It's commonly accepted knowledge that spies simply *don't* walk around openly in public!

An individual cover does more than merely shield the Agency, though. It protects you as the field agent as well.

The source of the incident you are tasked to investigate may very well be human occultists or even just plain, old criminals. You may not know for certain until you've completed your investigation. In either case, the culprits aren't going to take kindly to a government agent snooping around their affairs. More than likely, they will take direct action to prevent exposure.

On the more mundane side, the Agency's cover as an espionage organization is so widely accepted that Confederate forces and supporters now target our field operatives. This is an unfortunate consequence of the success the organization has had in promoting the deception. If it's known you're a member of the Agency, you may well find yourself under attack by pro-Rebel groups—even though you may have no interest in their activities!

So, as you can see, it's in everyone's best interests that you keep as low a profile as possible on an investigation.

Selecting a Cover Identity

When choosing an identity, remember that every person has some means of providing for his livelihood. Over time, that occupation shapes the person both physically and mentally. Miners tend to be strong of back and lawyers sharp of wit, not vice versa.

Now, that's not to say there aren't exceptions to this. Many an intelligent man has sought his fortune in gold and higher education does not prevent physical fitness. However, the general populace likes to fit people into preconceived archetypes. Those who don't fit are often remembered or commented upon.

This brings us to the first rule of cover identities: Don't stand out of the crowd if you can avoid it. Be as unremarkable as possible—as intangible to folks memories as a ghost if you will, hence our nickname as "spooks."

Sure, playing a wealthy Bavarian princeling is a lot more entertaining than an illiterate cowhand, but you can bet folks are going to be watching what the "rich ferner" is doing a lot more closely than the common cowpoke. Which means the cowpoke has more time to watch what everyone else is doing instead!

Now, since you've spent some of your valuable time learning about the region you're heading to, here's a good place to put that knowledge to work. If you know what the leading industry in the area is, you've got a line on a good cover occupation.

Chances are, if logging is the main source of income in an area, folks tend to see a lot of loggers pass through. One lumberjack looking for work, more or less, isn't going to draw a lot of attention. On the other hand, a deep-water sailor is!

Of course, there are other factors to consider. Remember we mentioned the physical aspects associated with various occupations. If you're small of frame or short-winded, it's unlikely you'll be able to pass yourself off as a veteran lumberjack. On the other hand, a lawyer with shoulders as broad as the Rocky Mountains is going to generate a lot of talk around a small town.

Play to your strengths as much as you can. In the long run, it will make your double life much easier to maintain in the long run.

Government Pamphlet 28-51A

Universal Cover Occupations

Some occupations are by nature transient and likely to pop up anywhere.

Journalists and writers are a good choice for this reason. These occupations allow an operative to poke around in other folks' business without arousing quite as much suspicion as, say, a nosy dock hand. For some reason folks who have nothing to say to a lawman open up like a book to one of these muckrakers.

Another travelling occupation is a snake-oil salesman. These shysters travel almost constantly and rare is the town that hasn't seen one or more within a few months. They also tend to be rather interested in local gossip, presumably looking to turn it to their own profit. The biggest drawback to this cover occupation is that criminal elements tend to consider them easy game since they usually have no close friends or relatives likely to come looking for them.

Itinerant or circuit preachers provide another option. They tend to be gossip magnets as folks trust them. However, for obvious reasons don't assume this cover without a solid knowledge of the chosen religion.

Assuming an Occupation

An operative's cover must pass a reasonable amount of scrutiny, otherwise, it's useless. There's more to portraying a member of a particular line of work than simply claiming the profession.

We mentioned earlier that certain occupations tend to produce a certain physical type. Working outside in the sun produces certain physical indicators that a clerk isn't likely to have. Conversely, an accountant is going to have cues to his profession that aren't likely to be found on a laborer.

Folks pursuing physical labor outdoors usually have tanned skin, at least in the face and hands. The hands of manual laborers are often heavily calloused and the fingernails chipped and dirty. These last are so common that many western frontier folk use them to determine if a man is a "tinhorn" or not.

Clerical workers are usually paler from working indoors. While their personal grooming, like shaving and nail manicuring, are expected to be better maintained, it's usual for these sorts of workers to have ink stains from writing.

Note this operative's use of a camera as a prop to bolster her cover identity as a journalist.

A good way to help flesh out a cover is to provide a few props appropriate to the profession. There are the obvious ones, like a lumberjack's axe or a photographer's camera, but as the saying goes, "The Devil is in the details."

In addition to the wood-cutting tools, the lumberjack is likely to have a well-worn pair of boots, a file for sharpening his axe, a chipped pocket knife, a kerchief for wiping sweat, and so on. A photographer is also going to have a soft cloth for his lens, flash powder, developing chemicals, and maybe even simple framing materials if he does freelance work.

Although it's a good start, appearance isn't everything. You should learn enough about your chosen cover profession to be able to converse on the basics of it. Otherwise, you risk exposure the first time it's tested.

The more you know, the better, but keep a sense of scale. To stay with the lumberjack example, while he's going to know the proper names for different axes, saws, files, and trees, it's the unusual member of the profession who understands the metallurgy behind the iron axe head or the inner workings of a paper mill!

Choosing an Alias

It might sound strange, but often choosing a name is the *last* part of coming up with a cover identity. Sure, it's completely opposite of the way things happen in life, but remember what we said earlier: The less you stand out, the better.

Most folks expect—even if it's not at the front of their thinking most of the time—for people in certain occupations to have a particular sort of name. For example, when you think of a doctor, you seldom imagine them named Chet or Blue, but those names are perfect for a range hand.

Now, once again, we're not saying there aren't any doctors named Chet—just that people tend to remember those that are. And people remembering is one thing an operative wants to avoid when under cover.

Another good rule of thumb is to choose an alias somewhat similar to your own when possible. That runs somewhat contrary to what an experienced detective or bounty hunter might think, since criminals on the run often use this practice when adopting an alias—

and it's often that very similarity that tips off their pursuers. However, the reason they do it is actually quite sound.

Choosing a false name that's close to your own real one helps lessen the chance you'll forget it or not respond to a greeting. Either of those are likely to raise suspicion or even expose you should they take place at the wrong time.

Another danger to a cover name is good old pen and ink. Many times out of habit, a new operative settling into a cover identity slip up when signing a document. About one pen stroke after she's already started the paper, she remembers she's writing her real one.

In general, it's a good idea to keep the first letters of the false name the same as the real one. Not only does that help you recognize it easily until it becomes familiar, but it also helps you when signing documents, ledgers, and the like by giving you a letter or two to recover.

The similar-alias method is practical for a field operative because she has an advantage that a criminal doesn't. No one is actively hunting for her by name nor is her face likely to be on a wanted poster.

She still needs to be careful about her cover, but, as long as she's *been* careful in the past, a similar alias isn't the problem for her that it is for a criminal.

Hiding in Plain Sight

We've spent so much time discussing a cover story and identity for your investigation, and likely you've gotten your fill of it at the Salem. However, when you get your first assignment, don't be surprised if your superior tells you to go in without a cover story, to let folks know—or at least strongly suspect—you're with the Agency.

While that seems to fly in the face of everything we've told you about maintaining a cover, there's a bigger picture to think of. We want people to believe the Agency is involved in counter-espionage operations and every so often we give them grain for the rumor mills! As long as the public thinks we're trying to keep our "spy" activities secret, it's unlikely they'll realize we aren't spying at all.

Besides, "Rebel infiltrators" are a convenient scapegoat for Event phenomena!

The Investigation

Once you've got your assignment, done a little preliminary research, prepared your cover identity, and actually arrived at the location of your mission, you're ready to dig into the meat of the investigation.

Odds are, your field office has given you the assignment because of unexplained—or outright supernatural—events have been occurring in the locality. Upon arrival, you need to overcome the urge to rush right to the scene of the latest sighting, murder, or what-have-you. Often patience is the hardest thing for a new agent to master, but trust us, it saves lives if you do—particularly your own.

Remember the first step in problem solving is gathering information. Work around the event, collecting facts on not only the occurrence itself, but the area in general. Circling it in this fashion, you're likely to uncover clues you'd miss by charging right into the scene.

With that in mind, there are a couple of routes to pull together information you should explore before heading to the actual scene of an Event-related sighting or occurrence.

Local Records

By "local records" we don't mean just official documents of the sort you find in courthouses and land claim offices—although those are a good source of background information. While you may have already covered these in your preliminary research, local official sources may contain newer versions of the same. Often updated copies take time to reach higher offices; for example, you may discover a change in land ownership that sheds new light on things.

However, once at the site of an investigation, you may find many more sources of documents and records that weren't available elsewhere.

People, especially businessmen, love to write things down. Store owners often extend credit accounts to customers, for example. Although it's likely to take some fast talking on your part, a review of those account records may reveal much about who's doing what, who has what, and who *doesn't* have money!

Pawnshops are another source of information of this sort. A quick review of the store's inventory may turn up items belonging to a recently deceased or missing person, and you can be sure that the pawnbroker has a record of who sold the item. Or, on a more mundane tack, you can get a good idea from here who's short on funds—often a good starting point for building a network of informants!

Other places to consider are local churches. Lacking a civil government facility, records of births, deaths, and marriages may be found here. The undertaker is also worth a visit when investigating a death or deaths. At the very least, he's going to know who paid for a coffin.

And, of course, any of the sources we mentioned as worth consideration during your preliminary research are prime sources on the site of the assignment. Local newspapers, in particular, may not be distributed outside the immediate area and are going to tell you much about recent events. Even a *lack* of reporting on the Event-related occurrence can tell you much.

But don't merely limit your research to the obvious. Cattleman's brand registries not only give you the brand itself, but also the name of the ranch and the owner. Telegraph offices record the date, time, recipient or sender, and destination or origination of any message, although seldom the message itself. Stage offices and train depots post schedules of arrivals and departures. And so on.

The possibilities are too great to list here, but evaluate the locality and adapt your research methods to capitalize the options it presents.

Interviews

Perhaps the single most important source of information you, as a field operative, have to draw upon are people. The inhabitants of your area of assignment are likely to have all the information you need to complete your investigation. If you're lucky, you find not only folks that provide eye-witness accounts of the occurrence, but also some that can give you local history, social information, and even just plain, old rumors and legends.

The trick is getting it out of them.

You might think that means convincing them to talk, and that is vital to an interview, but that's really only a part of the problem. The important part of conducting an interview isn't just asking questions—it's asking the *right* questions.

Getting Them to Talk

We refer to the first part of the interview as "approaching" the subject—or person you want to talk. There are nearly as many different approaches as there are people, which is good, since what works on one person might very well alienate another. What you have to do is find the right one for your subject.

Some folks break under pressure, while others clam up. A couple will sell their grandmother for a few double eagles, while just as many are insulted by the very thought of a bribe. Pick the wrong approach and you might end the interview before it even begins.

You usually have to spend some time just talking with the person about life in general just to get enough of a feel for her personality. Be prepared for it and be patient.

If you're in a saloon, pass the time with a drink or two—but don't start off buying unless the subject suggests it. Doing so too quickly puts some folks on their guard right away!

In addition to the subject's personality, you should also consider the category of person you're speaking with. By that, we mean is he a victim of an Event-related incident, a witness to the same, an informer, or accuser? Or, is he another type of subject altogether?

Each of these categories of people is liable to have different attitudes and motivations for speaking with you regarding an incident. These are going to not only play on the quality and bias of information you receive, but probably also the approach you select as we're about to discuss.

The Approach

We've divided up some of the most common methods into different categories and given you a brief run-down on each. We've also included a couple of personalities on which each is likely to work best. But in the end, it's up to you to make the right choice.

Friendly

This is exactly what it sounds like—a nice, easy-going approach. It's very simple to pull off, just talk to the person as if you're a friendly, but curious, cowpoke. Start off the conversation on neutral topics and slowly move to the target of your interview when you're sure the subject is ready to talk.

A word of advice, don't move too quickly with this approach. The trick is to get the subject to genuinely like you and trust you. Moving into the interview questions to fast may tip your hand and spoil the approach.

This is also a very easy approach to recover from if it's not working on the subject. It's not much trouble to go from friendly questions to one of the other approaches—but it's nearly impossible to work in the opposite direction! For that reason, we highly recommend if you plan on trying this method, do so first.

Friendly approaches are probably the best approach to start with. Assume the person *wants* to talk; many do and this is the best way to get them to do so. It's also a good strategy for shy or frightened folks, or those who don't quite fit in, like tinhorns from "Back East" in a frontier town.

Consider the situation of the interview and your cover as well. This sorts of approach is very appropriate if your cover is a journalist, a preacher, or maybe even just a member of the opposite sex. It's amazing what a smile from a pretty face and a kind word can do.

Sympathetic

This approach is a good one to take with a victim of an incident, but with practice, it can work just as well against someone who's guilty of breaking the law—or involvement with occult practices.

In the former case, sympathy requires little explanation. The person has suffered due to an encounter with an Event-based phenomena and is probably going to be very receptive anyone willing to believe their side. All it takes is a receptive ear and a few words of encouragement.

It's important in this case, though, to maintain what's known as "plausible deniability" in order to avoid violating Paragraph 6 of EO 347. That means, even when building trust with the subject, *don't* say anything that could later be used by the subject or a third party to prove the existence of Event 070363!

The second instance—sympathy towards the guilty—takes a little more effort. You, as the interviewer, explain to the subject that he's just a person who, under stresses greater than normal folks can be expected to bear, chose a path he otherwise wouldn't have.

If presented with confidence and sincerity, the guilty subject can be convinced that you not only understand how he came to enter the position he's in, but that you also intend to help him out of the predicament.

Of course, to do so, you need him to provide you with information...

A sympathetic approach can be difficult to master. It requires some skill in persuasion and acting—especially when dealing with someone whose actions are criminal or reprehensible. It's hard to be convincing when you're angry, outraged, or disgusted!

In the first case we discussed, it's often effective with victims of Event-related occurrences. This style builds well on a friendly approach.

In the latter, an operative may find it of use when dealing with a criminal element, or a reluctant participant in a cult or other group. And if the gentler approach fails, it's no problem to move to intimidation. However, it is *very* difficult to move from intimidation back to sympathy.

An operative negotiates a price with an informant.

Bribery

When interviewing less-savory members of society, occasionally you can loosen the tongue of an informant by judicious application of cash. Be wary when using bribery to obtain information, however; often, a greedy subject may fabricate information just to get paid.

Furthermore, the Agency does *not* budget for payment of informants. Such programs frequently lead to graft and mismanagement of funds. If you use this method, be prepared to either pay out of your own pocket or coordinate with your field office prior to beginning the investigation.

When paying a bribe, be careful to evaluate the value of the information fairly. Don't pay too much, but also be sure to pay an equitable amount for the quality of information and the danger the informant faced to obtain it. Paying too small a bribe is a sure way to lose an informant, and overpaying gets you a lot of trivial information and an empty wallet! A description of stage passengers may be worth a few dollars, while the password to enter an outlaw hideout is worth considerably more. But once you agree to pay for information, do so!

Don't insult the informant, regardless of your opinion of her, nor should you overreact to the information you obtain in this fashion—no matter how startling. On the other hand, you should consider it all important until you discover otherwise.

You must maintain control of the relationship with a subject of this nature. Otherwise, the informant may take unnecessary risks to gain more money—risks that could very well expose her and your investigation.

While you must remain respectful, don't tell the informant that she's indispensable. And never, never let the informant believe she's a part of the Agency; she's liable to brag to her friends—or even the very people on whom you're collecting information.

For all it's drawbacks, bribery does work *very* well with one cover story—that of a journalist. It's an accepted, and sometimes even expected practice for many members of this occupation.

Belittling the Subject

Surprisingly, this type of approach can be very effective when used against the right sort of personality. Some folks have such inflated egos that they will do most anything they can to avoid having them deflated—even spill the whole bag of beans.

The long and short of this approach relies on the operative's ability to convincingly demean the subject while tying his self-image to the desired knowledge. What that means is you express doubts to the subject that "a cowpoke like you *can't* know anything about..." inserting the appropriate desired fact.

If you've played your cards right up to this point, the blowhard may very well spout off about just how much he does know. From there, it's a hop, skip, and a jump to getting the braggart to prove it by telling you about it.

Now, it's nowhere as easy as it sounds, but if you're careful, you can work your way to another approach if you fail with this one. The trick is to be doubtful, but not insulting.

Young cowboys, upstart gunslingers, new deputies, and the like are the best targets for this approach. Understandably, some cover stories—say a preacher or a schoolmarm—aren't likely to use this one and remain believable.

Intimidation

This approach relies on a threat, or at the least an implied threat, to convince the subject it's a good idea to start talking. It's a hard approach to recover from if it fails, so use it carefully. We *strongly* recommend you try another approach if possible; this one is a one-shot pistol!

The exact nature of the threat depends on the situation. Some examples include imprisonment, loss of material wealth, public embarrassment, or even physical harm. The options are determined by the subject's predicament and the agent's abilities.

For this approach to work, the subject must believe the operative can actually bring about the consequences of the threat. It doesn't matter if the field agent is really able to do it or not, but rather that the subject is convinced she can. So, in other words, it doesn't matter if she's able to whip his backside up one side of town and down the other in a fist-fight, if he doesn't believe she can do it, he's not going to be intimidated!

In general, implied consequences are often better than outright threats. Most folks are able to imagine far worse things than you'll be able to come up with on the spur of the moment.

Intimidation is a good choice for hostile subjects, like criminals, captives, or just down-right uncooperative hardheads. Odds are you're already starting out on a bad foot with these types, so a more amiable approach is going to be a waste of time.

While nearly any cover story can pull off an intimidation approach under the right circumstances, authority figures usually have better luck. Lawmen, politicians, wealthy investors, and Agency operatives not undercover have the best luck with this type of interview.

Of course, it goes without saying that physically imposing folks have a certain advantage in intimating subjects...

Government Pamphlet 28-51A

Violence...or Rather the Lack Thereof...

One method that we can't speak strongly enough against is physical torture. While the importance of the Agency's mission may supercede ethical concerns for some operatives, the fact remains that torture is *not* a reliable method of obtaining information.

Once a person is subjected to direct physical pain, he may say anything to stop the injury. His concern is for the here-and-now—not what *may* happen to him in hours or days when his lie is exposed. The key to the approaches we've presented is that each, in one way or another, provides the subject with a reason to want to tell the interviewer the truth; torture just makes the subject want to get the torturer to stop as quickly as possible.

You can't rely on information gained through torture. Don't use it.

Closing the Approach

Actually, you *never* close the approach. Throughout the course of the interview, you may have to revisit and reinforce it if the subject begins to show signs of reluctance. Provided you chose the right one, a few nudges should keep the information flowing from your source.

Even once you've completed the interview, leave the subject in a state where, should you find it necessary, you can return. For the friendly approaches, that means end on a good note. For the aggressive ones, make sure the subject understands you intend to verify what he's told you—and you *will* be back if he's lying.

You might be surprised how many times you hear "Oh, did I forget to mention..." when the subject believes you're going to check his story!

Asking the Right Questions

Now that you've got your source talking freely, you want to make sure you get the information you need and not just, say, his grocery list. Or worse, a notebook full of confusing, and apparently contradictory answers.

The way you do that is make sure *you* ask the right questions—and that you don't ask the wrong ones. That's a skill that comes with experience, but here are a few pointers to help you get by until you accumulate that experience.

An agent in the Disputed Territories uses his cover as a Texas Ranger to "persuade" a local deputy to share information.

The Wrong Questions

We'll start with these, since it's easier to ask a wrong question than a right one. And the wrong one can trip up an interview as quick as any mistake in the approach.

The first type to avoid is a *compound question*. That's a question like "Were you at the saloon or the stage coach office when Sheriff Franklin was attacked?"

If the subject says "No," you've answered two questions with one stone. But, on the other hand, she can truthfully answer "Yes" and you're left guessing as to which one. You have to ask another question to sort it out, and if it happens often you're going to get frustrated with the subject (with good reason—anyone that repeatedly does that is trying to get your goat!) and possibly make mistakes in the interview.

The other type you want to stay away from is a *negative* or *leading question*. The question itself leads the subject to a particular response by the way it's asked. An example of this sort is "You didn't see anything at the old church, did you?"

This sort gives the subject an easy out by pointing them in the direction you apparently want her to answer. It can also lead to confusion. For example, if she answers "No" to the above question, does she mean "No, I didn't see anything" or "No..I did see something." Without further questions, you really can't be sure.

As a general rule, it's a good idea to avoid questions that the subject can answer with a simple yes or no. These aren't wrong in themselves; in fact, some questions have to be asked this way.

However, a yes-no question only eliminates one of two choices—either the subject answers in the affirmative or the negative. Whenever possible, you want to give the subject as much leeway in her answer as possible.

That's why you ask the *right* questions.

Narrative Questions

These are the type of questions you should ask in an interview. Narrative questions ask the subject to tell a story, if you will. An example of on is "Tell me what happened on the night you heard the howling near the McDermott farm."

Let the subject lead the answer where he wants at first. He may reveal a bit of information you had no idea existed—and thus couldn't ask about earlier! Take notes, if possible, because when he's done, you need to go back and fill in the blanks in his story.

Any journalist can tell you the important parts to any story are: Who, What, When, Where, and How. If, at the end of the subject's answer, you're missing any of those, go back and get them with additional questions like "Who was with you?" or "Where was the shadow?"

As each one is answered, it's a sound practice to ask "Who else?" or "What else?" to prompt the subject's memory of the event. If he's lying, he may suspect you know more than you do and you're checking his story. But, even if he's being completely honest, he may forget something. This sort of follow-up helps him recall.

You may need to prompt a subject's memory. There are a couple of good ways to do this. First, you can let the subject begin his answer where his memory prompts and work out from there. Another way is to choose a natural time benchmark, like dinner, lunch, or bedtime and work backward or forward as needed.

Repeat Questions

This one's pretty simple. Every so often during the interview, you might want to go back and ask a question the subject's already answered. Lies are harder to remember than the truth, and you can often trip up a deceitful subject by asking the same question later.

This works well when you sprinkle a repeat question or two into a long narrative answer.

Control Questions

Before you go into the interview, if possible, you want to have a few questions ready to which you already know the answers. We call these *control questions*, because they help make certain you're still in control of the interview. Whenever you suspect the subject is being untruthful, drop in one of these and see.

It's best to pick control questions the subject has no reason to suspect you know the answer to; otherwise, she'll play along.

Government Pamphlet 28-51A

While these are most often used to check a suspected liar's responses, you should drop one or two into all interviews. An sharp-eared and truly honest subject isn't as likely to notice a control question as she is a repeat one. Some folks get touchy when their honesty is doubted!

If you find a subject is lying, you need to go back to the approach you used to get her to open up in the first place. If it's sound, a little reinforcement should steer her back to the truth. On the other hand, if it's not, you may need to try another.

At the Scene

Hopefully, before you ever set foot on the site of an Event-related occurrence, you'll already got a good idea what you might be facing. That's why we've spent so much time going over preliminary research and interviewing subjects—to make sure you're as completely prepared as possible for what you're going to face.

Over time, the Agency (and the Pinkertons before us) has determined that, for some—as yet unclear—reason, most Event incidents are tied to human actions, either present or past. And, in most cases, the recent past. We suspect this somehow is also tied to the level of fear in the locality, but no solid evidence has yet been produced to prove this theory.

All conjecture aside, what this means to you as a field operative is that odds are whatever phenomenon you find yourself up against, it has its roots in the actions or history of the local populace. By building a sound base of facts prior to investigating the actual site, you are more likely to pick up on clues that would otherwise be overlooked.

Expect the Unexpected

This is the first rule of all Agency assignments. Or, maybe a better way to say that is "Have no expectations at all."

When your reach the end of this section, you're going to find our advice on eliminating threats rather sparse. That's because so many Event-related incidents are unique in nature; even those that seem similar to other encounters often have a unique—and dangerous—twist. Trying to fit an assignment into a cookie-cutter mold is a sure way to fail.

This field operative begins his investigation of an Event 070363 incident right at the source.

Government Pamphlet 28-51A

Approach the scene with as neutral a viewpoint as you can—while still juggling all the facts you've gathered through prior research. It's tough, remembering everything you've discovered so far without forcing an opinion onto the on-the-scene-investigation, but it's a skill you have to master. Going in with preconceptions and assumptions is a surefire way to overlook a vital clue, especially if it doesn't fit with your pet theory.

A good way to avoid this is to keep a notebook to refer back to after you've completed the investigation. Many field agents feel knowing the facts are safely recorded elsewhere helps them clear their minds for an on-site investigation. If you find this method works for you, however, be certain to take all necessary precautions to safeguard your notes according to Paragraph 6, EO 347.

Isolate Eye-Witnesses

Should you be lucky enough to arrive at a site shortly after the actual incident occurs, one of the first things to take care of are the witnesses to the event. It's important to quickly get these folks identified and separated, both from gawkers and other witnesses alike. Use your wits to come up with an excuse if your cover identity makes this tricky, but do it!

Obviously, you don't want witnesses speaking freely with the rest of the populace soon after an event. Until you've had time to develop a plausible explanation, a few loose tongues can do enormous damage to an investigation—and local fears! Since most Event phenomena fall outside the course of normal experience, most folks *want* a logical explanation and will bend over backward to believe one. By securing the witnesses, you give yourself time to come up with exactly that.

The other reason you need to separate them from spectators—and each other—is to keep their stories as pure as possible until you can sort them out. Give them free reign to discuss what they saw and facts get blurred. Pretty soon the witnesses are spouting descriptions of twelve purple monkeys delivering Smith & Robards catalogs instead of a stampede of perfectly normal longhorn steers.

Complete the rest of the on-site investigation, but interview the witnesses as soon as possible. Human memory is a faulty service at best; the longer you wait to speak to them, the

An operative scours a site for clues, leaving no stone—or splinter—unturned.

more unclear their recollections become. Soon, they'll be rationalizing what they saw their own and you'll never get a straight answer.

There's one more reason to speak to them quickly. An encounter with an apparently supernatural event often has an unsettling effect on the human mind. In the immediate aftermath, you may be able to sidestep any reluctance to speak the witness might have. Even the toughest cowhands get a little ruffled by the sight of a werewolf loping through the herd. Take advantage of it.

Secure the Scene

At the same time you're identifying and separating any witnesses, clear the site of any gawkers, passersby, or other folks not directly related to your investigation. Letting them wander free into the area runs the considerable risk of corrupting any clues left behind. At the very least, their own feet are going to obscure any tracks in the area.

Worse yet, since so many Event phenomena are related to the human element, some may be more than innocent busybodies; they may actually attempt to remove items from the scene or alter it in another way!

Touch Nothing...Yet

When you first enter the area, it's hands off. If possible don't even actually enter the area until you've observed it from several angles. You're just as capable of obscuring a vital clue as anyone else.

There is one exception: weapons. Don't leave a weapon lying around the incident scene or you might find yourself staring at the business end before you know it.

Use a Systematic Approach

You should scour every site the same way. There's some leeway in exactly how you go about searching the scene, but you have to do it the *same way each time*. Changing your routine leads to oversights and missed clues.

Start the investigation outside the actual incident site. Many field operatives use a series of concentric circles to cover the entire area, slowly moving in with each new revolution.

Examine it from different angles. What's invisible from the front may be apparent from a flank. One trap most people fall into is a form of tunnel vision—they observe on one plane and ignore what's over their heads and under their feet. Many Event-related entities and phenomena aren't bound by gravity or even solid objects; don't let your thinking be either.

Next note all possible means of entry and exit to the scene. If the entity is no longer there, it had to get out somehow. While some phenomena are capable of rendering themselves non-corporeal, most aren't. If you know how it got in and out, you've narrowed down where it came from and where it went.

By the time you're ready to enter the scene, try to have a good idea of how the entity entered and what it likely saw as it did. This helps look for other clues on the site itself.

Once you move into the actual scene, most of your investigation is an inventory of the site. That's right—it all boils down to what's there. Or rather: what's there; what's there that shouldn't be; and what's not there that should be. Each of those can tell you something about the incident.

Valuable objects are a powerful indicator. Event-related creatures are seldom drawn to an object for simply material value; few walking dead are concerned with rolling a victim for cash. Some items *are* attractive to these entities, however, and identifying their absence is a step towards understanding what you're facing.

Another example is blood. If you're checking a scene containing a badly mauled victim, there should be a fair amount of blood. If it's missing, there's a reason why. If it's there, there's a good chance you're going to find the tracks of the killer in it. We'll talk more about examining corpses and the like shortly.

One final word of advice: Take notes. On site is best, later if you must—but take them.

Cameras and Investigations

If you've got a camera (and it works with your cover identity) by all means, use it. Photographs are more certain than memory by itself.

However, photographs and notes are better than photographs alone, so don't neglect your notes in favor of technology.

Be sure to keep track of your plates and the angles and items photographed. Later on, trying to figure out what that strange object you're looking at doesn't help you accomplish your mission.

Another good tactic is to carry a small ruler to show scale in your photos. If that's inconvenient—or you just plain forget one—use another item of known size, like a bullet or pocket watch. That way, when you examine the photographs later you won't be looking for a lizard when you should be hunting a crocodile.

Also, if you're using a camera to record the site, be sure *you* develop the plates yourself. Even if your cover is a journalist, photographs sometimes reveal things not seen by the naked eye. Explaining those to a chemist is more work than simply carting the necessary chemicals yourself.

Finally—don't skimp on the flash powder; a shadowy photograph is worse than useless for our purposes

The Rangers clean up.

Sanitize the Site

After completing your examination and gathering any items or evidence of supernatural occurrences that you feel appropriate, the last step is to clear the scene of any signs of Event-related activity. Leave nothing behind to indicate that *anything* out of the ordinary occurred.

By this point, you should have some idea of what your explanation for the incident is; adjust the scene to reflect that. If that means removing or adding evidence, so be it. While you should try to avoid destroying any clues that point to guilty parties on a purely legal basis, EO 347 takes absolute precedence.

It's a good practice to carry a few items with you when investigating a scene to assist in this step. A pair of handkerchiefs or rags for cleaning, some alcohol as a solvent and odor remover, and a few false leads. Since our Southern neighbors are ready-made dupes for almost any unseemly affair, a few torn pieces of Confederate uniforms, Southern-made shell casings, or buttons are nearly always appropriate.

Human Remains

It's an unfortunate fact that many Event-induced incidents produce human casualties—often a fair number. However, a careful operative can deduce much about the attacker from a victim's remains.

If you're lucky enough to have a physican on hand who's cleared to EO 347 knowledge, she may be invaluable in an investigation. Often, she can tell more about a victim's attacker and the circumstances of the incident by examining a wound than a saloon full of witnesses.

Unfortunately, the few doctors in the Agency stay quite busy and can't be involved with every field operative that requests them.

However, while a physician's knowledge of the body is certainly a great asset in conducting an examination of such remains, a sharp-eyed investigator can learn a number of things without years of medical school. We included some of the most common in the following pages.

Time of Death

One of the things an operative without medical training can establish is a rough time of death. Now, we don't mean down to the minute—or even, in many cases, the hour. However, an attentive investigator can gain valuable information about the length of time a body has been dead with a cursory examination.

Approximately half an hour after death, skin takes on a purplish hue as gravity pulls the blood down from the surface. The skin becomes waxy, almost translucent, in appearance. Lips and fingernails go from pink to pale. Blood begins to collect in the parts of the body closest to the ground; however, at this point, the pressure on these areas causes the blood to disperse, leaving a pale spot at the point of contact. The eyeballs begin to lose shape and settle from fluid loss.

Rigor mortis—the stiffening of the corpse's muscles—sets in after about four hours. This may occur sooner if the victim struggled or the climate is hot, or later in cold regions. It starts in the smallest muscles first, like the face and neck. Over the next day or so, it spreads to the rest of the body and then recedes as the muscles begin to decay.

Also, by this time, the body is noticeably cooler to the touch. It loses heat at about 1° to 1 1/2° every hour, and our medical researchers tell us this drop is fairly constant.

Six hours or so after death, the blood in the lower portions of the body has begun clotting. Pressing against the discolored regions no longer causes the flesh to pale or blanch. The eyes become cloudy about this time as well, giving the corpse a "glassy-eyed" look. Contrary to what dime novels might have you believe, very few folks die with their eyes closed—unless they were sleeping at the time.

About 12 hours after death, rigor mortis has caused the body to stiffen completely, freezing the joints in place. If the temperature is warm enough to support flies, maggots begin to hatch from their eggs about this time as well.

Somewhere close to a day after death, the skin has a cool and clammy feel and around the head and neck it turns a greenish-red as decomposition begins. Rigor mortis begins to leave the small muscles of the body, leaving the face slack.

By about a day and a half, rigor mortis has departed altogether, and the body goes completely flaccid. During this time, larger insects may begin to feed on the flesh as well.

Decomposition progresses over the next few days, and, by three days after death, the corpse is truly unsightly. Gas begins to bloat the body, blisters form on the surface of the skin, and fluids forced out by the gas pockets begin to leak from every available exit. That's right, *every* exit.

After this point, it's even more difficult to determine the time of death. By three weeks, the skin begins to burst open exposing the muscles and organ. Where it doesn't burst, it sags and hair and nails slough off.

Exact dates are an impossibility at this point. However, it's safe to say that in warm, moist temperatures the body may be reduced to a skeleton within less than a month. In cold climates, the process may take twice the time.

Other Clues to Time of Death

A sharp-eyed operative may not even need to see the body to determine when the victim died. People leave signs of life constantly; when those signs end, it's usually safe to bet that life did as well. There's no secret to figuring these signs out, but here's a few examples to get your mind rolling the right direction.

Prepared, but uneaten, food may mean the event occurred around meal time. The type of food should help pin down exactly which meal; scrambled eggs and pancakes aren't a popular lunch for most. Dirty dishes can indicate the same thing—or poor housekeeping habits.

A candle burned down to the holder or a lamp out of oil means the victim was most likely alive at nightfall, but not come bedtime. On the other hand, a full chamberpot probably means the victim had gone to bed. Most folks take a stroll to the outhouse prior to bedding down to do their business—unless they're truly lazy. Likewise, the pot is empty first thing in the morning...for obvious reasons.

Clean clothing is unlikely to be worn by anyone who's worked a long day in the dust of the West, and even back East some dirt and stains accumulate. The shoes are maybe the best indicator for this. During the day, they accumulate a layer of dust, which most folks clean prior to retiring.

Was It Murder?

Agency medical researchers at the Denver facility spend much of their time examining unusual specimens. However, they also have more experience examining dead bodies than probably anyone else. Sure, the undertaker in Dodge City might *see* more corpses, but Agency specialists take the time to figure out what makes them cadavers in the first place.

These forensic medical experts have noted a number of facts about victims of violent deaths that can very possibly be of use to field operatives. Space prevents us from covering these in any great detail, but here are some tidbits most likely to be of use to an agent.

Hanging

This is a common method of execution, by legal courts and lynch mobs alike. When properly performed, the noose pulls tight against the back of the victim's neck, breaking it and causing nearly instant death. Of course, it's seldom performed properly by vigilantes and lynch mobs and the victim is left to strangle slowly.

Obviously, few folks die by accidental hanging, but occasionally an individual down on his luck might check out this way. A suicide note is a good sign of this, but it's also easy to forge one. It's tough to tie your own hands behind your back, so if the victim's bound, that's a clue it wasn't suicide.

You should also find a chair, ladder, or other spot for the victim to have jumped from. Not too many people have the strength and fortitude to hoist themselves up by the neck!

Finally, a noose makes a V-shaped rope burn on the neck. It's not unheard of for a murderer to strangle a victim and then fake a suicidal hanging. However, a strangling cord makes a straight-line rope burn, not a V-shape; look for it. If the murderer used her hands, there are most likely bruises on the neck corresponding to her fingers. Also, check the back of the neck—throttling often produces a pronounced bruise there.

Even if a hanging is staged afterward, those marks remain, and the characteristic "V" is *not* formed. It takes a live body to produce those.

Drowning

Most often, when a person drowns, they've gotten a fair amount of water into the lungs. This causes the body to sink under the surface. Later, when decomposition sets in, the corpse rises to the surface and floats face down.

Note, decomposition underwater generally takes longer than it does in the air. It's also influenced by water temperature, the colder it is, the slower it occurs. This makes it hard to get a good estimate on the time of death for a drowning victim.

It is possible to drown without getting water in the lungs; it happens about one time out of ten. In that case, the body doesn't sink—or at least not as far as one with water in the lungs. However, that also means that most of the time a floating body that isn't decomposing was dropped in *after* death.

In either case, the victim's mouth and nose may contain sand, dirt or weeds from the bottom of the pool or river, especially if there's a current. Also, a current may drag the body, causing bruises and scrapes on the face.

Knives, Razors, and ...Claws

Stabbing and slashing wounds to the back, stomach, or side of the body indicate an attack, especially if done through clothing. Murders using these types of weapons usually involve multiple stabs or slashes. The victim's arms and hands, particularly the palms, often have cuts and slashes from trying to fend off the attack.

In any case, a victim killed by such attacks is most likely going to lose a lot of blood. Absence of blood at the scene is a sign the body may have been moved. Absence of blood in and around the wounds themselves may mean the victim was killed and then cut. Or maybe something just collected the blood...

Should you suspect suicide, there are a few clues to look for. If a fellow decides to slash himself, he usually exposes the skin; he doesn't cut through clothing. Second, he's most likely to have targeted his neck or wrists. Finally, since this sort of thing isn't easy to talk oneself into, there are probably going to be smaller and shallower cuts around the final wound as the victim worked up his courage.

Firearms

Not too many Event-related creatures or entities rely on Colt Peacemakers to do their dirty work. However, since lots of normal, but no less evil, folks do, you're probably going to see a lot of gunshot wounds in the course of your assignments.

A few experts in European countries, claim they can tell the caliber of the weapon, and possibly even the very gun itself from a bullet fired from it. Unfortunately, that sort of detail is outside the realm of the ordinary operative's means—if it is even possible. Barring occult methods, of course, and those are too unreliable to rely upon with regularity.

However, one thing you can tell by the wound itself with some certainty—and ease—is the distance from which the gun was fired.

A wound where the gun was actually touching the skin causes a star-shaped tear around the entry point. This occurs because the gases released from the barrel are trapped inside the wound and expand under the skin. You may also find a small circular burn or abrasion where the barrel of the weapon touched the flesh.

Out to about half a foot or so, burning gunpowder causes a sooty scorching on the skin. This black residue can be smudged or even wiped off with little effort. Clothing may catch fire in this area due to the burning powder. Black powder or other low-quality gunpowder may enhance this effect, by the way.

At distances up to as much as two feet, unburned chunks of powder are propelled with enough force to actually penetrate the skin. This causes the area around the wound to appear dotted with tiny black marks that won't wipe off. Again, low-quality powder may produce a greater amount of this than standard loads. Also, a powerful cartridge like a Sharps .50 can cause this pitting at distances up to 3′ or further.

Beyond those distances, all you're looking at is a hole where the bullet entered. However, you can often tell a bit by its location alone.

We've talked about suicides a little in the other topics, so we'll hit on it here as well. As before, a suicide note may be a clue, but don't count on it. More important is the gunshot itself.

Most suicide victims choose to shoot themselves in the side of the forehead, mouth, or under the chin. The gun is either in

An Agency medical researcher begins a detailed autopsy.

contact or close contact with the body, which you can determine from the indicators above. Clothing is pushed aside, allowing contact with the skin. Finally, there is seldom more than one shot—very seldom.

Shots to the head from other angles usually aren't suicide; it's too awkward to manage. A gunshot to the eye is almost *never* a suicide. Evidence of a struggle is also a pretty good indicator that the victim didn't die by choice.

Government Pamphlet 28-51A

Finally, do you remember we mentioned securing weapons when checking a site? Here's one place it might prove helpful. At the site of a suicide you should most likely find the firearm; if someone else pulled the trigger, odds are he carried the weapon away as well.

Poisons

Toxic substances are a popular method of murder among those who don't want to "dirty their hands" with more direct methods. There are a few cases in Agency files of field operatives encountering Event entities that were innately poisonous. On the more mundane side, rattlesnakes are as common in the West as bullets on a battlefield and they're not the only poisonous snake in the bush, either.

Arsenic is tasteless and odorless, so it's easy to slip into foods. A victim may experience nausea, dizziness, convulsions, a dry mouth, vomiting, and numbness, while an odor of garlic might be detectable on her breath.

The average field agent shouldn't have to get this detailed!

Cyanide can be inhaled or ingested. A victim of this poison suffers an agonizing death suffocating while still able to breathe. Some, but not all, operatives can detect a faint almond-like odor on the breath of a cyanide victim.

Ingesting strychnine results in violent spasming convulsion in its victims. The body may thrash back and forth and then be racked by continuous seizures until death. Rigor mortis sets in almost immediately, leaving the victim's face distorted in agony and with eyes wide open.

Animal toxins usually spread from the point of the bite. If you suspect a venom to be responsible, look for a bite or sting—very few examples of contact poisons exist in nature. Usually the area around the bite is swollen and discolored with similar symptoms following the larger blood vessels toward the heart. Venomous animal bites are often quite painful, with the sensation centering around the bite itself.

Poisoned weapons generally follow the same trends as animal bites.

Unfortunately, toxins spread by Event-related creatures or entities often defy classification. One may paralyze a victim while the next turns him to soup. Like much supernatural phenomena, each case is often unique.

An Important Difference

By now, you might be wondering why we're concerned with suicide and that's a fair question. You remember we mentioned most Event activity is tied to human actions—usually unpleasant ones. Occasionally, the perpetrators of these acts are either overcome with guilt over their deeds or fear of the consequences of them and take their own lives.

Being able to tell a suicide from a murder may help point your investigation in the right direction. Instead of wasting time looking for a nonexistent murderer, you can focus on what drove the victim to take her own life. If you figure that out, you may have an important tool in cleaning up the situation.

Furthermore, suicides and murders seem to link to Event occurrences more often than nearly any other activity. However, the solution to the resultant phenomena may hinge on the difference, as we'll discuss in the next section.

Classification and Elimination

Once you've completed your preliminary research, conducted witness interviews, and investigated an Event site or three, you've probably dug up all the information on the incident you're going to.

The next step is to eliminate the phenomenon. Part of that is making a solid determination of what it is your facing.

Classifying Entities

In order to more clearly define what an operative might face in the field, the Agency has developed a method of classifying entities. There are four broad classes of Event-related manifestations and phenomena, each further broken into subclasses.

Thanks to the rather individual nature of Event incidents, the classes are rather general. However, with the application of the appropriate sub-class, you as a field agent should be able to use them to narrow your options.

Reporting and Classification

All after-action reports filed on completion of Agency assignments must use these approved classifications. Furthermore, the entity must be described in complete detail, including, but not limited to, it's apparent origin, abilities, weaknesses (if any), and the elimination method.

After-action reports are an important part of your mission as an Agency operative. Through them, other members of the organization can profit from your experience. In addition, after review by your field office, copies are forwarded to both the Denver Facility and the Director's own file storage in the Philadelphia field office.

Writing those pages of reports is tedious, but in their way, they are just as important as field work.

Class I, Humans

This class is composed of human beings—or at least mostly human beings—who either participate in Event-related activities or have been altered by them in some fashion.

Class I-a, Normal

These are purely human participants without any ties to the supernatural, the Event, or even the occult, guilty of criminal action that has caused Agency involvement. In other words, they're outlaws doing something that has been mistaken for a haunting or some other activity.

Members of a cult that do not manifest powers of a supernatural origin also fall into this subclass, as do charlatans claiming non-existent abilities.

This subclass of incident requires attention because they serve to heighten local fear levels and may precipitate a more serious event. Although legal means—or a plain, old gun—is usually all that's necessary to thwart these sorts, they can be dangerous.

Class I-b, Practitioners

Humans exhibiting arcane abilities make up this subclass. They include black magicians, so-called "hucksters," miracle-workers, and the like. Inventors working with sufficiently advanced technologies also fall into this subclass, as certain gadgets' abilities are nearly indistinguishable from the supernatural.

These individuals pose a serious threat to an operative and must be approached with caution, regardless of any apparent lack of hostility. Members of this subclass possess access to all the tools available to members of Class Ia and are augmented by Event phenomena as well.

Class I-c, Shapechangers

This group includes humans who've somehow obtained the ability to alter their form through means other than those available to Class I-b. In other words, werewolves and the like—that's right, werewolves.

Shapechangers tend to be very unpredictable in temperment as well as form. Their behavior can be very erratic, varying enormously between physical shapes. In some cases, alternate forms appear to have alter egos as well.

Worse yet, some of these can assume more than one other shape, so move against these with extreme caution.

Class I-d, Revenants

Revenants are humans who've returned from the grave in some fashion. Included in this subclass are not only the simple walking dead, but other corporeal forms of undead like vampires; non-corporeal entities are covered under Class III. These entities are, without exception, malevolent and considered an serious threat. Take immediate steps to eliminate them.

Also, Class I-d subsumes a group of revenants most commonly referred to as "Harrowed." These individuals *may* be redeemable, but only the Denver Facility has the necessary tools to determine that. If possible, return such persons to Denver. However, if you have any concerns about your safety or that of others, or the integrity of EO 347, eliminate the subject.

Class II, Non-Human Corporeals

This is the broadest of the categories in descriptive terms. Any entity that is not human, but has a physical form, is considered Class II. This class, as a whole, is least tied to human activities, and, as such, can complicate your investigative efforts.

The subclasses further break the category down according to the creature's physical form. The entity's form may provide insight into some of its abilities and perhaps even weaknesses, but don't count on it. You're often better off trusting your own observations on these.

Class II-a, Humanoids

These entities have a generally human form— that is, a head, torso, two arms and two legs. However, they may be considerably larger or smaller than the average human and physical features often vary greatly. Be careful to avoid mis-classifying a member of Class I-c as this subclass and vice-versa—it's easier than you'd think.

Many creatures previously thought legendary fall into this subcategory. The Indians' Wendigo are examples of this class, as are trolls and dwarves of European folklore.

Class II-b, Mammalian

Although the title of this category implies the entity is a member of the order of mammals, it's something of a misnomer. We don't expect you to actually attempt to scientifically classify an Event-spawned creature; specialists in Denver are still unable to do that in many cases.

Rather, members of this subclass generally *appear* to be mammals at a cursory glance; in other words, they have fur and maybe they resemble an existing animal. Beyond that all bets are off.

You may encounter six-legged mountain lions, rabbits with antlers, or wolves with prehensile paws. All of those belong to this subcategory.

Class II-c, Reptilian

As above, don't be too concerned trying to decide if it's truly a reptile. If it's covered in scales, it goes in this subcategory. Often members of this group reach large size—the Maze dragons of California, for example. But be wary; venom is common among smaller Class II-c creatures.

Class II-d, Avian

Here we diverge a little bit from the pattern we've set. *Any* non-human, corporeal creature capable of winged flight belongs to this group. (Should you encounter an entity capable of non-winged flight, by the way, label it normally with a note to its special ability.)

Hence, the winged creatures found in the Dakota Badlands known as "Devil Bats" are considered Class II-d and not Class II-b, in spite of their fur.

Your primary concern is if it has wings. Those not only give a good indication it can fly, but also limit it's ground movement. Few Class II-d entities enter normal-sized buildings.

Class II-e, Insectoid

If it looks like a bug, it's Class II-e. We're not concerned if it has six, eight, or even ten legs; it's Class II-e. These entities are usually smaller than human-sized, although there are unconfirmed rumors of enormous spider-like creatures in the Confederate southwestern states..

Venom is fairly common to this subcategory, as is an ability to move along vertical surfaces. For very small members, a common tactic is to swarm a victim.

Oh, they tend to move very quickly, as well.

Class II-f, Other

That's right—there are some things prowling about out there that don't even fit into these broad descriptions. Label them Class II-f and give a detailed description in your report.

The legendary "Mojave Rattlers" belong to this class, for example, so that should give you an idea of the variety of entity you may end up facing.

Class III, Non-coporeals

Entities of this category lack substance in the physical world, at least by default. They are unaffected by corporeal barriers and most normal weapons. This state of being makes them quite troublesome to field operatives, as most natural laws—and sometimes even common sense—don't seem to apply to them.

Class III-a, Repeaters

It's questionable that entities of this subcategory are truly entities, and are more likely purely Event phenomena. These incoporeal entity do not exhibit any free will or awareness. Instead, they follow a single repetitve pattern; for humanoid phenomena of this sub-category, it's usually the events of a tragic or violent death.

Class III-b, Apparitions

These entities, unlike Class III-a, are both aware of their surroundings and free-willed. They are fully incoporeal, but usually have some indirect means of interacting with the physical world. Apparitions usually resemble a deceased person's physical appearance, but often are

A Class III entity manifests near the site of its death.

capable of altering it or even rendering themselves completely invisible as well as intangible. These entities are the closest in nature to ghosts of folklore and legend.

Class III-c, Transitionals

Members of this sub-category are probably the most dangerous of the incoporeals. They possess all the abilities of Class III-b, but they also appear capable of assuming a tangible physical form at will. Fortunately, there are few recorded instances of Agency operatives encountering entities of this sub-category.

Class IV, Constructs

In keeping with its assumption of investigations of new technologies, the Agency added Class IV to its categories. This class is used to qualify purely technological phenomena that nonetheless fall under its purview.

Note that this category is used for those investigations which uncover *only* an advanced device—for example, a stolen weapon being used by someone other than its designer. Should the operative find a renegade scientist is involved, it should be listed as a Class I-b.

Class IV-a, Manually Operated

Weapons, remotely-controlled devices, and other inventions that require a human operator fall into this class. This sub-category includes vehicles of a mechanically-advanced nature.

While that technically includes steam wagons and velocipedes, in general, field offices don't require written reports unless the device differs in a substantial way from the standard models. Steam tanks or any flying contraption do, however, require complete documentation.

Class IV-b, Self-Motivating

Any human-constructed mechanical device capable of functioning for extended periods without human supervision falls into this sub-group. The automatons employed by the Wasatch railroad are prime examples of this category.

Operatives uncovering creations of this class are strongly encouraged to attempt to capture them intact, if they can do so without undue risk. The Denver Facility is very interested in learning what makes these things tick.

Be warned, however—many of these devices not only resist capture, but may be booby-trapped to prevent duplication by competitors!

Class V, Undefined

In the rare instance you encounter an entity or Event phenomena that can't be adequately cataloged under any of the proceeding categories, use this one. However, be sure to provide an *extremely* detailed description and, better yet, physical samples, if possible.

Threat Levels and Prioritizing

In general, the Agency expects field operatives to deal with any entity encountered during the course of an investigation. However, we do recognize that on occasion a situation may arise that is outside the ability of the agent to handle alone.

In those instances, field operatives can request support from the supervising field office. Special Threat Teams—more commonly known in the Agency as "cleaners"—are assigned to each Region for exactly this sort of contingency. Each Eastern Region has two such teams, while the Western Bureau maintains one team in each Region and an extra team attached directly to the Denver Facility.

When requesting field office support, in addition to the entity's Class, send the following color codes to better enable the office to prioritize its resource allotments:

Green: Entity poses no threat to human life now or in the foreseeable future. Probability of Event exposure due to activity is slight.

Yellow: Entity poses moderate threat to human life. Probability of Event exposure due to activity is moderate.

Red: Entity poses definite threat to human life. High probability of Event exposure.

Black: Entity responsible for attacks on humans. Event exposure is probable barring Agency intervention.

Eliminating Event Phenomena

You've completed all the steps of your assignment up to, and including, classifying the phenomenon or entity you're facing. All that's left is to eliminate the source.

And that's the tricky part.

The problem in dealing with Event-related incidents is that nearly every one is unique in some fashion. So much so that trying to give you a pat set of instructions on how to eliminate them would more than likely get you killed because it would fail the first time you went into the field.

However, we can point you in the right general direction.

Trust Your Facts

If you've been following our pointers, you've spent a lot of time gathering information on your assignment—not just the incident itself, but affairs, rumors, and the history surrounding it. Use it.

Like we said, most Event phenomena are based in human actions. You've got a good chance of finding the key to eliminating the source of your incident in your research. That's the main reason we've so emphasized the investigative side of your field assignment—not just because we're sticklers for detail!

Myths and Legends

Surprisingly, folklore seems to actually be on target much of the time when it comes to Event phenomena. Or at least in the same county, if not square on the bullseye.

Before you leave the Salem Academy, we try to give you the most common legends and myths found in the occult to give you a hand here. If your research doesn't give you any clues to the entity's weakness, plumb your memory for possible folkloric methods of its destruction.

You may very well have to weed out useless details but once you have, it *might*, just *might*, give you a shot.

A Few Proven Solutions

Now that we've given you the necessary caveats, sometimes you're just plain caught empty-handed as far as a plan goes. In that case *some* idea is better than none at all.

Class I-d entities are usually fairly resistant to physical damage. However, these undead creatures usually have a specific body part that is vulnerable to attack. In the most commonly encountered form—the so-called "walking dead"—this is usually the head. Kill the head, and you kill the revenant, at least in that case.

A field agent tests a Class I-c entity's vulnerability to silver.

Unique Class II creatures are often susceptible to normal means of attack, although size, natural armor, speed, or a host of other abilities may make inflicting it difficult. Use dynamite if necessary.

Class III entities seem to maintain a link to the physical world, an "anchor," if you will. This item is usually something of either importance in the apparition's life or involved in its death in some fashion. Their manifestation can often be affected by acting on or through this anchor.

Last Resort

When all else fails, remember this: There are almost always two solutions to a investigation. The first is the one we've been talking about throughout this pamphlet—that's the Agency's preferred method by far. But there is usually a second approach, and that's the one used by cleaner teams.

The Special Threat Teams don't investigate haunted houses, they burn them to the ground.

Remember, the good of the Union outweighs individual rights.

Plausible Explanation

The very last thing you are responsible before wrapping up your assignment is presenting a plausible explanation for the incident. Just killing the zombie—again—isn't enough, you've got to explain to the witnesses that it wasn't *really* a zombie, but something totally ordinary. It's not that hard, but there are always a few complications. Here are the most common.

The Press

While it might seem journalists are a hindrance to this step, if you can manipulate them correctly, they can actually do your job for you. If you've been sanitizing any incident sites properly, you've already begun building the foundation for a good story. Provide the muckrakers some of the "clues" you've discovered and let them run with the doctored evidence. Remember, most folks are going to look for the believable answer, not the supernatural one.

The exception to this are the yellow-journalism rags, like the *Tombstone Epitaph*. They'll print anything. However, few readers believe what they publish, so play on that. Let them find ludicrous facts, or just outright lie to them. The more outlandish the story, the more foolish the publisher looks.

Recalcitrant Witnesses

In spite of how good your story is, you may find yourself faced with victims or witnesses that insist on denying it. This is a difficult situation, to say the least. The Agency tries to work within the strictures of the Bill of Rights at all times, but EO 347 is our final authority.

If necessary, you are authorized to slander, discredit, or even blackmail such individuals into silence. Don't expose the Agency in pursuit of these tactics, however, as that only exacerbates the situation.

Your last recourse lies in the hands of law enforcement. Remember we mentioned a few Confederate artifacts were a good idea to keep on hand? It doesn't take much effort to fabricate a treason or conspiracy charge if you're careful enough—and clever.

Appendix A: Field Communications

Corresponding with your field office or another operative isn't as simple as sending Aunt Emily a letter or telegraphing back East for a bank draft. Normal methods of communicating over distances aren't secure enough to safeguard Agency operations in accordance with EO 347.

There are two primary methods the Agency recommends field operatives employ to ensure the security of their messages. In fact, when possible, we advise you use both!

Dead Drops

Although its name suggests some particularly nefarious method of transferring messages, a dead drop is nothing more than a previously agreed-upon location where operatives leave and receive correspondence.

It's called a "dead drop" because the message leaves the courier's hands, and is, in effect, "dead" until picked up by another operative. This method protects either the originator or the recipient from exposure should the other be discovered with the correspondence.

The Agency often prefers to conduct equipment transfers in this manner, so as to protect the identity of undercover operatives.

Selecting a Dead Drop Site

The more out of the way, the better when it comes to dead drops. You don't want a curious passerby stumbling onto a sensitive message. However, you need to balance this against the difficulty posed by retrieving the packet.

For example, placing a dead drop atop the Capitol Dome makes it unlikely anyone is going to come across it by accident, but the agent retrieving it is going to attract a *lot* of attention—assuming she doesn't break her neck in the process!

The Agency has developed equipment to assist in preparing dead drops. Hollow railroad spikes, waterproof bags, and even false bolts are among the most common items of this sort.

Using the Dead Drop

First, both parties using of the drop must be aware of its location. That's common sense, but sometimes it gets overlooked. It's best to arrange this prior to departing on the mission. The Agency does have several preset drop sites in most major cities; check with your field office for locations.

Next, part of the idea behind the dead drop is to prevent either party using it from being seen together, you need to arrange a signal for when a message is dropped. A chalk "X" on a fence, a specific flower arrangement displayed in a front window, or similar methods all work, but these must also be agreed upon prior to beginning the investigation. When using one of the prearranged drop sites, check with your field office—most already have established codes associated with them.

Dead Drops and Seccurity

Dead drops are used primarily to protect the operative and/or informant involved. When properly selected, they also provide *some* security for the message or equipment being transferred. However, they are effective in this capacity only as long as they remain undiscovered.

For that reason, Agency policy requires all Event or EO 347 related correspondence passed through dead drop methods—or in any fashion outside an Agency office, in fact—to be encoded in some fashion.

An agent retrieves a packet from an underwater dead drop site.

Codes and Ciphers

The primary purpose of a dead drop site is to protect the correspondents. However, it provides no protection for the information once it's exposed.

For that reason, the Agency requires any official correspondence outside an office to be encoded with a recognized cipher or code. The Agency has several ciphers commonly used to encrypt correspondence. We'll address the two most common: the Stager and the Vigenère.

The Stager Cipher

On the surface, the Stager Cipher is nothing more than rearrangement of the words of a message in a predesignated pattern. However, it remains our most effective code to date.

The message is laid out in rectangular table by columns. Any empty spaces at the end of a column are filled by designated "null" words. The operative then rearranges the message according to a specific "route" taken through the column. At the beginning of the coded message, the operative includes a single word that tells how many columns he used and further more identifies the route he used to arrange the message.

Stager Cipher Example

An operative wants to encrypt the following message:

"Believe investigated incident related to night rider activity in assigned locality."

The operative uses the pattern called "Willow" to set up the code. Willow uses four columns to set up the table, so laid out with the null word "fig" included, it looks like this:

Believe	investigated	incident	related
to	night	rider	activity
in	assigned	locality	fig

Following the Willow pattern, the operative begins at the bottom of the first column, reads up, then down the second, up the third and down the fourth, starting with the code name.

The coded message, then, reads:

"willow in to believe investigated night assigned incident rider locality related activity fig"

Reading the first word, tells the recipient the pattern and columns used, so she merely puts the words back into their original order.

Your field office can supply not only the proper code names and patterns, but also null words and any code words commonly used to replace names and other proper nouns.

The Vigenère Code

This is a favorite of the Rebel military, but it works well enough, so we're not going to let a little thing like that stop us. Especially since you can set this one up fairly easily in the field.

Government Pamphlet 28-51A

The first row of letters is called the plaintext, the first column the key column. A key phrase is chosen and used to filter the message into the code by cross-indexing the first letter of the message with the first letter of the key phrase Then, take the letter found at the intersection of the corresponding row and column.

Vigenère Code Example

Here's a quick example of how to encode messge using this code

The note the operative wants to pass is:

> *"Meet at church at dawn."*

The key phrase used is the operative's name, James Thomas. The operative's name is the common default when communicating with a field office; that way the code can be used without prior arrangement. However, others may be assigned by the office beforehand.

To encode the message, all spaces are dropped and all letters are made lower case. Then, the key phrase is repeated in whole or part as many times as necessary to fill out the message:

> *meetatchurchatdawn*
> *jamesthomasjamesth*

And the letters are cross-indexed. Matching "j" with "m" produces "v", then "a" with "e" is "e," etc. The final phrase now reads:

> *ueqxsmjvgruqafhspu*

To decipher it, the recipient locates the first letter of the key phrase on the key column, reads across the row until she reaches the first code letter. Then she goes up that column to find the first plaintext letter of the message. She repeats with the second letter, and so on, until she's finished the message.

Obviously, without the key phrase this is gibberish. The only reason we've been able to decipher the Confederate codes is that they seldom change their key phrases!

Vigenère Code Table

	a	b	c	d	e	f	g	h	i	j	k	l	m	n	o	p	q	r	s	t	u	v	w	x	y	z
a	a	b	c	d	e	f	g	h	i	j	k	l	m	n	o	p	q	r	s	t	u	v	w	x	y	z
b	b	c	d	e	f	g	h	i	j	k	l	m	n	o	p	q	r	s	t	u	v	w	x	y	z	a
c	c	d	e	f	g	h	i	j	k	l	m	n	o	p	q	r	s	t	u	v	w	x	y	z	a	b
d	d	e	f	g	h	i	j	k	l	m	n	o	p	q	r	s	t	u	v	w	x	y	z	a	b	c
e	e	f	g	h	i	j	k	l	m	n	o	p	q	r	s	t	u	v	w	x	y	z	a	b	c	d
f	f	g	h	i	j	k	l	m	n	o	p	q	r	s	t	u	v	w	x	y	z	a	b	c	d	e
g	g	h	i	j	k	l	m	n	o	p	q	r	s	t	u	v	w	x	y	z	a	b	c	d	e	f
h	h	i	j	k	l	m	n	o	p	q	r	s	t	u	v	w	x	y	z	a	b	c	d	e	f	g
i	i	j	k	l	m	n	o	p	q	r	s	t	u	v	w	x	y	z	a	b	c	d	e	f	g	h
j	j	k	l	m	n	o	p	q	r	s	t	u	v	w	x	y	z	a	b	c	d	e	f	g	h	i
k	k	l	m	n	o	p	q	r	s	t	u	v	w	x	y	z	a	b	c	d	e	f	g	h	i	j
l	l	m	n	o	p	q	r	s	t	u	v	w	x	y	z	a	b	c	d	e	f	g	h	i	j	k
m	m	n	o	p	q	r	s	t	u	v	w	x	y	z	a	b	c	d	e	f	g	h	i	j	k	l
n	n	o	p	q	r	s	t	u	v	w	x	y	z	a	b	c	d	e	f	g	h	i	j	k	l	m
o	o	p	q	r	s	t	u	v	w	x	y	z	a	b	c	d	e	f	g	h	i	j	k	l	m	n
p	p	q	r	s	t	u	v	w	x	y	z	a	b	c	d	e	f	g	h	i	j	k	l	m	n	o
q	q	r	s	t	u	v	w	x	y	z	a	b	c	d	e	f	g	h	i	j	k	l	m	n	o	p
r	r	s	t	u	v	w	x	y	z	a	b	c	d	e	f	g	h	i	j	k	l	m	n	o	p	q
s	s	t	u	v	w	x	y	z	a	b	c	d	e	f	g	h	i	j	k	l	m	n	o	p	q	r
t	t	u	v	w	x	y	z	a	b	c	d	e	f	g	h	i	j	k	l	m	n	o	p	q	r	s
u	u	v	w	x	y	z	a	b	c	d	e	f	g	h	i	j	k	l	m	n	o	p	q	r	s	t
v	v	w	x	y	z	a	b	c	d	e	f	g	h	i	j	k	l	m	n	o	p	q	r	s	t	u
w	w	x	y	z	a	b	c	d	e	f	g	h	i	j	k	l	m	n	o	p	q	r	s	t	u	v
x	x	y	z	a	b	c	d	e	f	g	h	i	j	k	l	m	n	o	p	q	r	s	t	u	v	w
y	y	z	a	b	c	d	e	f	g	h	i	j	k	l	m	n	o	p	q	r	s	t	u	v	w	x
z	z	a	b	c	d	e	f	g	h	i	j	k	l	m	n	o	p	q	r	s	t	u	v	w	x	y

Appendix B: Recruitment

One of the less exciting parts of an agent's job is recruiting long-term informants an new members to the organization. However, it's an extremely important aspect that deserves mention in this field guide.

Informants

A reliable long-term informant is a valuable asset, not just to the field agent recruiting her, but to the organization as a whole. On the other hand, an unreliable one is a danger to the whole Agency.

In order to bring trustworthy informants into the fold, you need to understand what motivates them and how to keep them in the dark about the Agency's real mission.

Motivation

When we said "informant," probably the first thing that leaped to your mind was a paid snitch. That's certainly one type of informant; greed is a powerful motivator. There are other kinds, though, and often they're more reliable than someone you have to bribe to get the time of day from.

The first is the honest-to-God patriot who believes in the Union's cause. This sort of informant is willing to provide assistance to the Agency simply because he feels it's his duty. These are probably the most reliable of all information sources. They gain nothing by providing false information.

The other type is a coerced informant, a source who cooperates because she believes the operative or organization may take some sort of action against her if she doesn't. Often, these informants are Rebel sympathizers or criminals who fear official sanction for their action, but simple public embarrassment may be enough of a threat.

A willing informant is always preferred over an unwilling one. Even a bribed source is better than one working against his will. The coerced informant is likely to attempt to sabotage an investigation.

Of course, the bribed source may fabricate information to get the payoff!

Protecting the Informant

Once you've cultivated a reliable informant, you must protect them from exposure. Odds are, if they're worth the effort to bring into the fold, they've got access to information the Agency can't get on its own. If they're revealed as Agency collaborators, that access is likely to be lost and they may be in danger as well.

Don't let the informant approach you; you may be watched. If you have to meet at an unscheduled time, use a cover identity and have a good excuse for meeting the source.

Never let an informant feel he's in control of an investigation; it may fuel his ego, prompting him to take foolish risks.

All informants must be assigned a code name or number for use in reports and other documents to protect their identity.

New Agents

This one's tougher.

Basically, we're looking for sharp eyes and sharp minds. With tightly closed mouths. Try potential recruits out on an investigation or two and see how they handle the situation.

By the way, physical ability is a plus, but we're more concerned with wits than brawn.

If you find a good shooter without the brains to back it up, you may want to consider using them as a freelance troubleshooter. We can always use another good gun-for-hire on call.

Appendix C: Case Study

Okay, we've gone through the whole course of an investigation and then some—save those unpleasant reports—so we thought a good way to end this pamphlet is with the examination of a successful investigation.

The Assignment

Martin Ross, an operative assigned to the New York City Ward, was tasked to investigate a number of unexplained murders in the city that had been taking place for almost four months. The victims were all found badly mauled and apparently partially devoured. The attacks all took place inside the victims' homes—in many cases behind locked doors. All the murders occurred in a relatively small area near the city zoological gardens.

The Investigation

Ross had been assigned to New York for nearly a year, so his preliminary research was small. In it, however, he noted each attack took place on nights of a full moon. He also noted the attacks were in a relatively small area surrounding the city's zoological gardens.

Under the cover of a journalist, Ross interviewed several witnesses and learned that the victims had literally been torn limb from limb. In some instances, the witnesses claimed to have heard a growling prior to or during the attack. Finally, one of the subjects recalled hearing a noise on the roof following an attack.

Next, he arranged to view a couple of the attack sites, again under the guise of a journalist. He noted each room showed signs of damage—scratches in the paint, torn curtains, gouged furniture—indicating a struggle had occurred. He also found that each room in which an attack took place contained a fireplace.

Following up the comment by the last subject, he inspected the chimney of each fireplace. Not only was the flue of sufficient size to allow a man-sized creature to climb up or down, each had also been recently cleaned. Furthermore, the sides of the flues all showed deep and recent scratches, indicating that something had indeed climbed through them.

Solution

Compiling his findings, Ross reached a conclusion. The attacker had entered the homes through the chimneys. Each chimney had recently been cleaned, which meant a chimney sweep had recently visited each home. A quick check revealed all the victims had contracted a single company to do the cleaning.

Since the attacks had been going on for only a few months, he reasoned the attacker was a fairly new employee of the firm. A brief interview with the firm's manager confirmed this, and secured the name Conrad James.

Finally, the savagery of the attacks, the correspondence of each with a full moon, and the physical evidence of apparent claw marks on the scene convinced him that Conrad was Class I-c entity—a werewolf, to be specific.

Resolution

The next full moon, Ross caught the creature leaving its residence and dispatched it with a silver bullet. He then situated Conrad's body to look as though he'd been the victim of robbery.

Next, he traveled to the zoo, where he unlocked the cage of a new exhibit, a gorilla. He tore a piece of his own clothing and placed it in the cage. Finally, he wounded the creature with his pistol and rushed to the police station to report he'd been attacked by a creature, but had chased it into the zoo.

Case closed.

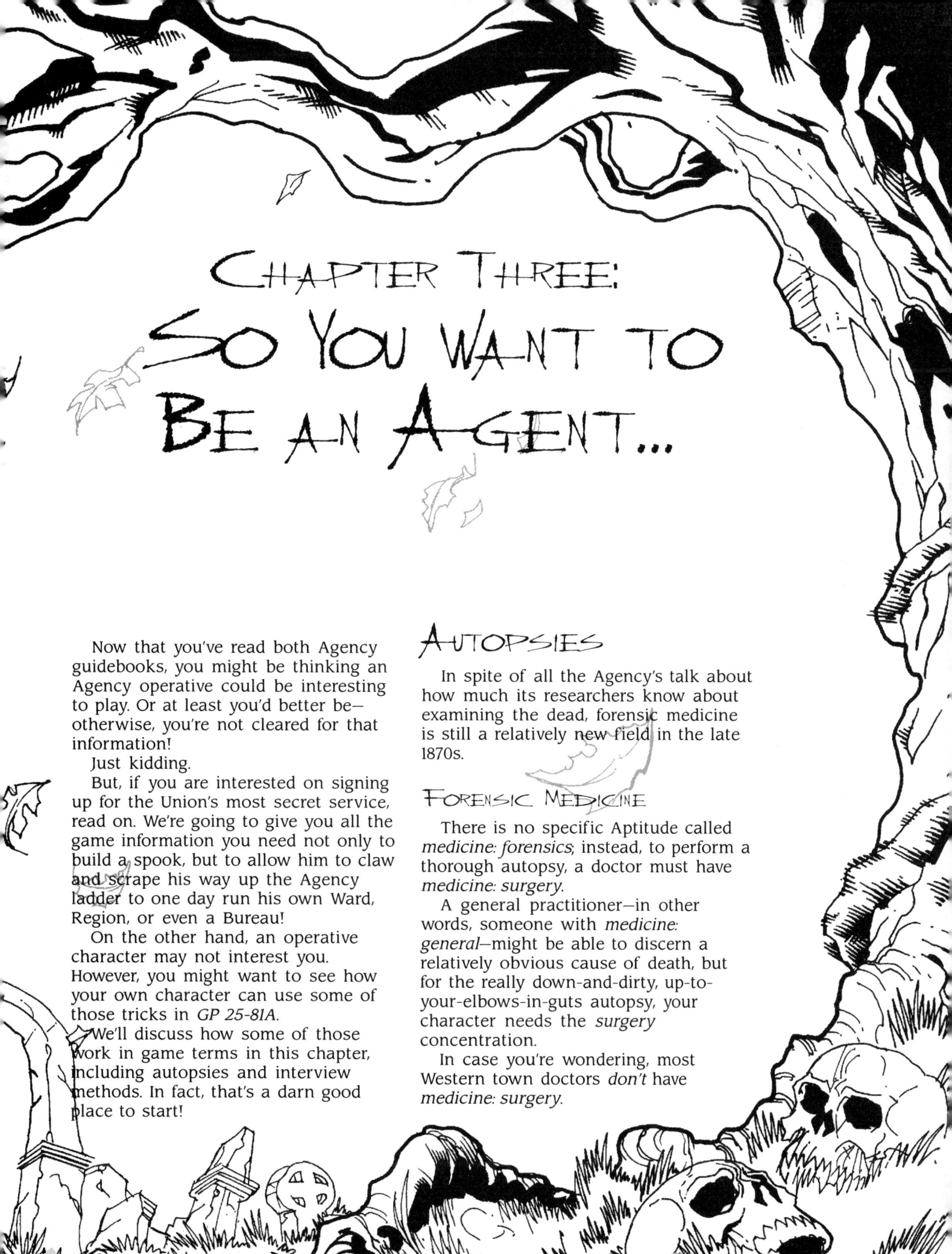

CHAPTER THREE:
SO YOU WANT TO
BE AN AGENT...

Now that you've read both Agency guidebooks, you might be thinking an Agency operative could be interesting to play. Or at least you'd better be—otherwise, you're not cleared for that information!

Just kidding.

But, if you are interested on signing up for the Union's most secret service, read on. We're going to give you all the game information you need not only to build a spook, but to allow him to claw and scrape his way up the Agency ladder to one day run his own Ward, Region, or even a Bureau!

On the other hand, an operative character may not interest you. However, you might want to see how your own character can use some of those tricks in *GP 25-81A*.

We'll discuss how some of those work in game terms in this chapter, including autopsies and interview methods. In fact, that's a darn good place to start!

AUTOPSIES

In spite of all the Agency's talk about how much its researchers know about examining the dead, forensic medicine is still a relatively new field in the late 1870s.

FORENSIC MEDICINE

There is no specific Aptitude called *medicine: forensics*; instead, to perform a thorough autopsy, a doctor must have *medicine: surgery*.

A general practitioner—in other words, someone with *medicine: general*—might be able to discern a relatively obvious cause of death, but for the really down-and-dirty, up-to-your-elbows-in-guts autopsy, your character needs the *surgery* concentration.

In case you're wondering, most Western town doctors *don't* have *medicine: surgery*.

CUTTING AND LOOKING

Actually performing the surgical aspects of autopsy—and we're not going into all the gory details here—requires the doctor to make a Fair (5) *medicine: surgery* roll. However, all that gets is a nice big "Y" incision on the torso of the cadaver and...

Oh, wait, we said we weren't going into *those* details, didn't we? Well, let's just say that first roll is for basic procedures; the physician doesn't actually discover anything about the cause of death from it.

Actually determining specific information takes another *medicine: surgery* roll, but based on *Cognition* instead of *Knowledge*. The exact TN is determined by the Marshal on a case-by-case basis, and discovering in-depth information might take a raise or two.

For example, figuring out the victim was killed by a stab wound to the gut is probably a Foolproof (3) TN. But, determining he suffered a stab from a long, bayonet-like object might take a Fair (5) or even Onerous (7) roll. And, discovering it was actually an enormous insect's stinger is likely to require a raise on that Onerous (7) TN!

AUTOPSY BY THE SEAT OF THE PANTS

Now, like we said, to perform an autopsy the character needs *medicine: surgery*. But, a really desperate investigator can recruit the town doctor—or even dentist!—to do an impromptu one.

The physician simply rolls his *medicine* Aptitude with the normal -4 modifier, so he's got a fair chance of catching the obvious clues, but he'd better know his stuff to find the really obscure ones!

Of course, a character can even try this without *medicine* at all, but all she's liable to get for her trouble is a bloody mess—and a lot of explaining to do to the authorities!

THE LIMITS OF MEDICINE

Forensic medicine isn't that far along in the Old West. Very little is known about ballistics, identifying remains, or, to be honest, medicine in general.

If it helps put things into perspective, fingerprinting is just a novelty for some Englishman in India at this point in history. He calls it "dactylography," and he's just begun using it to make sure workers don't claim their paychecks twice. It's years from application to criminal science.

In short, don't expect your surgeon to be able to run blood tests, check for nitrates on a cadaver's palms, or identify a corpse through DNA—or even dental records! He's pretty much stuck with good old visual observation.

Unless he's got a really neat gizmo or two...

INTERVIEWS

Back in *GP 25-81A* we threw out some really basic approaches for your operative to use when conducting an interview. All well and good, you're probably thinking, but how do I use that in game terms? That's a fair question, so here's the answer.

RUNNING THE APPROACH

An approach is nothing more than an opposed test of wills between the operative and the subject. Of course, you and the Marshal may want to roleplay out the approach—it is more fun that way.

Not counting bribery—which is its own reward—we gave you four different styles of convincing a subject to talk to you: friendly, sympathetic, belittling, and intimidation.

Now, if you've been playing *Deadlands* for a little while, or you've just got a sharp eye, you notice those match up fairly well with certain Aptitudes. Friendly corresponds with *persuasion*, sympathy with *performin': actin'*, belittling with *ridicule*, and intimidation with *overawe* (and maybe *bluff* depending on the circumstance).

Each of those is opposed by a specific Aptitude of its own. Roll out the contest as normal. At the Marshal's

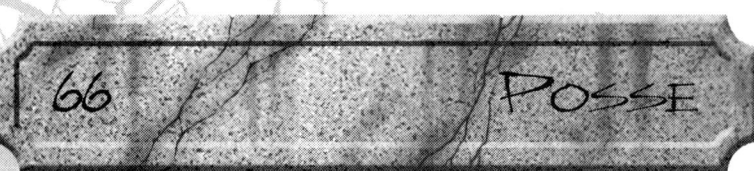

discretion, if you've picked the right approach to use, you may receive a bonus to your roll as well. Depending on the subject and the circumstance, this bonus may be +2 to +5, or more.

Pick the wrong one and you may get a penalty of the same amount.

If you lose, your approach failed. You can't try that method again on the subject until at least a day has passed. If you win, he'll talk, but won't reveal too many secrets. On a raise, he'll tell you most anything, and on two or more, he's liable to give you his mother's maiden name—and her current address!

Some folks might be particularly closed mouthed. Trying to pry Confederate secrets out of a Texas Ranger isn't going to be easy. He's probably going to get +5 or more to any obvious attempt to do so!

Questions, Questions

As to the questioning phase, you're on your own. However, should you think the subject is lying, you can make an opposed roll of your *scrutinize* versus his *Smarts* or *performin': actin'*. On a raise, you know for sure if he's telling the truth or trying to pull the wool over your eyes. Not what the truth is, mind you, just that she isn't telling it.

By the way, if you ran a successful approach, you get +2 to this roll as well.

Basic Training

Every new operative attends the Agency's Salem Academy for a two-month training period. There, they get a few very basic skills to prepare them for the horrors of the Weird West. Granted it's the bare minimum, but the Academy intends for it to be only a foundation for later development, not a crash course in everything Agency.

To reflect this, upon leaving the Academy, an operative must have at a minimum the Aptitude levels we list on page 68. If she has less skill than that, she simply doesn't graduate the course.

These aren't free Aptitude levels. If you're making an Agency operative, you must spend at least these minimum points to represent time at the Academy.

You're welcome to purchase *higher* levels in the Aptitudes, of course.

Freelance troubleshooters or potential recruits obvious don't have to purchase these levels. However, if they later attend the Academy, they must meet these minimums if they don't already have them prior to entry.

An experienced field operative that didn't attend the Academy doesn't *have* to take these minimums. Of course, the only ones who fit that bill are former Pinkertons grandfathered into the Agency upon its creation. We'll talk more about them in a minute.

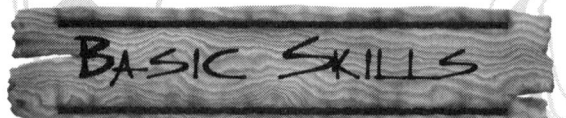

BASIC SKILLS

Skill	Minimum Level
Academia: Occult	3
Professional: Law	2
Scrutinize	2
Search	2
Shootin': automatics	2
Streetwise	1

BELONGIN'S

All new operatives are assigned a set of credentials, a badge, a Gatling pistol and a speed load cylinder for it. To reflect this equipment, all operatives must purchase a 3-point *belongin's: Agency equipment* Edge during creation.

The operative is responsible for these items and can't allow them to fall into the hands of anyone outside the Agency. Losing a badge or credentials is a serious mistake, and we'll discuss that under **Advancement** later.

However, the Agency understands Gatling pistols do breakdown, get swallowed by Rattlers, fall into the Grand Canyon, and so forth, so it makes allowances for this. Gatling pistols or speed load cylinders lost in the line of duty *are* replaced by the Agency. The operative must fill out approximately 10 pages of reports—in triplicate—explaining the circumstances of the loss. Additionally, an agent can't request a replacement while still on assignment—he has to wait until the mission is complete.

Pawning Agency equipment is a *very* bad idea, by the way!

OBLIGATIONS

All Agency operatives work for the organization full time. When a spook gets an assignment, he doesn't have the liberty of simply refusing it—he has to go. More often than not, these assignments are dangerous and require a lot of effort to complete. Furthermore, he is required to follow the orders of his superiors in the organization.

This constitutes a 3-point Hindrance, *obligation: Agency*. All operatives, regardless of background or position have this obligation.

Of course, he can always quit the organization, and we'll talk about that in a moment.

OLD-TIMERS

Operatives who were brought in from the Pinkertons when the Agency was first formed usually haven't been to the Academy. That means they *don't* have to have the minimum basic skill levels we just talked about.

However, if they want to progress through the ranks of the organization, it's a good idea for them to pick them up. We'll explain why that is under **Advancement** below.

Pinkerton carry-overs are still issued a Gatling pistol and credentials, so they must purchase the 3-point *belongin's* Edge we discussed on page 68.

On the other hand, since these operatives have been working on Event-related incidents for a little while, they *must* take the *veteran of the Weird West* Edge to reflect their experiences. That also means they can start with *rank (Agency)*, but they still must meet all the Aptitude requirements as normal. More on that under **Advancement** as well.

CLEANERS

Members of the Special Action Teams are all experienced operatives. They must have all the common basic skills we discussed. However, they get the most dangerous missions and their work is even more sensitive than the usual operative. As such, cleaners have the *obligation: Agency* Hindrance at 4 points instead of the usual 3.

Like other Agency characters, they are issued Gatling pistols and badges, so they have to purchase the *belongin's* 3 Edge to reflect this.

Lastly, all starting cleaner characters are *veterans of the Weird West* and have *rank (Agency)* 1.

I QUIT!

Every so often, an operative decides he's had enough of facing the unknown with a piddly little Gatling pistol and files his walking papers.

The Agency does allow spooks to leave the organization, but it requires them to swear to secrecy on what they now know. In effect, this is a 3-point *oath* to never reveal the Event–enforced

AGENCY CREDENTIALS

Each field operative carries a nice little two-fold leather wallet containing her Agency badge on one side and her identification on the opposite fold.

The Identification carries a paraphrase from EO 347 that directs Union law enforcement agents and military forces to provide the operative with "all due assistance in pursuit of his/her duties." Although it doesn't reference the EO 347 directly—that is forbidden, after all—it does bear the Official Seal of the Office of the President.

As we mentioned earlier, even though it provides them to all operatives, the Agency strongly discourages field operatives from whipping out their credentials at the drop of a hat. New field operatives who use their credentials often find their superiors do *not* bail them out of the trouble blatant badge-flashing might cause them!

by lifetime imprisonment for treason if broken!

ADVANCEMENT

Not all agents are created equal, to paraphrase an old adage. And, since we're spouting cliches, we might as well add, "The cream rises to the top."

What we're getting at is that the Agency has a system of advancement in which operatives can rise to higher levels of authority—and responsibility—within the organization.

AGENCY RANK

An operative's level in the Agency is represented by the Edge *rank (Agency)*. There are five levels to *rank (Agency)*, just like the regular Edge. However, unlike other Edges, though, this one usually can't be purchased at creation.

Technically there are six levels to *rank (Agency)*. Most starting spooks actually have *rank (Agency)* 0 but it doesn't provide any benefits to the hero, so you can even leave it off the character sheet if you want.

Ex-Pinkertons and cleaner operatives are exceptions to this, and of course your Marshal may make more if he likes. However, in no case should a starting character have more than one level of *rank (Agency)*.

Most of the time, though, *rank (Agency)* must be earned through play. And how do you do that?!

Minimum Skills

First, the Agency has developed a set of tests to ensure an operative has the necessary abilities to progress to the next level. If the spook doesn't pass them, he can't get the promotion, although he can later retake them.

In game terms, this just means there are certain minimum Aptitude levels your character must have for each level.

The table below details the Aptitudes and the minimum level your operative must have in order to be eligible for the next level of *rank (Agency)*.

Agency Advancement

Aptitude	Rank				
	1	2	3	4	5
Academia: occult	3	4	4	5	6
Disguise	1	2	3	3	3
Professional: law	2	3	4	4	5
Scrutinize	3	4	4	5	5
Search	2	3	4	4	4
Shootin': automatics	3	3	3	3	3
Sneak	2	3	4	4	4
Social*	2	3	4	4	4
Merits**	3	6	12	25	50

*The operative must have any two of the following Aptitudes at the noted levels: *bluff, overawe, perfomin': actin', persuasion,* or *ridicule.*
These are explained under **Merits and Demerits.

Note that if you're making a starting cleaner or ex-Pinkerton with *rank (Agency)*, the character must have these minimum levels as well.

Your Permanent Record

The Agency isn't so caught up in bureaucracy that it promotes agents based solely on their test-taking ability. It also tracks the field performance of its operatives through a system of merits and demerits.

Merits

For every properly completed mission (i.e., the phenomenon is eliminated and the incident covered up by the field operative) the agent is given 1 Merit. Some truly extraordinary missions may result in an award of 2 Merits, or maybe even 3, but these are very, very rare and along the lines of rescuing an important official or defeating a phenomenon capable of affecting an entire territory or state.

You should keep track of your character's Merit points somewhere on your sheet. They are cumulative, by the way, so you need to earn 3 Merits to be eligible for *rank (Agency)* 1, 3 more (for a *total* of 6) for *rank (Agency)* 2, etc.

If your hero is either an ex-Pinkerton or cleaner and starts with *rank (Agency)* 1, while he must purchase the skills indicated on the **Agency Advancement** table. However, he receives his first three Merit points for free. Don't say we never gave you anything!

Demerits

On the other hand, if an operative makes major errors, he receives Demerits. These are subtracted directly from his Merit total when determining his eligibility for advancement. The amount of Demerits awarded depends on the severity of offense.

Failure to complete a mission may not automatically net a Demerit, but badly botching one surely will. Losing credentials is an automatic 1 Demerit

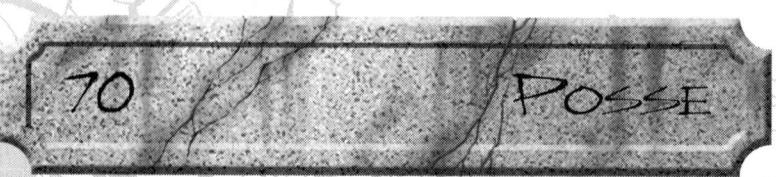

and selling your Gatling pistol is worth 3 Demerit points. Note these are for *first* offenses; repeat offenders get more Demerits for habitual mistakes.

If your agent drops below the minimum Merits for his *rank* in this fashion, he drops to the next level!

WHAT'S IT GOOD FOR?

First, unlike other Edges, you don't have to pay three times the value to pick up *rank (Agency)*, just a number of bounty points equal to the level you're going to.

Your character gains *friends in high places (Agency)* equal to her *rank (Agency)* to represent her authority within the organization. She also gets Requisition Points equal to 10 times her *rank (Agency)*. She can request all kinds of nifty equipment with these; see **Chapter Four** for more info.

RANK TITLES

Rank	Title
0	Field Operative
1	Operative
2	Field Agent
3	Agent
4	Special Agent
5	Assistant Director

On the opposite end of the scale, she's also going to accrue additional responsibilities according to her *rank*. For example, *rank 3* or *4* agents are usually tasked with administering Wards and *rank 5* with Regional offices.

It's possible for your operative to become head of one of the Bureaus, but that's entirely up to your Marshal to work out as best suits her campaign.

BRINGIN' HOME THE BACON

The other way *rank (Agency)* improves your operative's life is by increasing the amount of pay he receives for doing his job.

In addition to monthly pay, operatives are also eligible to be reimbursed for expenditures, or if they're clever enough to ask in advance, set up an expense account for these costs before they ever leave the office.

REWARDS

The Agency has, not surprisingly, adopted the Pinkerton policy of not allowing its operatives to accept rewards, bounties, or other outside payments. The Director feels such financial enticement may lead to a conflict of interests for agents.

Should it be necessary for the operative to take pay to maintain her cover, she can, but she must keep a detailed log of all received payments. At the end of the mission, she's expected to turn them over to her field office.

Violation of this policy nets an operative at least 1 Demerit, and maybe more, depending on the severity of the violation.

MONTHLY PAY

An operative receives pay according to his rank, as detailed on the table below. Cleaners receive an additional $25 a month "hazard pay."

MONTHLY PAY

Rank	Amount
0	$70
1	$80
2	$90
3	$120
4	$150
5	$200

REIMBURSEMENT

Finally, the Agency understands an operative may be required to spend money above and beyond simple needs to accomplish a mission. With that in mind, the organization has developed a few guidelines for reimbursing agents for expenses incurred in the line of duty.

After any mission, your agent may request repayment of expenses up to his monthly pay amount provided he produces ample documentation of those expenditures (Marshal's decision) and succeeds at a Fair (5) *persuasion* roll. Any more than that, and he's out of pocket—and luck.

EXPENSE ACCOUNT

Prior to a given mission, your operative can request a larger amount of funds, but it's a little tougher. He must provide written justification—in triplicate—to his field office. Then, your operative needs to make a *persuasion* roll against a Onerous (7) TN. Each success and raise nets your character an advance equal to his monthly pay amount—which he does have to repay.

The maximum amount he can receive in this fashion is four times his monthly pay and it *cannot* be combined with a post-mission request for reimbursement.

Going bust on either roll not only nets your spook no money, but his supervisor suspects he's attempting to defraud the Agency and slaps him with 1 Demerit!

NEW EDGE

Here's a new Edge that's useful for operatives and sawbones alike.

STRONG STOMACH   1

The character has a cast iron stomach when it comes to gore. Maybe she's an ex-surgeon or has just seen one too many murder victims, but whatever the case, it just doesn't have that strong of an effect on her anymore.

Whenever she fails a *guts* check because of blood, dead bodies (not *undead* ones, though), she can ignore any result that causes her to lose Wind or run away. She still suffers any other penalties, if applicable.

NEW APTITUDE

This Aptitude is particularly appropriate for operatives or spies.

PROFESSIONAL: CRYPTOLOGY

Associated Trait: Knowledge

This is the know-how to use codes and ciphers to encrypt a message. We don't mean the ones we showed you in *GP 25-81A*; those are freebies. This Aptitude is for other codes your character might encounter later on in his career.

Professional: cryptology rolls are based on the *Knowledge* Trait when your character is encrypting or decrypting a known code or cipher. If he's trying to break an unknown one, though, the Aptitude is based on *Smarts* instead.

Your Marshal assigns the TN to the roll based on the complexity of the given code.

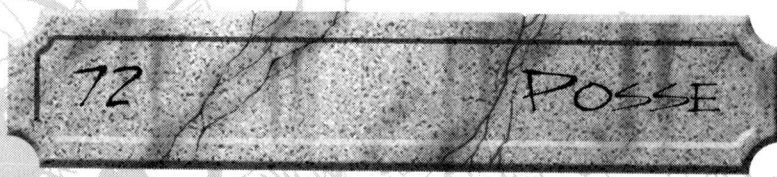

Agency Technician

Traits & Aptitudes

Deftness 3d8
  Shootin': automatics 3
Nimbleness 2d6
  Climbin' 1
  Drivin' 2
  Sneak 1
Quickness 3d6
Strength 3d6
Vigor 4d6
Cognition 2d10
  Scrutinize 2
  Search 2
Knowledge 4d10
  Academia: occult 3
  Area Knowledge:
    Denver 2
  Demolitions 1
  Language: English 2
  Mad Science 4
  Professional: cryptology 2
  Professional: law 2
  Science: engineering 3
  Science: chemistry 3
Mien 1d6
Smarts 2d12
  Streetwise 1
  Tinkerin' 4
Spirit 1d8
  Guts 2
Wind 14
Pace 6
Edges
  Arcane background:
    mad science 3
  Belongin's 3:
    Agency
    equipment
  Mechanically
    inclined 1
Hindrances
  Curious -3
  Obligation -3: Agency
  Tinhorn -2
Gear: Gatling pistol, spare cylinder, Agency badge & credentials, photo-reactive goggles, basic tool kit, box of 50 shells, $100

Personality

Okay, maybe this is my first field assignment, but I'm no babe in the woods—you don't have to worry about me. I've read several after-action reports back in Denver. I know the gist of how things work out here.

Sure I asked for this assignment! We don't get the chance to participate in many investigations in the SRF. Besides, the opportunity to field test some of my equipment in a real-world environment was just too much to pass up.

I'm certain the modifications I made to the photo-reactive goggles will allow them to detect cross-pollination of fibers in a live environment. Of course that's important! Okay, maybe not on this exact investigation, but in the future I'm sure it will be.

Quote: "Pay attention, agent, or you'll never learn how to use this equipment!"

CLEANER

TRAITS & APTITUDES

Deftness 2d12
  Shootin': automatics 4
  Speed load: pistol 2
Nimbleness 3d8
  Climbin' 1
  Fightin': brawlin' 4
  Sneak 3
Quickness 4d10
  Quick draw: pistol 2
Strength 4d6
Vigor 3d6
Cognition 2d10
  Scrutinize 3
  Search 3
Knowledge 2d6
  Academia: occult 3
  Area knowledge 2
  Demolition 2
  Disguise 1
  Language:
    English 2
  Professional:
    law 2
Mien 1d6
  Overawe 4
Smarts 3d6
  Ridicule 2
  Streetwise 1
Spirit 1d8
  Guts 4
Wind 14
Pace 8
Edges
  Belongin's 3: Agency
    equipment
  level-headed 5
  rank (Agency) 1:
    Operative
  veteran o' the
    Weird West 0
Hindrances
  Big Britches -3
  Obligation -4:
    Agency
    cleaner
  Self righteous -3
Gear: Agency duster (-4 AV), boot knife
in right boot, explosive putty (1 oz),
Gatling pistol, spare cylinder, Agency
badge & credentials, quick-draw
holster, 3 boxes of 50 shells, $175

PERSONALITY

If I'm here, you've got problems—big problems. They don't waste my particular skills on the run-of-the-mill Event phenomena.

But don't sweat it. Me and the rest of the team will straighten things out here just as soon as you tell us what's going on.

See, we're kind of like the Agency's gun. Aim us, pull the trigger, and we make trouble go away.

Just one last question: Is there someplace we can lay our hands on a case of dynamite? We didn't have time to restock our supply when our orders came down.

Quote: "There's nothing to see here. Or at least there won't be in about 30 seconds..."

MEDICAL RESEARCHER

TRAITS & APTITUDES

Deftness 4d6
  Shootin': automatics 2
Nimbleness 2d6
  Climbin' 1
  Fightin': knife 2
  Sneak 1
Quickness 3d6
Strength 1d6
Vigor 3d6
Cognition 4d10
  Scrutinize 2
  Search 3
Knowledge 2d12
  Academia: occult 3
  Area knowledge 2
  Language: English 2
  Language: Latin 2
  Medicine: general 5
  Medicine: surgery 5
  Professional: law 2
  Science: biology 2
  Science: chemisty 2
Mien 1d8
  Persuasuion 2
Smarts 2d10
  Streetwise 1
Spirit 3d8
  Guts 3
Wind 16
Pace 6
Edges
  Belongin's 3: Agency
    equipment
  Keen 3
  Strong Stomach 1
Hindrances
  Curious -3
  Obligation -3: Agency
  Stubbron -2
Gear: Gatling pistol, spare
  cylinder, Agency badge
  & credentials, doctor's
  bag, box of 50 shells,
  gold pocket watch, paper and
  pencil, $138

PERSONALITY

Trust me, very little surprises me any more, young man.

Well, to be honest, the time that cadaver sat up and attacked young Wilson, *that* was a little...shall we say, unexpected.

Nonetheless, I've seen corpses diced, sliced, chopped, grated, and even sautèed on occasion. I've worked on bodies that were little more than pulp and bone splinters held together in a bag of skin.

I worked battlefield surgery in Gettysburg, Cold Harbor, and too many other killing grounds to remember.

Now, since I've joined the Agency, I've plunged my arms up to the elbows into the remains of some abomination ne'er dreamt of—even in the imagination of God himself, I'd wager.

Now exactly what is it you expect I'll find so "unusual" about this case?

Quote: "He's dead, James—shoot him in the head before he gets back up!"

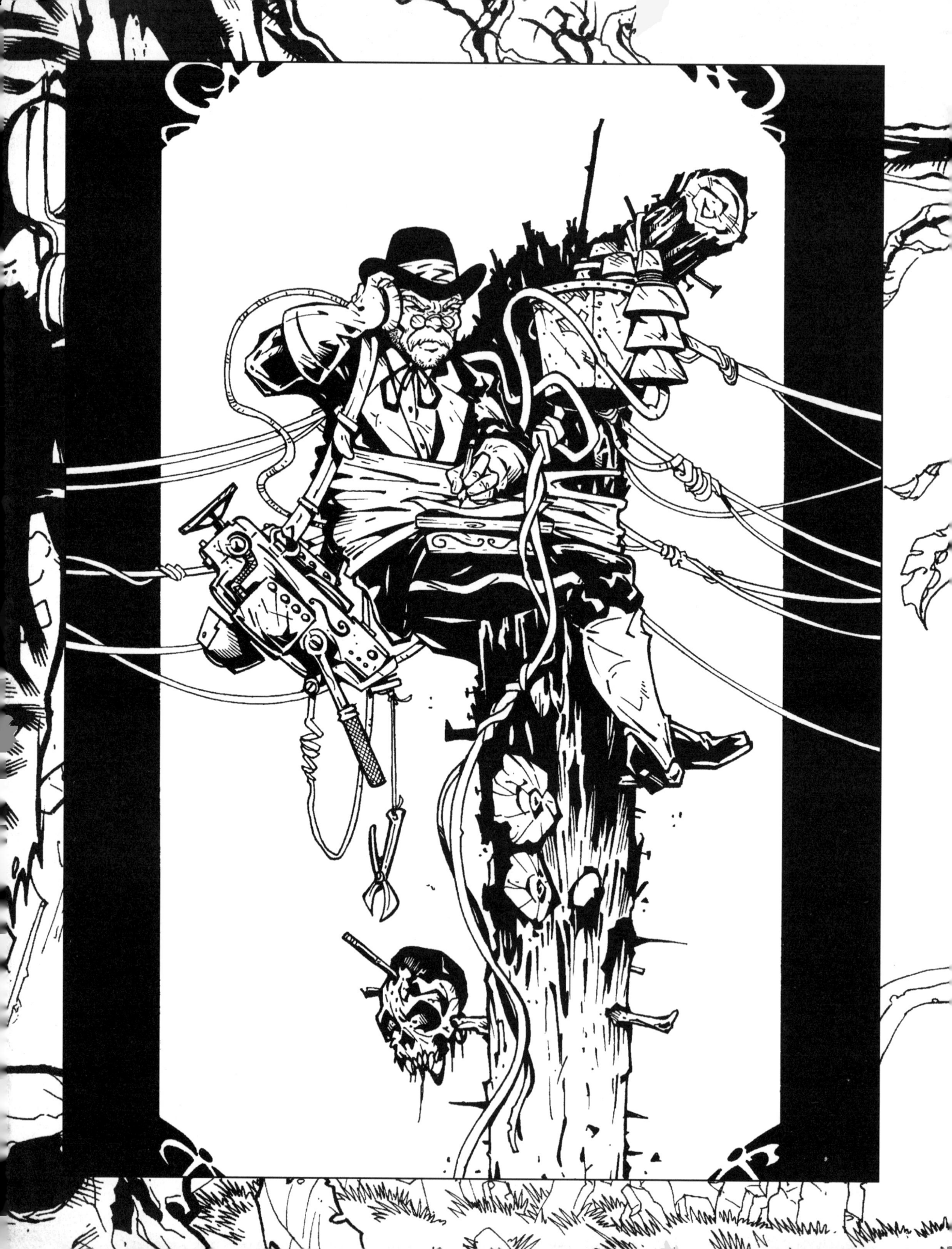

CHAPTER FOUR: TOOLS O' THE TRADE

What self-respecting Agency operative would go on a field mission without getting his hands on the best possible equipment the organization had to offer—or at least would offer *him*?

Not one that wanted to live to see his next assignment, that's for sure!

Every self-respecting operative starts her career with a Gatling pistol. That weapon is purchased with the *belongin's* Edge during character creation as we explained earlier. From time to time—okay, *most* of the time—the field operative is going to want more than just a simple fast-shooting pistol.

REQUISITION POINTS

That's where the operative's rank comes in handy. Once the character has proven herself a reliable field operative, the Agency is willing to loan additional special equipment for her investigations.

Each piece of equipment has a Requisition Point value. An Agency field operative has 10 Requisition Points equal for each point of *Agency rank*.

For example, Leslie, an Agent (Rank 2), has 20 Requisition Points to spend on equipment. She can spend all of her points on a single powerful item, or split them among a number of smaller ones. Starting spooks (*rank 0*) have *no* Requisition Points!

One important note: Equipment gained in this fashion is *not* the property of the operative. The Agency only loans the equipment to her on a temporary basis, usually, the course of a single investigation. At the end of that time, she's expected to return it in good working order.

An agent that consistently breaks—or worse, loses—equipment is going to have to do some fast-talking to convince her superior to let her have more on her next assignment!

Some items, like bullets and explosives are expected to be destroyed in the course of their normal usage. The Agency doesn't hold an operative liable for these expendables, although it does require the requisitioning agent to provide a full and detailed report as to the circumstances of the item's expenditure.

Supervisor Approval

Regardless of the operative's rank, all requests for equipment must meet with supervisor approval. Usually, the character's word is good enough, but for some unusual requests or investigations, the operative's boss (in the guise of the Marshal) may simply deny the equipment. If that's the case, the operative's Requisition Points can be reallocated to another item or items.

This shouldn't happen too often, though, but don't be too surprised if your request for an ectoplasmic calcifier is turned down—especially if your assignment is to track down a werewolf!

Another potential hurdle is availability. Not every field office has every device on hand. Your Marshal has the final say here as well, but he'll be fair.

Equipment

Not that we've already given you the basics on how your operative goes about requesting equipment—whether or not his request is honored—we're going to show exactly what's available in the Agency equipment lockers.

Equipment Descriptions

Each piece of equipment has a short paragraph or two detailing the device's description, function, and game effects. Additionally, every device has two entries: Requisition Points and Reliability. Mad science gizmos contain a third entry: *Hand*.

Requisition Points is the number of Requisition Points the operative must allot to obtain the item. In general, devices developed through mad science are rare and more difficult to obtain, thus costing more Requisition Points.

Reliability is a measure of a gizmo's chance of malfunctioning. How this works is detailed fully on pages 167-168 of the *Weird West Player's Guide*, but the higher the number the more reliable the device.

You'll notice most Agency gizmos have a high reliability rating; that's because the organization exposes its mad science gizmos to strenuous testing prior to releasing them into the field. If the device has a rating of **NA** in *Reliability*, it is a normal (albeit unique and advanced) piece of equipment and not subject to malfunctions.

119

Hand is only present on mad science gizmos. This entry is for those mad scientists keeping score at home and interested in developing the gadgets on their own. Obviously, in order to develop a piece of Agency equipment, the inventor must have gotten a look at an example—or have a really good imagination!

Equipment Lists

We've broken the list down into sections by the general purpose of the items in question, like Communications, Surveillance, and Weapons. Within each section, you'll find both normal and exotic (i.e. mad-science created) equipment.

Communications

These are pieces of equipment and tools designed to either enable faster or more secure communication between Agency operatives. Often communication equipment is used in conjunction with other types of devices to enhance its effectiveness. Dead-drop and concealed compartments are good choices for combinations of this sort.

Code Wheel

Requisition Points: 2 points
Reliability: NA

In the Operations manual, we showed you a couple of different ciphers regularly used by operatives to encode messages. The code wheel is simply another method of encrypting communications.

These devices are flat disks with two or more rows of alphabets inscribed along the outer rim. Each alphabet is on its own free-turning wheel, allowing the user to spin them to different alignments.

To use the wheel, the operative lines up the letter *A* on the inner wheel with a designated letter—or even number—on the outer one. Then, the message is translated by substituting the replacing each letter in the message with the matching one on the outer wheel.

To properly translate the code back into its original message, the recipient must have access to an identical code wheel and know the index letter or number used by the encrypting operative.

This device allows for fairly rapid encoding and decoding of a message. As long as the operative has access to the proper code wheel and knows the index letters, use of a code wheel requires only a Foolproof (3) *Smarts* roll.

Conversely, breaking a code wheel encryption isn't terribly difficult either. Unless other steps are taken—such as using a Stager cipher—a nosy cowpoke need only make a Fair (5) *professional: cryptology* roll (based on *Smarts*) to decipher the message.

The code wheel is actually just a version of a cipher known as a *cesarian* code—legend has it that Julius Ceaser was the first person to employ such a method of encryption.

Invisible Ink

Requisition Points: 4 (per vial)
Reliability: 18
Hand: Pair (Alchemy)

A determined spy can fabricate invisible ink with lemon juice, however Agency researchers have developed a slightly more complex formula for the organization's use. Better yet, prying eyes can't reveal what it hides with a mere candle flame either! Only with application of the proper reagent or use of photochemical goggles (covered on pages 88-89) does the ink become visible.

Each vial holds enough ink to scribe approximately 8 full handwritten pages. Along with each vial, a requesting agent receives enough of the reagent compound to reveal the same amount of writing, allowing her to send and receive messages in this manner.

Agency operating procedures still require encoding the message using at least a Stager or Vigenère Table, even when using invisible ink.

MICRODOTS AND VIEWER

Requisition Points: 3
Reliability: NA

Using a technology pioneered by Confederate spymasters, the Agency has developed special image-reducing cameras. With these devices, field offices can prepare minute replicas of most documents and maps. Operatives can then better secret these miniature documents from casual searches.

Each microdot is less than 1/10" square and can hold the image of a single 8 1/2" x 11" document. An operative can request up to 20 pages of documents be reduced for each 1/2 Requisition Point spent on microdots.

To properly view the tiny image, the operative needs a special, high-powered lens resembling a standard, if somewhat large, magnifying glass. The microdot viewer is included in the Requisition point cost.

An operative can make a microdot in the field using the viewer, but it requires a blank microdot—which she can request prior to the mission—the microdot viewer, and a camera of some sort. By reversing the viewer's lens and making a Hard (9) *professional: photography* roll, she can make a microdot.

VOICE PROJECTORS

Requisition Points: 13
Reliability: 19
Hand: Flush

These devices are based on a relatively new scientific theory known as the "Identity Field Theory" which states that certain properly prepared ghost rock nuggets keep some, as yet unexplained, connectivity. Voice projectors use this link to conduct sound waves over a short distance allowing operatives to maintain contact during surveillance operations.

The device consists of a pair of receiver/transmitter units. Each unit consists of two small cones—one an earpiece and the other a mouthpiece—each containing a piece of ghost rock covered by a rubber diaphragm and connected by a length of wire.

Each pair of units is matched and a single treated ghost rock nugget is separated and inserted into the mouthpiece in one unit and the earpiece in its counterpart unit. The rubber diaphragm inside the mouthpiece vibrates when an operative speaks into it and these vibrations are transmitted via the connectivity of the ghost rock nugget to the earpiece in the other, much in the way a pair of cans with a string work.

The projector has a maximum range of 150', but using the device at any range greater than 50' requires the operatives to make an Onerous (7) *Cognition* roll to understand a transmitted message.

CONCEALED COMPARTMENTS

These are items with small hidden compartments suitable for smuggling a message, map, or other item into an area. Often, this sort of equipment is used in conjunction with microdots to maximize the potential of each method.

FALSE COINS

Requisition Points: 2 each
Reliability: NA

Agency operatives have access to carefully manufactured hollow coins. The coin faces screw tightly together, concealing a tiny interior compartment. For practical purposes, only $5, $10, and $20 coins can conceal compartments of any useful size.

Each coin can hold a single carefully folded note or map up to 4" square. This is very useful for smuggling messages or passing information to another operative clandestinely. Alternately, a coin can contain up to 1/2 oz. of explosive putty (see page 85) but this makes the coin slightly heavier than normal .

The reproduction is excellent. Fortunately, if a recipient aware of the nature of the coin, she can easily detect it. However, anyone examining the coins casually will only note the differences on an Incredible (11) *Cognition* roll.

An operative carrying false coins should exercise caution, otherwise she might mistakenly pass the bartender one of the coins!

False Playing Cards

Requisition Points: 3 per deck
Reliability: NA

False playing cards are one of the most unexpected methods of concealing documents or maps. These cards are actually two ply; the face and the back are connected by a thin, gummy adhesive, allowing information and/or map segments to be secreted between the two pieces.

Detecting a false deck is difficult, normally requiring an Incredible (11) *Cognition* roll. However, card sharps seem to have an unusually good eye for catching out-of-the-ordinary decks. An Onerous (7) *gamblin'* roll tells a sharp-eyed card player something's up, so operatives should be careful about using these in a "friendly" game in the saloon!

Hollow Fountain Pens

Requisition Points: 2
Reliability: NA

This item is rather self explanatory—a seemingly normal fountain pen with a portion of its length hollowed to hold messages, or items. The pen is even constructed with a smaller ink compartment so you can still use it to sign your John Wesley!

Any number of items can be hidden in the pen; common sense should tell you in most cases—and when that fails, your Marshal will! Some examples are: lockpicks, two .22 caliber cartridges, 1 oz. of explosive putty, and so on.

Although a searcher might check for a secret compartment inside a fountain pen, there is *no* chance of discovering it unless the cowpoke specifically looks for it. However, if he does, finding it's as easy as shooting fish in a barrel; in this case, no roll is needed.

Hollow-Heeled Shoes

Requisition Points: 4 per pair
Reliability: NA

Hollow heels are available for nearly any sort of heeled foot gear, from traditional Western boots to ladies' formal shoes. The heel compartments are usually 2" square and 1" deep, but this depends largely on the type of foot gear. A high-heeled slipper has a narrower, but deeper compartment. Nonetheless, all have close to the same amount of storage space.

As with the hollow fountain pen, what does fit and what doesn't should be pretty obvious; a few rounds of ammunition does, a Peacemaker doesn't! In general, the heel compartment can hold about 3 times as much as the fountain pen can—in other words, 6 small bullets, 3 oz. of explosive putty and so forth. Of course the operative is free to mix and match what she puts in the heel.

Hollow Keys

Requisition Points: 2
Reliability: NA

Keys are usually the tool used to open locks protecting items of value, so who would think the key itself was the safe? Hopefully nobody!

The compartment in a hollow key is pretty darn small—only a single tightly rolled piece of paper about the size of one piece of paper money can be fit into it. However, unlike the other common smuggling devices employed by the Agency, the hollow key only opens when turned in a certain fashion. In effect, it's a miniature safe!

Detecting a hollow key is nearly impossible. Only someone who's been exposed to one in the past is likely to examine it. Even then, it takes a Hard (9) *search* roll to discover the compartment.

Opening the mechanism requires only a Foolproof (3) *lockpickin'* roll.

Covert Operations

This section deals with equipment designed to help an operative in pursuing an investigation without alerting any suspects to his actions. These gadgets help spooks get around security measures or into places they're not wanted.

It's not uncommon for these devices to be used in what may be perceived by non-Agency members as somewhat less-than-legal operations either! For that reason, the Agency advises utmost discretion when employing these items.

Automatic Key

Requisition Points: 13
Reliability: 17
Hand: Three of a Kind

Looking rather like a spring-loaded six-shooter with some sort of overly complicated dentist's probe protruding from the barrel, the automatic key is a locksmith's worst nightmare.

Using a complicated system of coil, the automatic key adjusts to the tumblers or wards of a keyed lock. A series of watchsprings mounted on the frame then rapidly gyrates and twists the probe within the lock, causing the tumblers to fall and the disk to spin removing the bolt from the striker panel.

The whole process takes only moments. Even better, an automatic key works whether or not the character has the *lockpickin'* Aptitude. However, some knowledge of locks does help the spook avoid accidentally damaging the automatic key through misuse.

The automatic key opens any keyed lock unless it fails its Reliability check. Thanks to the springs and tightly-wound coils, if the automatic key doesn't spin the lock, it usually suffers some sort of internal damage!

The Marshal may apply modifiers to the Reliability roll depending on the complexity of the lock; complex locks reduce the Reliability, while simple ones increase it. Also, if the spook using it has the *lockpickin'* Aptitude, she can add her level to the device's Reliability. Note that in any case, the automatic key can never have greater than a Reliability of 19.

Disguise Kit

Requisition Points: 7
Reliability: NA

This is exactly what its name implies. It not truly a gadget, but rather a collection of makeup, wigs, false beards, moustaches, and other accessories to assist an operative using the *disguise* Aptitude.

The kit also contains a few hard-to-come-by articles of clothing, including uniforms for both Union and Confederate officers, a selection of rank and branch insignia for said uniforms, and replica badges for both Union and Confederate law men (including U.S. Marshals and Texas Rangers).

While any operative can use the kit, it works best when the spook is skilled in the *disguise* Aptitude. It provides a +4 bonus to all rolls under that Aptitude if the operative has at least one level in it; unfortunately, it only provides a +2 bonus for default rolls.

The kit is fairly large and comes in a plain, medium-sized steamer trunk.

Letter Extractor

Requisition Points: 5
Reliability: 18
Hand: 3 of a Kind (Alchemy)

Another of the Secret Service's spy gizmos occasionally used by the Agency is a nifty gadget called the letter extractor. Unlike the document reproducer, Agency operatives find more opportunities to employ this device. The ability to open and reseal envelopes is surprisingly useful in many field operations.

The letter extractor is a wonder of alchemy, and actually composed of two separate devices. The first, the de-adhesor, consists of a squeeze bulb attached to a long, thin razor-like blade. Inside the squeeze bulb is a unique chemical concoction that causes normal adhesives—of the sort used to seal letters, for example—to break down on contact. Pressure on the bulb forces the liquid onto the razor blade which is then carefully inserted into the envelope flap. The chemical even works on sealing wax, allowing an operative to remove the seal without breaking it!

The second portion, the re-adhesor, is a spray bottle, similar in appearance to a lady's perfume aerator. The compound in the re-adhesor combines with the de-adhesion chemical to form a new adhesive. Thus, the new seal is only formed where the old seal existed, making detection of the surreptitious opening quite difficult.

Using the de-adhesor requires an Onerous (7) *Deftness* or *lockpickin'* (operative's choice) roll. Failure indicates a portion of the envelope or flap has been slightly torn. Resealing the envelope does not require a roll.

A cowpoke must make a Hard (9) *Cognition* roll to notice his mail's been pilfered. However, if the snooping operative failed the roll to open the envelope, the rightful owner gets a bonus to his roll equal to the amount by which the spook missed her *Deftness* TN.

Rocket Grapnel

Requisition Points: 5
Reliability: 18
Hand: Two Pairs

This handy device allows an agent to launch a small grappling hook from her favorite firearm. The grapnel is actually a tiny rocket that affixes to the barrel of the spook's gun—models are made to fit everything from a derringer up to a Sharp's Big .50. A special underpowered cartridge touches off the rocket when the hero pulls the trigger.

The rocket is strong enough to carry the grapnel and a small cord up to 50' straight up or 75' horizontally. Once it snags something at the other end, the operative can then use the small cord to pull a longer rope through and climb up or across as the situation requires.

Hooking the grapnel on a suitable target requires a *shootin'* roll for the appropriate firearm. The base TN is Fair (5) and the grapnel has a Range Increment of 10.

The gadget comes with two rocket motors and two suitable blank cartridges. Reloading takes 2 Action cards.

Dead-Drops

Normally, an operative uses a dead-drop to pass along sensitive information without risking exposing his contact. If so, he usually employs some method of encryption to code his message.

However, a dead-drop can also be used for a limited transfer of other equipment or to establish a hidden cache of vital supplies.

Technically, dead-drops are a form of communication. However, since they so often require specialized devices and practices, we've given them a separate category.

Ground Stakes

Requisition Points: 1
Reliability: NA

Ground stakes are roughly the size of railroad spikes, but with a screw-off cap and hollow compartment inside. Operatives place messages or maps inside and hammer the stakes into the ground at a designated location.

The top of the stake can be left exposed, or covered with a layer of dirt to further conceal its position from prying eyes. Often, in the latter case, the operative marks the location with a thin coat of photoreactive dust, allowing another to quickly detect it with a pair of photochemical goggles on pages 94-95.

A ground stake can hold a surprising amount of goods, including 10 rifle bullets, a single-shot derringer or 6 oz. of explosive putty.

The stakes closely resemble railroad spikes and a favorite drop site for these devices is along a rail line. This allows the operative to provide exact directions to the stake's location. For example, "The stake is planted on the northern side of the 238th railroad tie west of the Ogden Denver-Pacific station."

Hollow Bolts

Requisition Points: 1
Reliability: NA

Hollow bolts are a smaller version of ground stakes. Unlike ground stakes, however, hollow bolts can create a "moving dead-drop," allowing operatives to send and receive short messages or microdots clandestinely over long distances.

Like the name suggests, these are large screw-like fasteners with a hollow compartment reached by removing the cap. Agents commonly replace a normal bolt on a train car or stagecoach with these bolts, and use them to send a message to operatives in other localities. Field offices often use them to communicate with operatives as well; the method is more secure than a telegraph and with a little notice, the operative can meet the arriving train or coach and remove the bolt.

Locating the bolt requires an Incredible (11) *search* roll unless the searcher knows exactly where to look.

A hollow bolt has no more space than a hollow key; in other words, a single piece of paper is about all it can hold.

Waterproof Drop Bags

Requisition Points: 4
Reliability: 19

Waterproof bags are one of the most common methods of transferring large quantities of documents or small equipment caches. These bags are about the size of a pair of saddle bags, but, at an empty weight of 5 lb., are considerably heavier. The bags have a rubberized coating and a lining of lead pellets to weight them down in water.

Each bag can hold as much as a medium-sized saddle bag. Also, the bags come in joined pairs.

The Reliability score pertains to the likelihood of the bags leaking when submerged and allowing water damage, not to a mad-science malfunction.

Demolitions

Although the Agency prefers to work without resorting to flashy methods, there are some problems that just can't be solved without the judicious application of explosives—or a blowtorch!

Explosive Putty

Requisition Points: 3 per ounce
Reliability: 18
Hand: Flush

Explosive putty is a handy little invention that combines the combustibility of a ghost rock/gunpowder combination with the malleability of modeling clay. It's easy to conceal and even easier to use. And, better yet, it's more stable than dynamite!

No wonder it's a favorite tool of many field operatives.

Each ounce of explosive putty does a mere 1d8 damage with a Burst Radius of only 1 yard. Each additional ounce added to the mass adds another 1d8 to the damage, but nothing to the Burst Radius.

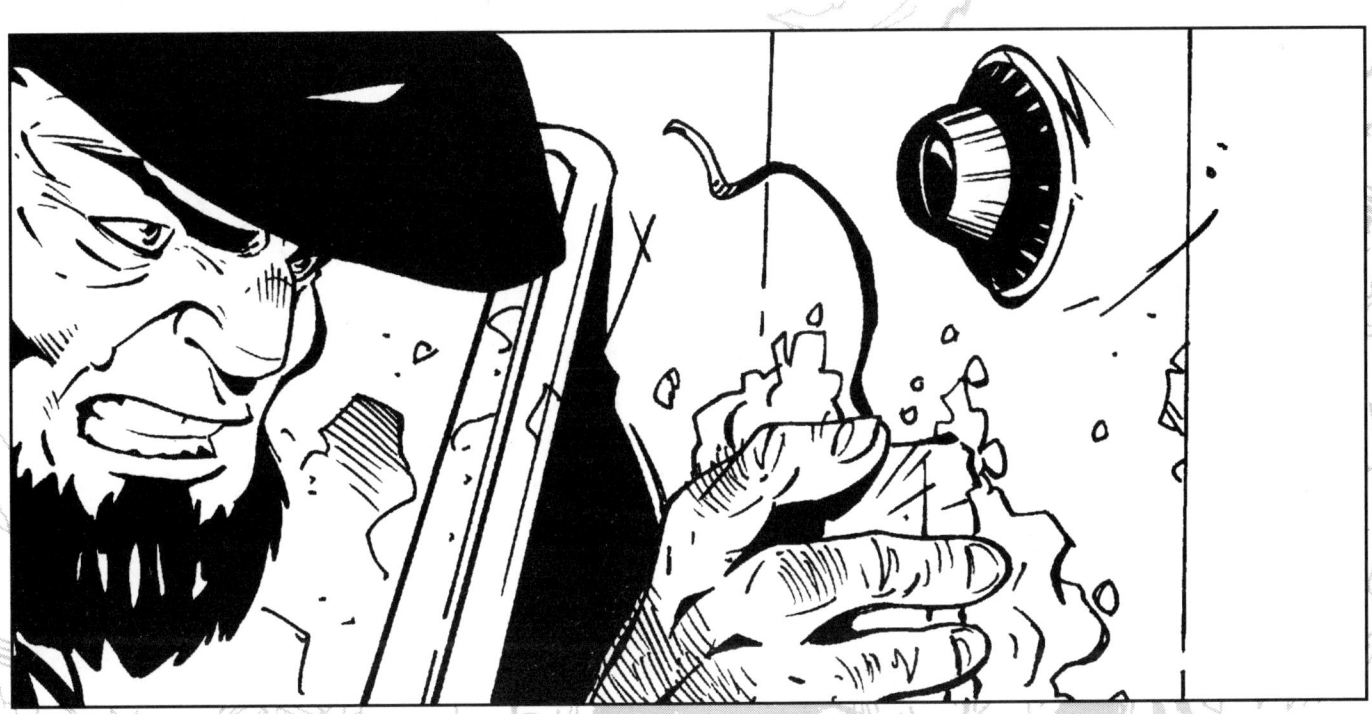

Pretty weak compared to an old-fashioned stick of dynamite or vial of nitroglycerin, but the putty has some advantages those traditional demolition tools don't.

First, an operative can use the putty as a shaped charge. By carefully forming the putty into a desired shape, the spook can direct more of it's power against a particular object. For every success and raise he gets on a *demolitions* roll against a Fair (5) TN while shaping it to the desired object, the putty gains AP 1. Shaping a charge only works when the putty is placed against an object—no AP putty-grenades!

Third, the putty can only be detonated by fire. Dropping the putty—or even a stray bullet hit—has no chance of accidentally detonating it. Most often a spook uses a fuse to set off the explosion, but in desperate situations he can touch it off directly with a match, but this exposes him to the explosion.

Finally, the spook can even form the putty along a door, wall, safe, or similar object so that it cuts a section of it away, such as a hinge, a safe's lock, or even just a door in a wall. The operative has to make an Onerous (7) *demolitions* roll to accomplish this.

Each ounce of putty can be stretched to cover an area up to 1' long by 1" wide when used in this fashion. However, putty formed this way looses much of its explosive force. The total damage done is equal to the number of ounces per foot of length. In other words 2 ounce of putty stretched over 2' does 1d8 damage total, but the same 2 ounces over only 1' does 2d8. For simplicity's sake we don't recommend you break it down into fractional amounts; stick with whole number multiples for these calculations.

Make sense?

In the last situation, the explosion must actually penetrate the wall or other surface; see *Smith & Robards*, page 37 for details on blowing holes in walls. However, the explosion only needs to do enough damage to blow a single 2' by 2' hole—in other words, the minimum damage. Also, the operative can also

shape the charge as detailed above to improve its efficiency.

Here's an example:

Arthur wants to cut a 2' by 2' hole in a brick wall so he can extract a safe that has thus far defeated his attempts to crack it. He needs a minimum of 8 ounces of putty—enough to line four 2' sides. Brick is fairly tough (Armor Value 3, Durability 5), so he decides to use 2 ounces per foot to up the damage to 2d8. He also figures it's a good idea to shape the charge as well.

Arthur first makes the *demolitions* roll to place the putty properly and gets a 7, easily succeeding. Next, he rolls to shape the charge to make it armor piercing—and gets a whopping 17! That's a success and two raises, making his charge AP 3.

His charge should now easily cut through the brick.

FLASH BUTTONS

Requisition Points: 2 per button
Reliability: 18
Hand: Flush

These buttons are made of a specially treated and hardened type of explosive putty. There's not enough putty in the buttons to do any real harm, but they are great for momentarily distracting opponents.

When jerked forcibly from an operative's clothing, a tiny fuse ignites and causes the tiny charge to detonate in less than a second. In game terms, the button detonates as soon as the spook pulls it loose and throws it. Holding one of these beauties after pulling it loose is a bad idea!

The button causes a loud pop and flash, rather like a potent firecracker. Anyone within 1 yard of the button must make an Onerous (7) *Vigor* test or loose her next Action Card.

The TN is reduced by one step for every additional yard a cowpoke is from ground zero, so at 2 yards from the explosion, the TN for the *Vigor* roll is only Fair (5) and so on. Folks more than 3 yards from the button when it pops might take notice of the spook's cute fireworks, but suffer no real effects from it. Of course, the operative should take care to protect himself form the blast or lose any advantage he might have gained gathering his wits!

The button can't be thrown farther than 5 yards; it's just not a good projectile. Tossing it effectively requires *throwin': unbalanced* and misses deviate 1d4 yards in a clockface direction determined by a d12 roll.

POCKET BLOWTORCH

Requisition Points: 6
Reliability: 18
Hand: Three of a Kind

This gizmo resembles a pocket fountain pen under casual observation, but is in reality a powerful cutting tool. A tiny reservoir of ghost rock vapors is contained within the body of the pen, and the writing tip is actually a focusing nozzle for the vapor. Turning the tip allows a thin stream of vapor to escape, which the spook then ignites with a match or other source of flame.

The cutting flame is only 2" long, but very powerful. It is capable of cutting a 6" inch line through 1/2" steel in 15 seconds. The reservoir holds enough fuel for 1 minute of cutting; after that, the pen must be refilled before it can be used again.

In extreme circumstances an operative can use the torch as a weapon. Since it's unlikely the hero has *fightin': pocket blowtorch*, she's probably going to have to default to another *fightin'* concentration or her *Nimbleness*.

The blowtorch is AP 2 and does 2d6 damage, but provides no Defensive Bonus. Don't add *Strength* to the damage roll; all the damage comes from the flame not the force with which the spook uses it.

OBSERVATION

This group of devices are intended to give field operatives a much-needed edge in keeping subjects (or things!) under surveillance. They include gizmos that enhance the senses, devices to intercept messages, and inventions that assist in discreetly following a subject.

FEAR DETECTOR

Requisition Points: 12
Reliability: 16
Hand: Flush

The fear detector is one of the most exotic pieces of equipment readily available to Agency operatives. Technicians at the Denver facility have been working on its development for nearly five years. Allan Pinkerton himself directed the facility to undertake the research that has resulted in the detector.

Pinkerton noticed early in his career that supernatural occurrences were more likely to occur in a region where the populace was already in a heightened state of fear. Although the Agency still doesn't understand this link today, Pinkerton felt his operatives would benefit from a gadget which provides them at least a clue as to the level of mental tension in an area.

The exact workings of the device are secret, known only to the technician who developed it and perhaps Pinkerton himself.

123

An oddly-shaped piece of metal, not unlike a tuning fork rests atop the body of the gadget. A single tube of liquid is embedded in the wood of the detector's body and changes color according to the level of fear in a one mile-wide area.

In order of least tension to highest, the colors progress as follows: Yellow, Green, Blue, Indigo, Violet, and finally Black. Any operative finding himself in a "Black" area is advised to proceed with utmost caution. It's not a bad idea in the other regions either, come to think of it.

According to some field operatives, striking the tuning fork atop the device seems to temporarily mute the level of fear in the immediate locality—affecting an area around the device of about 10 yards across.

Agency technicians deny these claims, and warn that such activity may damage the detector.

Homing Slugs

Requisition Points: 9
Reliability: 18
Hand: Straight

Homing slugs allow a spook to follow a target at a distance, even out of eyesight. Although simpler than the voice reproducers, the slugs are another application of the Identity Field Theory.

The device consists of a small slug of ghost rock, usually mounted in a metal sheath, and a compass-like instrument. The compass needle has another piece of ghost rock, taken from the same nugget as the slug. The two pieces are attracted to each other, causing the needle to point in the direction of the slug.

The effective range of the device is roughly 5 miles, but the compass provides no indication of the distance to the slug, only its general direction.

Only one slug is matched to a compass; multiple slugs would cause confused readings as the needle is pulled between the different directions.

Homing slugs have a number of uses. Besides merely trailing devices, some operatives have used them to assist in guiding them to a safe house or a campsite in the wilderness after dark.

A variation is available that can be fired from a modified bullet. This isn't much use against human subjects, as the bullet tends to pass on through the body, but for large abominations it works quite well. This special modified bullet costs an additional 2 Requisition points (bringing the total to 11) and reduces the Reliability to 15. The bullet is available in virtually any caliber, but always does 1 die less damage than a normal round of the same caliber.

Infrared Goggles

Requisition Points: 12
Reliability: 18
Hand: Flush

Smith & Robard's produces a set of light-enhancing goggles for general purpose, but sometimes Agency assignments require a spook to hunt abominations where *no* light shines. For those instances, there are infrared goggles.

Using a sequence of specially treated lenses, these goggles make differences in surface temperature, rather than light, visible to the wearer. They're not much use for reading in the dark, but they do give a spook the ability to see living creatures in absolute darkness.

In game terms, the wearer suffers *no* penalties to combat rolls with most creatures, even in total darkness. However, when the wearer is working with inanimate objects that have no temperature difference with the surrounding air, she suffers the full effects of penalties to her vision.

Infrared goggles can also assist in tracking an animal (or barefoot human) in the dark. As long as the trail is not older than 5 minutes, the wearer can add +2 to her *trackin'* rolls to follow the creature.

Intense heat sources like open flames (even a match!) are nearly blinding to anyone wearing infrared goggles. When exposed to such, the wearer must make an Onerous (7) *Vigor* roll or be blinded for 1d6 rounds.

A word of warning: Not every horror of the Weird West is warm-blooded—or even living—so operatives relying too much on these devices may one night run into a nasty surprise!

Listening Cone

Requisition Points: 2
Reliability: 19
Hand: Pair

This tiny invention is little more than a small brass cone the size of a shot glass, with a pair of rubber diaphragms inserted into the narrow end. Spooks use it for listening at doors, thin walls, and other barriers behind which folks hide to discuss nefarious plots. The wide end goes on the barrier and the narrow end into the operative's ear.

The device gives a +2 to *Cognition* rolls to overhear sounds behind the barrier.

Photochemical Goggles

Requisition Points: 8
Reliability: 18
Hand: Straight

These goggles allow a spook to detect the presence of different chemicals by enhancing each compound's reflective properties.

Photochemical goggles have a variety of lenses and filters attached to a rather ungainly headpiece that straps to the wearer's head. To use the goggles, the operative simply begins trying different combinations of lenses and filters until the correct combination is found.

The difficulty depends on how common the chemical being sought is, how quickly it breaks down, and the amount in which it is present.

The wearer must make a *Knowledge* roll against a TN which the Marshal determines using the factors above. For example, table salt is fairly easy and has a Foolproof (3) TN, while human body oils require an Onerous (7) TN, and ectoplasm has an Incredible (11) TN. The wearer can make only one such attempt; if he fails, either he's unable to locate the correct combination or the compound just isn't present.

The Agency has developed several compounds to use with the goggles, including inks, marking powders, and so forth. Detecting one of these known compounds requires only a successful Foolproof (3) *Knowledge* roll.

A pair of goggles comes with 16 oz. of a simple marking powder. Photoreactive invisible ink must be requested separately; see pages 78-79.

Sound Magnifier

Requisition Points: 7
Reliability: 19
Hand: Three of a Kind

This device resembles a standard phonograph. A large, trumpet-like cone is attached to the main box by a swivel. A rubber tube, similar to that found on stethoscopes, emerges from the back of the magnifier.

The cone captures sound waves emanating from a target location and directs them into the main box. There, a series of rotating diaphragms relays, clarifies, and magnifies the sound waves several times over, allowing a spook to eavesdrop on faraway conversations.

To operate the sound magnifier, the spook inserts the listening tube into an ear. Next, he turns a hand crank on the side of the box to start the rotation of the diaphragms. Then, he points the cone at the desired location and the magnifier begins capturing sound.

The magnifier targets an area 10' in diameter; sounds outside that area are not affected by its enhancing effects. The gizmo has a range of 200', but does require an unobstructed line of

SUITCASE CAMERA

Requisition Points: 11
Reliability: 18
Hand: Two Pairs

This is an improved version of the briefcase camera used by Union espionage agents to gather information. It's more reliable, but, as a result, also a little larger. The suitcase camera is about the size of a small travelling bag.

The camera contains enough plates for a dozen photos. Taking a picture with the camera requires the spook to make a Fair (5) *professional: photography* roll. Failure indicates the image is blurry, while going bust on this roll ruins the plate.

Of course, the plates must be developed to be of any use; a cowpoke making a Fair (5) *professional: photography* can do so easily with access to a darkroom.

The gizmo is fairly well disguised, and a casual observer won't notice anything amiss unless she succeeds at a Hard (9) *Cognition* roll.

TELEGRAPH TAP

Requisition Points: 15
Reliability: 19
Hand: Two Pairs

A telegraph tap allows an operative to cut into a telegraph line at any point along its length to intercept and send messages. The tap consists of a set of wire cutters, a receiving coil, and a set of ear phones.

A tap can receive and transmit messages. The user can choose to stop to allow the message through interrupted, alter it slightly, or stop it completely. This device is handy not only for monitoring the communications between individuals under observation, but also to aid in media control. A few changes to a pesky Epitaph reporter's story turn it from a dangerous exposè to a nationwide cover story!

In any case, to make proper use of this device, the character must make a Fair (5) *trade: telegraphy* roll.

Also, it's likely the agent must climb a telegraph pole to tap into the line, so a few points in the *climbin'* Aptitude or at least a good set of lineman's gear is handy as well!

sight to function. Even so much as a closed window stops the magnifier's amplification.

In game terms, any character using a magnifier can hear sounds at the target location as if he were standing there himself. For whispers or other faint noises, the spook gains +5 to his *Cognition* roll to hear them.

Trans-Mnemonic Olfactory Cataloger

Requisition Points: 9
Reliability: 17
Hand: Straight

By nature, humans don't have the most effective sense of smell. The trans-mnemonic olfactory cataloger, or "sniffer" as it's commonly known, serves as a crutch for an operative's underpowered nose.

The sniffer is a box the size of a brief case. On one side there is a small, spring-powered fan and the other is covered in small push-buttons and corresponding bulbs.

The fan pulls in the surrounding air and exposes the scent particles to a wide array of chemical samples and allows them to interact. Those to which the scent particles have a positive reaction cause a specific bulb to light on the outside. Noting the lit and unlit bulbs, the operative then compares the result to a fairly comprehensive list of known smells and their reactions.

If she's lucky, the scent has already been cataloged and identified. If not, she notes the combination and lists the reactions in case it is encountered again.

Most areas have a variety of scents and the sniffer filters each one, analyzing them in order from strongest to weakest.

WEAPONS AND ARMOR

The armory is the first stop most new spooks head for with their requisition forms. And while veteran operatives usually prefer more indirect methods of dealing with their targets, even they find the need for some increased firepower from time to time.

Luckily for both groups, the Agency has a wide variety of mechanisms of mayhem to support their needs.

ARMOR

What good is the best surveillance equipment and biggest guns if you're not alive to use them? All the smarts in the world won't stop a bullet when the chips are down—or a claw, come to think of it.

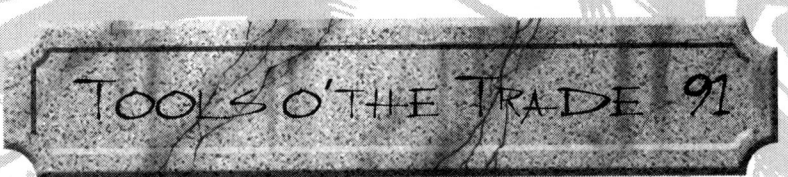
Once a field operative has a few missions under his belt, the Agency's selection of protective gear becomes a lot more attractive.

Agency Black Duster

Requisition Points: 4
Reliability: 19
Hand: Pair

This article of clothing is likely responsible for the new nickname for Agency spooks out West—"men in black." So many experienced operatives are enamored with this long black coat that it's become a trademark.

First off, the duster has heavy cloth strips and light chain armor pieces sewn into the lining to provide some protection for the wearer's upper body. These strips give the spook light Armor -4 in the guts and arms. The leather strips do not cover the legs, allowing the wearer to move freely.

Perhaps more importantly, the duster is cut along the sides to allow the spook to draw her weapon easily (no penalty to *quick draw*).. Furthermore, the pockets have slits so the operative can sneak her hands to a holstered weapon without them leaving her pockets.

There are numerous interior pockets where the spook can hide small items as well. Any cowpoke searching the wearer without removing it gets a -2 to all *search* rolls to find any item that reasonably could be hidden in the coat.

Impenetrable Vest

Requisition Points: 6
Reliability: 19
Hand: Two Pairs

"Impenetrable" is probably as misleading a title as the technicians could have given this vest. "Bullet-Resistant" or "It-Won't-Hurt-Quite-As-Much" would have been a fair deal closer to the mark.

The impenetrable vest is really anything but. It provides the hero's guts hit location with Armor Value 1 against all attacks—which means most (if not all!) bullets are going to be slowed down, rather than stopped, by it.

However, the impenetrable vest isn't designed to be a suit of armor. It's meant to provide some protection against attacks while not revealing its true nature to the observer. In this it succeeds quite well.

On the outside, the impenetrable vest looks exactly like a normal vest and is available in a variety of styles, from leather trail clothing to posh wool or tweed. It's also available as a girdle for operatives wishing to maintain a more feminine appearance.

WEAPONS, FIGHTIN'

Sometimes the black hats get the drop on an operative, or perhaps the Gatling pistol just isn't handy, or maybe the operative needs to take a captive while he's still among the living for questioning. Whatever the reason, spooks occasionally have to rely on brute force. For those occasions, the Agency provides a few special toys...

BLACKJACK

Requisition Points: 1
Reliability: NA

No matter how slimy the cultist, how low-down the outlaw, or even how bad either smells, there are times when it's necessary to take them alive. For those occasions, it's hard to beat a good, old leather pouch filled with lead shot!

Blackjacks do *only* brawling damage. This weapon is best used by smacking it against some poor sod's noggin. In that case, the wielder does normal brawling damage, but gets to add 3d4 to his *Strength* roll. For hits to other locations, it adds a measly 1d4.

Since the weapon requires a called shot to the noggin to be truly effective, it's best used in an ambush or surprise back attack. In those circumstances, the wielder gets a +2 bonus to her *fightin'* roll, bringing the total modifier, after the called shot penalty, to -4.

The blackjack doesn't have its own *fightin'* concentration; instead, it uses *fightin': brawlin'*.

A blackjack is only effective against living, human targets. It's pretty pointless to try to knock out a walkin' dead anyway!

BOOT KNIFE

Requisition Points: 2 per boot
Reliability: NA

No, we don't mean a holdout knife stuffed into a boot sheath—although some operatives do carry those as backup weapons. These boot knives are actually built into the sole of the shoe and are spring-loaded so the spook can extend and retract the 2" to 3" blades with a little bit of toe dexterity or perhaps a special heel tap.

A boot knife does STR+2 damage, but unlike normal kicks, this is true wounding damage, not a brawling attack. Although the *fightin': boot knife* concentration exists, the blade can be used with the *fightin': brawlin'* concentration, but at a -2 penalty due to its awkwardness.

GARROTE

Requisition Points: 1
Reliability: NA

This nasty weapon is a favorite of street thugs and assassins across the globe. A garrote is nothing more than a strangling cord, usually with a pair of small handles attached to each end so the wielder can get better leverage.

A garrote has no effect if used anywhere but the neck; even then, the wielder must get behind the victim before dropping the cord around his neck. However, if these conditions are met, the victim is likely to find himself in a whole heaping pile of trouble!

The wielder uses the *fightin': brawlin'* concentration to attack. To hit the neck, she suffers a -6 modifier to her roll. However, if she's attacking by surprise, she gains a +2 bonus to her own roll. This brings her total penalty up to only -4.

On each of her following Action Cards, she rolls a contest of her *Strength* against her opponent's *Vigor*—but she gets a +5 to her roll! If the victim fails, he takes Wind equal to the amount by which he lost the contest. Once he reaches 0 Wind, he drops unconscious and is at the spook's mercy.

The victim can attempt to break free on each of his own Action Cards by winning a contest of his *Strength*, *fightin': brawlin'* or *fightin': martial arts* (his choice) versus his attacker's *fightin': brawlin'* or *Strength* (her choice). He must get a raise on the roll to break free. However, until he does so, he can take no other action; he can't even cry out for help!

Garrotes can be concealed in a variety of places: hat bands, belts, trouser legs, etc.

SLEEVE DAGGER

Requisition Points: 3
Reliability: 19

Some gamblers keep cards up their sleeves; an Agency operative is likely to keep a knife up his!

This device is a forearm-mounted, spring-loaded knife that an operative can trigger with a flick of the wrist, instantly dropping the knife into his palm. If the situation demands, he can even shoot the knife at a nearby opponent!

Activating the knife is a Fair (5) *Deftness* roll. If successful, the spook instantly readies the knife; no *fast draw* roll is necessary.

If he chooses to fire the knife at his target instead, he must have the *shootin': sleeve dagger*. The spring is weak, giving the dagger a maximum range of 5 yards. Beyond that, it clatters ineffectually against its target, dealing no damage.

Spooks who fire the dagger in this fashion often find themselves weaponless! For that reason, it's best to use this tactic only as a last resort.

Thanks to the tight-fitting sheath, any cowpoke looking for one of these weapons on a spook must succeed at a Hard (9) *search* roll.

SWORD CANE

Requisition Points: 3
Reliability: NA

This weapon is fairly common, even among certain civilian members of society's upper crust. Still, that makes it no less effective when push comes to shove.

The sword cane consists of a long blade concealed within the body of a cane. A twist of the handle and the operative can draw 2 1/2' of sharpened steel with which to defend himself!

Unlike similar weapons, the Agency version has a reinforced body, allowing fighters trained with it to use it in their off hands in a defensive roll. This method is detailed on page XXX, under the description of *fightin': Agency sword cane* Aptitude. A cowpoke with the *fightin': sword* Aptitude can use the blade easily enough with no penalty. However, she doesn't get the bonus from the cane body.

WEAPONS, RANGED

Fighting hand-to-hand is fine if you've got no choice, but it's awful easy to get killed that way. Fortunately, most Agency operatives are canny enough to stand back and plug a target with lead whenever possible. Here's some weapons designed with that in mind.

AGENCY CARBINE

Requisition Points: 20
Reliability: 17
Hand: Straight

Field operatives noted that while the stopping power of a rifle round was helpful in pursuit of their duties, normal rifles fired too slowly. A commercial Gatling rifle was available, but spooks found the weapon too long and not as reliable as they'd like.

The Agency carbine is a smaller-caliber version of that design with shorter barrels and minor modifications to make it more trustworthy.

It has four revolving barrels and a top-mounted circular magazine. The magazine contains a clockwork mechanism to rotate the barrels as each round is fired. The carbine also has a spring built into its receiver to assist in the rotation, or to operate the weapon should the magazine fail.

The Gatling carbine requires *shootin': automatics* to fire properly. Swapping magazines takes one action, provided a loaded magazine is ready and at hand. Otherwise, it can be reloaded at a rate of 1 bullet per action.

Agency Shotgun

Requisition Points: 20
Reliability: 17
Hand: Flush

This is the Agency's version of the Gatling shotgun. Like the more common Smith & Robards' version, a belt feeds the paper shotgun shells to the weapon's receiver. However, the weapon also uses four revolving barrels to improve the cartridge feeding and ejection process.

Not only does it fire faster than the civilian version, the Agency model is noticeably more reliable—a vital trait for most field operations that require this gadget's awesome firepower!

The Agency shotgun lets a spook lay down a terrible amount of lead shot in a relatively short time. For this reason, it's a favorite with Agency cleaners. Unfortunately, it also packs a kick like a stampede of buffalos.

Each time after the first an operative fires more than one burst from an Agency shotgun in a single round, he suffers a cumulative -2 penalty to his *shootin': automatics* roll. The +2 bonus for firing a shotgun still applies, so the first burst is fired at a total +2 bonus, the second burst at 0 bonus, the third at a total of a -2 modifier and so on. Spending an Action card to recover control removes those modifiers as does the start of a new round.

Reloading the shotgun takes 2 actions if a loaded belt is handy; if not, the belt can be reloaded at the rate of 1 shell every 2 actions. Of course, the firer can also load one shell into the weapon and fire it single shot as well. Loading a single cartridge like this takes 1 action.

As with other Gatling weapons, a spook needs *shootin': automatics* to properly fire one of these thundersticks.

ECTO-PLASMIC CALCIFER

Requisition Points: 23
Reliability: 13
Hand: Full House

This is one of the most unusual items in the Agency's arsenal. Originally developed by a member of the Collegium, the Ghost's operatives in Gomorra got their hands on a prototype and shipped it back to Denver for study. The Agency technicians are no slouches themselves—especially when most of the really hard work's already been done—and in a short while the Denver facility had produced a few test models for special missions.

The device itself resembles a souped-up flamethrower with a single large tank and electrical coils wrapped around the firing nozzle.

It's exact mechanism isn't clearly understood yet, even by the techs that build it. Although it appears to be firing a stream of burning electrical charges, it actually sprays an electrically-charged solution. The liquid is a colloidal suspension of ghost rock particles mixed with a saline solution and a jelling agent for adhesion.

Against normal folks, the calcifier is fairly useless. Sure, it coats them with a disgusting goo and makes their hair stand on end, but that's about it. Not exactly the best weapon for a shoot-out with the James Gang.

Where the gizmo proves its worth is against non-corporeal targets, primarily Class 3 entities. The electrical charge, combined with the colloidal solution, can somehow render these targets temporarily corporeal—and vulnerable to normal attacks! This state wears off quickly, so the spook had best have another weapon close at hand to dispatch the abomination.

The operative makes an opposed test of her *shootin': ectoplasmic calcifier* Aptitude (yep, that's right—it has it's own *shootin'* concentration) against the entity's *Spirit* Trait. If she gets even a single raise, the target becomes corporeal for 1 round, plus 1 round for each raise beyond the first.

The tank holds enough liquid for 10 shots, but can only be refilled at the Denver or Boston facilities.

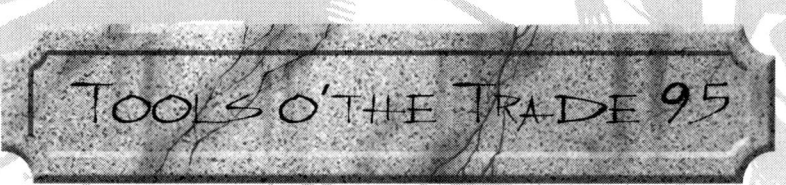
At present, the Agency has only successfully built 5 such gizmos. Needless to say, the organization is rather tight-fisted with these devices. Any operative requesting one needs a darn good reason for the Agency to agree to issue one.

PISTOL CANE

Requisition Points: 8
Reliability: 18
Hand: Three of a Kind

Building on a couple of designs recently released by the famed Smith & Robards company, Agency technicians have invented a concealable firearm that can be fired without attracting too much attention.

The cane has a long pistol barrel concealed in its length and a firing mechanism in the handle. The barrel is so long because it incorporates a series of sound baffles, greatly reducing the noise of the shot.

Even though the cane fires a pistol round, it uses the *shootin': rifle* Aptitude due to its odd construction. The cane holds a single .44 pistol cartridge and takes one action to reload. As it lacks any real means to draw a bead, the firer suffers a -2 to his *shootin'* rolls with the cane.

Shots fired form the cane are fairly quiet. A nearby bystander must make an Onerous (7) *Cognition* roll to hear the firearm. That TN raises by a level for each 5 yards the listener is from the firer.

Unlike Smith & Robards' rifle cane, the pistol cane is sturdy enough to use as a light club in melee without damaging its firing mechanism.

RING DERRINGER

Requisition Points: 5
Reliability: 18
Hand: Pair

It's just plain common sense to carry a backup gun in the Weird West. Too bad most of the black hats know that

as well. Many a spook has had a plan fail when a thug discovered his boot pistol or wrist derringer. You know what they say about hiding in plain sight...

The ring derringer looks like a rather large signet ring. The operative fires it by pressing a small stud on the ring itself. It only holds a single .22 bullet and many gunmen scoff at the tiny round. Those folks would be wise to remember the words of an old sheriff who said, "You ever been shot by a .22, pardner?"

The ring derringer has its own *shootin': ring derringer* Aptitude. On top of that, it's so inaccurate that the firer takes a -2 modifier for any shot other than one in direct contact with his target. And thanks to it's non-existent barrel, the tiny firearm is unlikely to hit a target at any real distance.

A ring derringer holds only a single round, but let's be honest, if a spook taking of these to a shootout, he deserves what he gets! Reloading it takes a single action.

On the plus side, the derringer can be fired in conjunction with a normal punch, giving a nasty surprise to the victim! If the spook makes a successful *fightin': brawlin'* roll, the derringer round hits as well--and in the same hit location as the punch.

The punch does brawling damage, but the bullet inflicts normal wounding damage on top of that. Better yet, if the spook's careful, onlookers may think the sharp crack came from the punch and not some hidden weapon!

WRIST-SPRING DERRINGER

Requisition Points: 5
Reliability: 19
Hand: Pair

The ring derringer is all well and good for emergencies, but for those times when a spook needs a little more firepower while still maintaining a low profile, the Agency offers the wrist-spring derringer.

A normal derringer attaches to a spring-loaded shaft strapped to the operative's wrist. A deft twitch of the wrist and the pocket pistol springs into the owner's palm, and, thanks to the specially-constructed mechanism, another sends it back into the sleeve as appropriate.

The entire contraption is easily hidden beneath a normal jacket or dress sleeve. A curious cowpoke must succeed at an Onerous (7) *search* roll to find the pistol—unless he already knows it's there, of course!

The mechanism adds +4 to the operative's *quick draw: pistol* Aptitude (or default!) when using the derringer, so even a wet-behind-the-ears tinhorn has a good chance at getting the drop on a hardened gunslinger! Of course, the greenhorn's still got to *hit* her target once she's gotten the gun out...

COMBINATION DEVICES

The old wisdom is that it's foolish to put all your eggs in one basket. Now, most of the time, that makes perfectly good sense—especially if some of those eggs tend to explode when dropped, like certain Agency equipment does!

However, there is a certain advantage to carrying a multipurpose device like those below. If for no other reason, at least when she's searched for weapons, the spook only has to worry about hiding one gizmo instead of five!

DESIGNING NEW COMBINATIONS

Below, we've listed three of the most common combination devices found in the hands of Agency operatives. By no means are these the only ones possible. In fact, Agency technicians can throw together most any amalgam of gizmos and gadgets the operative can imagine.

There are a couple of restrictions on what's possible, however.

First, no gadget in the combination can have a Requisition Point value higher than 9. Once you get into double digits, the item is too large or complex to tinker with that much.

Second, if any mad science gizmos are included, the device has a Reliability score equal to the lowest Reliability of any of its component gadgets.

In addition to the advantage of keeping the gadgets in a single, easy-to-carry package, combining them in this fashion has one other bonus. Total the Requisition points for all the pieces of equipment combined into the device and then reduce it by 1.

Sure, it's a little more time consuming for the technicians to fit all those gadgets together, but it saves the Agency a little bit on materials.! After all, those technicians are salaried workers. So what if they have to put in a little over time?

Now, on to the gadgets!

AGENCY WALKING STICK

Requisition Points: 12
Reliability: 16
Hand: Three of a Kind

Using the pistol cane as a base, the "Agency walking stick," as some spooks call it, is one of the most versatile combination gizmos commonly encountered.

The cane portion is a silenced firearm, just like normal pistol cane (see page 100). A twist of the handle causes a spring-loaded blade to emerge from the tip turning it into a fencing weapon, that while not as fearsome as a regular sword cane is still very capable of inflicting a lethal wound if properly used.

Firing the weapon requires *shootin': rifle*, while the sword uses *fightin': sword*.

Needless to say, the tip and blade must be removed before firing the pistol. The Agency designers were clever enough to build a fail-safe into the weapon; it simply won't fire with the tip in place. This protects the careless spook from a nasty backfire!

If both tip and handle are removed, a pair of lenses (kept in a compartment inside the handle) can be attached to either end. This turns the cane barrel into a powerful telescope. An operative using the telescope gains +5 to *Cognition*-based rolls to observe distant objects or people.

The handle, when removed from the cane can be fitted with one of the lenses making a magnifying glass. The glass gives an investigator +2 to all *search* rolls to find minute clues. By itself, the handle is actually a listening cone (see page 94).

The Agency walking stick is a popular piece of equipment for operatives Back East.

False Pocket Watch

Requisition Points: 19
Reliability: 17
Hand: Straight

To the casual observer, this device is nothing more than a gentleman's fancy pocket watch and chain. Beneath its gold-plated exterior, though, the watch is a complete operative's tool kit.

The back hides a false compartment holding 2 oz. of explosive putty and the watch stem holds a double-headed match for its ignition. The face comes off and on the reverse is a small code wheel. A quick twist and tug on the watch chain exposes a wire garrote.

The very outer rim of the watch pulls away to expose a spring-powered cable saw capable of cutting through a typical jail-cell bar in less than a minute. (This saw accounts for the extra Requisition Point cost.)

Finally, the clip on the watch chain is actually a homing slug. An operative can quickly detach the clip and use it to fasten the slug to her target. The minute hand on the watch serves as the locator arrow, pointing the direction to the slug, just like a normal homing device (page 93).

As handy as the pocket watch is, it has one failing. With all the gadgets crammed into its small case, there's no room to put a real time piece!

Field Boots

Requisition Points: 20
Reliability: 17
Hand: Two Pairs

Unlike the other combination devices we've detailed, the Agency's field boots look more at home on the range than a fancy eastern smoking room. At a glance, they're nothing more than a simple pair of boots complete with spurs that any cowpoke might put at the foot of his bunkhouse rack after a day riding the range..

Both boots house spring-loaded boot knives. To help distract a sloppy searcher, the technicians also included a normal boot sheath, complete with knife in the right boot.

The left boot has a hollow heel compartment, which is filled with 3 oz. of explosive putty. The top of that heel is a striker pad, capable of producing enough sparks to ignite a fuse—or the putty directly.

The right heel can be turned into a tiny foot-powered air pump by twisting the heel just so. A tiny air hose runs to the spur on that boot, which is, in reality, a small saw blade.

The spook can detach the saw from the boot and, by holding the mechanism by its frame, use it to saw through rope, wood, or even stone. It cuts 1" of rope in 15 seconds, 1" of wood in 30 seconds, and 1" of stone in 5 minutes. The saw blade wears out after 5 minutes of use, but the other spur is a replacement blade.

Finally, the outer soles of the boots are reversible and have a completely different pattern and shape on the opposite side. When using these soles to confuse her trail, the operative gives any tracker a -2 modifier to his *trackin'* roll.

The Requisition Points on this item include the cost of the air-powered saw and the reversible soles.

WHAT ABOUT A FLAMETHROWER?

Obviously, this list isn't inclusive. We've tried to include as many unique devices and gizmos as possible without turning the book into an equipment supplement. Undoubtedly, we've missed some. Hopefully it isn't the very item your character was hoping to request for his next mission!

If it's a mad science gizmo listed in another of our books (*Weird West Player's Guide*, *Smith & Robards* or even the upcoming *Collegium* sourcebooks), chances are the Agency's tinkering with it. Even if they don't have a perfected model, the Denver techs are always looking for a willing operative to field test a prototype.

For gizmos like that, the operative can place a request with his field office. It's up to the Marshal whether or not the gadget is available. If it is, determine the Requisition Point value by dividing the dollar value by 100 (rounding up in this case).

You'll find that this makes some gizmos hard to come by for all but the highest ranking operatives. That's because the organization just doesn't keep a large stock of this equipment on hand.

And, in case you're wondering why bulletproof vests cost so much by this method, it's because the Agency feels they tend to make field operatives think with their trigger finger, not their head. Body armor is usually reserved for direct action missions—undertaken by higher ranking operatives with lots of experience under their belts.

ALL I WANTED WAS A ROPE...

Okay—all these nifty gizmos are neat, but there are sometimes when an operative doesn't need anything quite so extravagant. After all, sometimes a good old stick of dynamite will do the job as well as the same amount of explosive putty

Like say when the spook needs to seal up that old "haunted" mine...

The Agency recognizes this fact, but it's not the local mining company store. It doesn't have the resources—or desire—to keep every single item an operative *might* need on hand, particularly when a short walk down the street to the general store can supply it.

Instead, an operative can request funds to purchase these more mundane pieces of equipment from her field office. For each Requisition Point she allocates, her superiors front her $5 in cash for outside purchases. Now, by "outside purchases," the Agency means real equipment, not a bottle of the "good stuff" and a bath at the local hotel! She has to provide a detailed list of exactly what she plans to purchase and why it's necessary to her assignment. This money is intended to be used as an expense account—see page 72 for details on how to get one of those.

At the end of the assignment, the Agency expects the spook to return the equipment (or what's left of it) to the local field office. Any operative unable to account for the funds is going to find herself in hot water with her superiors. At the very least, she's going to accumulate a Demerit or two. The Agency takes a very dim view of graft and abuse of funds!

AGENCY SHOOTIN' IRONS

Weapon	Shots	ROF	Range	Damage	Reliability	Hand
Agency Walking Stick	1	1	10	3d6	16	3 of a Kind
Agency Carbine	30	3	10	3d8	17	Straight
Agency Shotgun	20	3	10	2d6+4d6	17	Flush
Ectoplasmic Calcifier	10	1	5	Special	13	Full House
Pistol Cane	1	1	10	3d6	18	3 of a Kind
Ring Derringer	1	1	1	2d4	18	Pair
Wrist-Spring Derringer	2	2	5	3d6	19	Pair

WHY IS IT SO EXPENSIVE?

You might be wondering why it's a great deal more expensive to pick up normal goods through the Agency supply channels than an exotic piece of equipment like, say, a steam wagon.

First, the Agency has a fair-sized stock of mad science gizmos ready to go. Those gadgets are largely a renewable resource for the organization. Other, less exotic, equipment isn't. The Agency doesn't run a warehouse for dry goods, after all.

Second, when an operative wants something from the local general store, his superiors not only have to pony up real cash, they've got a lot of paperwork to fill out to explain the expense. The Agency is tight with its cash.

And trust us, they *don't* like paperwork anymore than the field operatives!

FIGHTIN' WEAPONS

Weapon	DB	Damage	Reliability
Agency Walking Stick	+2	STR+2d6	16
Boot Knife	—	STR+2	—
Blackjack	—	Special	—
Garrote	—	Special	—
Sleeve Dagger	+1	STR+1d4	19
Sword Cane	+2/+3	STR+2d8	—

POOLING REQUISITION POINTS

If you're is playing in an Agency campaign, you might very well have several field operatives in your posse.

For those missions involving more than one spook, the organization allows the operatives to pool some of their Requisition Points. This often lets the heroes acquire gadgets of a much higher value than their rank would normally allow.

Why trust a bunch of newbies with tools you wouldn't risk on a single operative?

Simple: It's likely at least one of the greenhorns is going to make it back. Hopefully, he'll bring the pricey equipment back. But if not, at least his superiors can take it out of his hide!

Seriously, though, the Agency has found that a group is a better risk when it comes to valuable devices than the lone wolf. Unfortunately, the need for secrecy and the scarcity of operatives often makes the group operation a rare bird in the Weird West.

When pooling Requisition Points, the operatives can add half of their available points (round down) to a group pool. Then, they can use the points from this pool to purchase equipment for the entire team.

While this isn't that great a deal when only two spooks are involved, it does let three or more operatives purchase equipment normally unavailable to them.

For example, three Field Agents (rank 1) can each add 5 Requisition Points the pool. This is enough to get them a set of voice projectors or a pair of infrared goggles—gadgets none could afford on their own.

The Marshal's Handbook

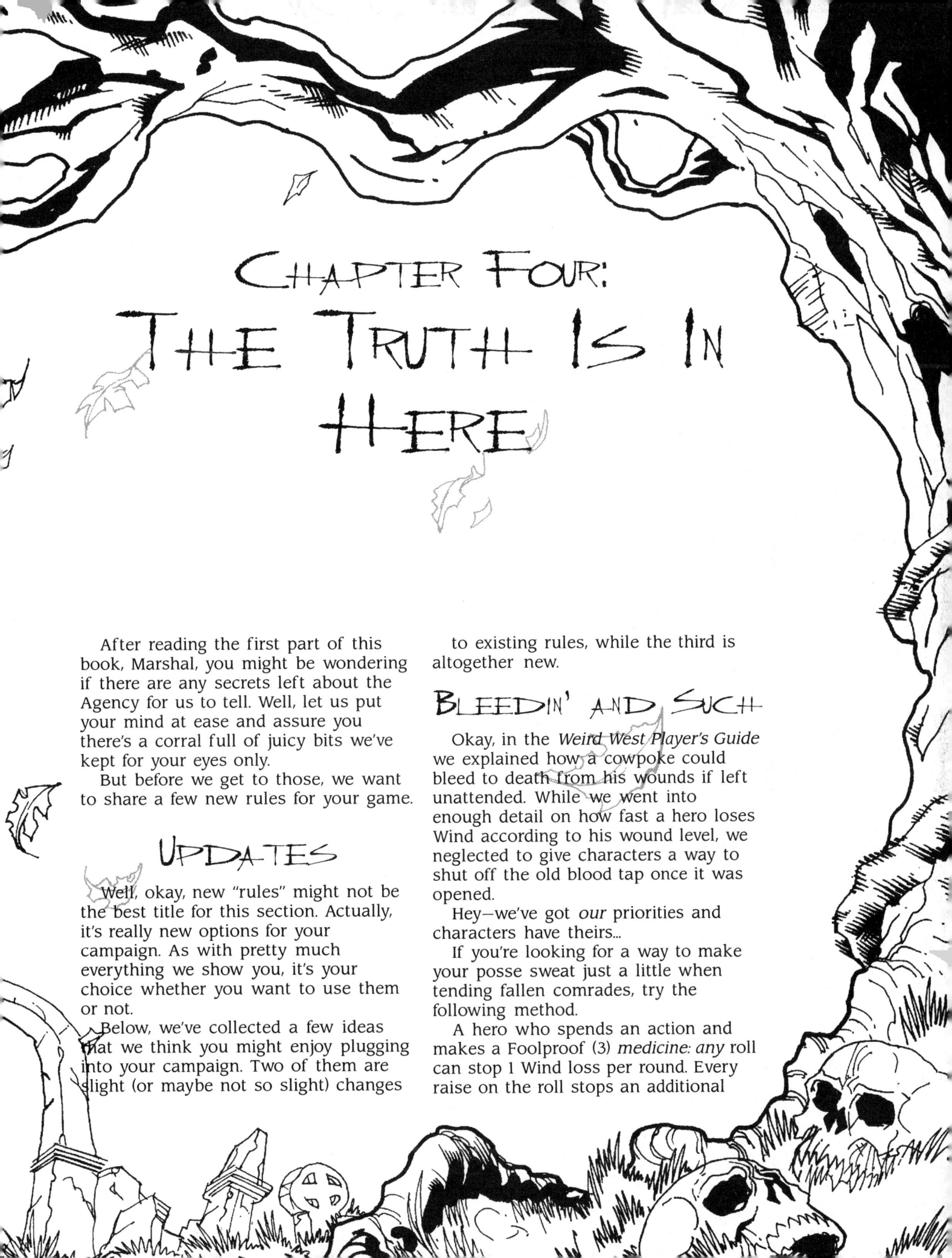

CHAPTER FOUR:
THE TRUTH IS IN HERE

After reading the first part of this book, Marshal, you might be wondering if there are any secrets left about the Agency for us to tell. Well, let us put your mind at ease and assure you there's a corral full of juicy bits we've kept for your eyes only.

But before we get to those, we want to share a few new rules for your game.

UPDATES

Well, okay, new "rules" might not be the best title for this section. Actually, it's really new options for your campaign. As with pretty much everything we show you, it's your choice whether you want to use them or not.

Below, we've collected a few ideas that we think you might enjoy plugging into your campaign. Two of them are slight (or maybe not so slight) changes

to existing rules, while the third is altogether new.

BLEEDIN' AND SUCH

Okay, in the *Weird West Player's Guide* we explained how a cowpoke could bleed to death from his wounds if left unattended. While we went into enough detail on how fast a hero loses Wind according to his wound level, we neglected to give characters a way to shut off the old blood tap once it was opened.

Hey—we've got *our* priorities and characters have theirs...

If you're looking for a way to make your posse sweat just a little when tending fallen comrades, try the following method.

A hero who spends an action and makes a Foolproof (3) *medicine: any* roll can stop 1 Wind loss per round. Every raise on the roll stops an additional point of Wind. The angel of mercy can attempt this roll on as many actions as she wants to in a round and the results are cumulative.

The only real danger is going bust while stanching the bleeding. This causes the casualty another wound in the hit location being treated. Maybe the inept sawbones tied the tourniquet too tight, or maybe she just poked the wound with a stick.

For example, Jason has taken a Serious wound to his guts and a Critical wound to his leg. He's losing blood to these holes faster than a sieve and is suffering 3 Wind loss a round.

Sister Cabrini sets about bandaging his wounds. She spends her first Action card and gets a 6 on her *medicine* roll. This reduces Jason's Wind loss to 2 a round. On her second, and last, Action in the round, she rolls again and gets a measly 4 on the roll. However, this is enough to stop an additional 1 Wind, and Jason is only going to lose 1 Wind next round.

Assuming she continues to treat him on the next round, it's pretty likely she'll be able to completely stop his bleeding.

Massive Damage

Marshal, if you've found your heroes running into a room with a lit stick of dynamite in hand once too often for your liking, you'll probably like this next option. Particularly if those same heroes walk out of the wreckage in the next round with only a Light wound or two and a few less chips.

On the other hand, if you like the cinematic feel of the way of dealing massive damage described in the *Weird West Player's Guide*, by all means, keep using it. The method we're about to detail is completely optional.

Attacks and other events, like falling, that cause massive damage now inflict their full damage to 1d6 hit locations. It is possible for the attack to inflict its damage to the same location more than once.

In the case of explosions, the number of hit locations affected is reduced by 1 for each burst radius crossed. An explosion with a burst radius of 5 yards, for example, would affect 1d6 locations, within 5 yards, 1d6-1 locations between 5 and 10 yards, 1d6-2 locations between 10 and 15 yards, and so on. It is possible for an explosion to affect zero areas—your cowpoke just got lucky!

Armor

Since damage is applied to specific hit locations under this new system, if you choose to use it in your game, armor works normally against massive damage. In other words, positive AVs lower the die type and negative AVs subtract from the damage.

Grim Servant of Death

This is one of our favorite Hindrances—when it's roleplayed properly. However, there are a lot of *grim servants of death* running around that are neither grim nor servants of death. Here's a suggestion from fan Stephen Joseph Ellis for making the Hindrance both.

Whenever a *grim servant of death* spends a Fate chip other than a Legend Chip to avoid damage, an innocent bystander or, lacking that, another posse member takes one-half the wounds he prevented!

Perhaps the bullet whizzes by the *servant's* head to strike the local schoolmarm, or the noseferatu he just dodged lands on a friend. Either way, he's going to find his welcome wearing out fast in any town he spends much time in.

Of course, if no one's around to take the wound, it's merely cancelled as normal.

Note that a *grim servant* doesn't get a Fate chip reward when his Hindrance makes someone else's life miserable—or even shorter! He only gets the reward for roleplaying his Hindrance well, or when the effects make *his* own life Hell.

Otherwise, these characters run the risk of recycling Fate chips endlessly in combat.

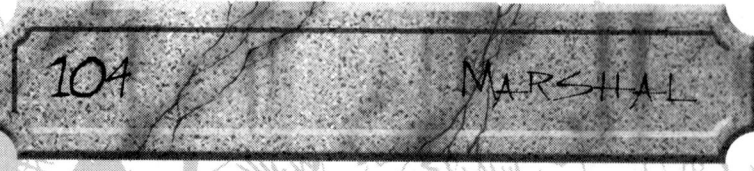

{"image_type":"decorative banner","text":"104","secondary_text":"MARSHAL"}

Running an Agency Campaign

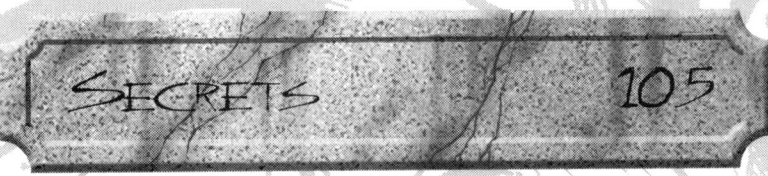

Now that we've thrown out all this new info for the Agency, you might find yourself swamped with players wanting to try it out with an Agency character. Honestly, we hope so!

However, as you've probably noticed, an Agency character is probably going to have just a slightly different outlook on things than your average cowpoke. Sure, they want to solve any mysteries they come upon or put any of your helpless abominations into Boot Hill—or at least they should, it's their job, after all. But, if they're paying attention to their mission, they're likely to go about it in a different way than the rest of the posse.

The Single Agent

If you've only got one or, maybe, two spooks in your campaign, you really don't have to do much to work around the characters. An agent is supposed to keep a low profile and meld with the civilian populace. Drawing too much attention to himself defeats his whole purpose.

Hopefully, your player running the lone Agency character catches on to this pretty quick. We tried to nudge him in that direction with the section on *GP 28-51A, Agency Field Operations* back in the **Posse Section**. Sometimes players can be cantankerously slow on the uptake though, and if so, just have his character's supervisor pass him a copy to read—again.

Ideally, the operative should provide you with a "man on the inside"—someone to help guide the posse to where *you* want them to be. In other words, with an operative, you never really have to work too hard to come up with a hook to get the posse involved with an adventure. Just give the poor sap an assignment and let him do all the work.

That way, the real work lays on the operative's player to manipulate the posse to fulfill Agency goals without giving away too much. Pretty sweet, for a Marshal, huh?

The Agency Campaign

The other possibility is that you end up with a whole stampede of players wanting to run spooks or at least freelancer troubleshooters. If so, that's great; it means we did our job right!

For you, it means less work as well, because now the posse's actions are pretty much directed by the beck-and-call of its superior agents. In other words, *you*, Marshal. Makes getting them involved in an adventure easier than falling off a log in a flash flood!

Of course, a campaign centering around a group of field agents is going to feel a little different than a regular visit to the Weird West. Instead of everyday heroes facing down horrors at High Midnight, you've got a group of agents undertaking the seemingly impossible mission of the Agency.

It takes an astounding amount of teamwork to pull off an operation successfully. Not only does the posse have to figure out how to overcome the local terror(s), it also has to do so in such a fashion that it can maintain a feasible cover story.

The possibilities for amusement abound—at least for you, Marshal!

INVESTIGATION

One thing you want to include a lot of in an Agency-oriented campaign is good, old-fashioned detective work. Think of an Agency mission as equal parts mystery and spy novel. Spooks should be just that, ghosts in the background—not dynamite-packing exterminators blasting everything in sight!

Odds are, if you've got a group that wants to play spooks, you're looking at a bunch of players that want to face a challenge with their brains and not their brawn.

By all means, cater to them! Everyone will have more fun that way.

ESPIONAGE

While the Agency isn't technically an espionage service, it operates like one in most respects. It keeps a low profile and its operations are considered top secret. Playing up this element of an Agency mission can go a long way toward heightening posse tension. Especially when the players realize that virtually everyone is a security risk to their mission!

You can add to the spy-versus-spy feel of the Agency by occasionally pitting the players against some of the more organized, occult-oriented groups in the Weird West. The Church of Lost Angels, Hellstromme and his lackeys, Kang's army, the Freemasons, and Black River are all excellent opponents.

You can even send them down South to really capture the sense of "danger at every turn" common to espionage stories. There, they can infiltrate a Texas Ranger operation—or even head further south into Mexico to spy on Santa Anna's Army o' the Dead.

A Little Help

If you're not sure about designing an adventure like this, take a quick read through the **GP 28-51A** section on field operations. There's a carpetbag full of hints for a player to use when investigating a strange event, but you can use them to help build your adventure as well. As a plus, if the players are doing their homework on their characters, they'll see the rewards.

Another good source for ideas on designing a more investigation-heavy campaign is your local library. There are any number of excellent mysteries available to fuel your imagination. Better yet, you'll probably even find books there specifically written to help a starting mystery writer get rolling. These are invaluable aids and chock full of ideas and facts sure to get the old stewpot of your imagination brimming over with schemes.

An Agency-centered campaign offers a new twist on the already twisted *Deadlands* setting. We think it's more than worth a try!

Secrets of the Secret

Okay, here's what the Agency doesn't know—or at least doesn't want their own people to know—about what's been going on since Gettysburg.

Whipping Boy for the Reckoners

President Grant was right all those years ago when he observed the Union seemed to catch the worst end of the Hell stick on the battlefield. More zombies do come down with a post-life hankerin' for Yankee brains than Confederate ones.

It's not because of any difference in taste—or size either, if you're reading this North of the Mason-Dixon line! Plain and simple, the Reckoners want the Civil War to drag out as long as possible. Occasionally, they throw a little weight on the Southern side to make sure.

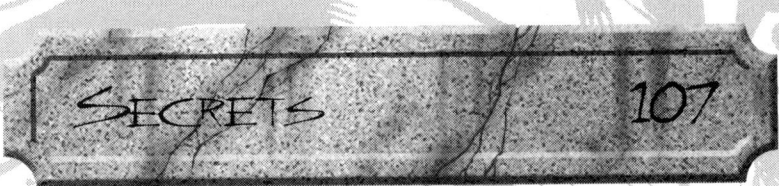

A continual state of conflict does a lot of the Reckoners' work for them. Obviously, it keeps folks on edge, particularly in the highly-populated east where most of the fighting takes place. It also provides a heap of dead bodies on a regular basis that can be used for any number of purposes—walkin' dead, 'gloms, or just plain spreading disease.

But, obvious benefits aside, the continuance of the War provides to *major* benefits to the Reckoners.

The Devils' Cabana Boys

The first reason is that it allows the governments of North and South to exert powers that would never be accepted in peacetime.

Both governments have dedicated fairly powerful organizations to covering up the Reckoning. In a roundabout way, this actually helps the Reckoners. Too much exposure makes a source of terror commonplace. To a degree the activities of the Agency and the Rangers are actually *aiding* the Reckoners. In time, it's likely both these groups will even become a source of suppressed fear as tales of men-in-black appearing and other folks disappearing begin to circulate.

But that's years away...

Things That Make You Go Boom!

And second, with the War first and foremost in folks minds, the fact that most mad science gizmos are weapons instead of automatic butlers and such goes largely unnoticed. Technology moves ahead by leaps and bounds in times of war, at least with respect to weapons. The longer the War lasts, the closer science gets to the Reckoners' final goal—nuclear ghost rock bombs.

As before, those bombs are years, even centuries away. But they are coming.

And the Reckoners know how to be patient...

LAFAYETTE BAKER

Baker was not blind to the events of the Reckoning. His position as head of the National Detective Police gave him access to a good deal of information about the unexplained and terrifying details of several encounters with abominations and the undead. He, like Grant and Lincoln, felt the public wasn't ready to face the facts and worked to keep the terrible truth from the world.

It galled him immeasurably when Lincoln hired Pinkerton to investigate the strange events. He took it as the highest insult to his abilities.

However, contrary to the rumors, Lafayette Baker had nothing to do with Lincoln's assassination. His men had become complacent with their duties and had slipped off to a local bar once the play was under way that night. However, he was never able to prove his innocence to the public's satisfaction as everything he did to exonerate himself was simply warped to fit the popular theory of conspiracy.

Over time, he found himself despised by nearly everyone in the Union, and continually compared unfavorably to Allan Pinkerton He grew to associate that name with all of his problems, and eventually convinced himself that the man was plotting his downfall.

In 1868, he faked his own death with a non-lethal dose of arsenic and a few other pharmaceuticals, so that he could go into "deep cover" and strike back against his hated foe. He's spent the last decade shadowing Pinkerton and his operatives building a plan.

Now he's ready to strike back...

BAKER'S SCHEME

Baker has built a small cadre of loyal operatives of his own. These men number less than 10, but the former spymaster doesn't need anymore for what he plans—the exposure and destruction of the Agency and, by association, Allan Pinkerton.

Ultimately, he intends to expose the Agency's true agenda, thus rendering it incapable of fulfilling it. Faced with failure, he believes the government will disband it and Pinkerton will once again fall from public grace.

Experience tells him that no amount of evidence he could produce would sway the public to believe his "wild" claims. Therefore, Baker assigns his men to follow an Agency field operative and complicate her mission, hopefully to the point of failure—disastrous failure.

Unfortunately, Lafayette Baker has complications of his own.

FLY IN THE ARSENIC

Over the years, Baker has continued to slide down the slippery slope of paranoia. The man has become convinced that someone is out to poison him, to make a reality of his falsified death.

To avoid this fate, he has slowly inundated himself with enough poison to kill all the locust in Kansas. While this has made him virtually immune to nearly every poison imaginable, it's also pickled his brain like a cucumber. Baker isn't a few cards short of a deck, he's down to pair of Jokers!

Unfortunately, this hasn't dulled his predatory cunning one wit. It has, however, dulled his perceptions to the point that he doesn't realize he has become a tool for the Reckoners themselves. His "men" are actually abominations that merely wear the faces of humans as a disguise.

They do, of course want to complicate the Agency's mission, but not for the same reason as Baker. To that end, the monsters do more than merely shadow Agency operatives and foil or expose their investigations. And, if the opportunity presents itself, they brutally murder the spooks, leaving another mess for the Agency to explain.

The abominations are careful to strike when the operatives are alone, but preferably where their remains will soon be discovered by others. To date, the Agency is completely unaware of either Baker's existence or the fact that an organized group is eliminating its operatives.

Profile: Lafayette Baker

Corporeal: D:2d8, N:2d6, S:1d8, Q:3d6, V:4d10

Climbin' 1d6, fightin': brawlin' 2d6, lockpickin' 3d8, sleight o' hand 4d8, shootin': pistol 3d8, sneak 4d8

Mental: C:2d12, K:2d8, M:2d8, Sm:3d10, Sp:2d4

Academia: occult 2d8, bluff 3d10, disguise 6d8, guts 2d4, overawe 3d8, performin' 4d8, persuasion 4d8, professional: law 2d8, scrutinize 4d12, search 3d12, streetwise 4d10

Edges: Keen 3, "the voice": soothing 1

Hindrances: Delusion (Pinkerton hates him) -3, greedy -3, oath (Destroy the Agency) -4, vengeful -3

Pace: 6

Size: 6

Wind: 14

Special Abilities:

  Grit: 2

  Immunity: Thanks to years of ingesting poisons, Baker gets a +4 to all *Vigor* rolls to resist a poison. If it normally doesn't allow one, he can shake it off on an Incredible (11) roll.

Gear: Wrist-spring derringer, bulletproof vest (under clothing), disguise kit.

Description: Baker constantly remains disguised, often changing his appearance two or three times a day. His natural hair color is dark brown and he has bluish-gray eyes. A decade of ingesting poison has given his lips a faintly blue shade and his breath is almondy. His nails are also cracked and discolored from his constant intake of poison, so he frequently wears gloves to hide them.

Profile: Baker's Men-in-Black

Corporeal: D:3d8, N:2d10, S:4d10, Q:4d8, V:3d10

Climbin' 3d10, dodge 3d10, fightin': brawlin' 5d10, quick draw 3d8, shootin': automatics, 6d8, sneak 5d10

Mental: C:2d8, K:2d8, M:1d10, Sm:3d8, Sp:3d10

Academia: occult 4d8, guts 4d10, overawe 5d10, ridicule 4d8, scrutinize 3d8, search 4d8, streetwise 4d8, trackin' 3d8

Pace: 12

Size: 6

Wind: 20

Terror: 5

Special Abilities:

  Fearless

  Gatling Pistol: as normal gadget.

  Immunity: Men-in-Black take *no* damage from Agency operatives, neither normal nor magical. They take half damage from all other attacks. They can only be killed as listed in **Weakness** below.

  Memory Blank: Non-Agency personnel have difficulty remembering men-in-black. A cowpoke must make an Incredible (11) *Smarts* roll to recall any details about a man-in-black.

  Shadow Walk: The men-in-black can *shadow walk* as per the hex. No roll is necessary, only two shadows man-sized or larger within 100 yards of each other.

  Unnatural Voice: The abomination's unearthly toneless voice gives it a +2 to all *overawe* rolls.

  Weakness: All men-in-black carry a badge inscribed "National Detective Police" in one of their pockets. Removing this from their person destroys them.

Description: Men-in-black are near perfect matches for the average civilian's idea of an Agency operative. They wear all black clothing, including their long dusters, carry Gatling pistols, and say little. Their skin is almost unnaturally pale, however, and their eyes have coal black irises.

The Pinkertons Today

Robert, Allan Pinkerton's son, currently in charge of the Pinkerton Detective Agency, knows almost as much as his father about the Reckoning. Only a few other detectives in the organization do, however.

As noted, the Agency does from time to time employ Pinkertons to assist on operations, but either they keep them safely away from any revealing events or they use hand-picked detectives from the small cadre of those in the know.

No one remaining in the Pinkerton Detective Agency knows the real identity of Andrew Lane, although Robert suspects there's more to the man than his father has told him.

Back in 1871, Allan Pinkerton staged a fire in his company's central archives—but not before he and a trusted few of his men removed all the records of their supernatural investigations. These files are now safely stored in the Chicago Regional office.

Of course, Marshal, if you'd like to complicate the Agency's already difficult mission, maybe a couple of those files were misplaced in transit.

THE GHOST

Andrew Lane is no longer handling the Western Bureau, thanks to recent events in Gomorra. In a climactic battle against the powerful manitou Knicknevin, the mysterious Austin Stoker freed the Ghost's own manitou to fight against its hated brother.

Unfortunately, the Ghost has been unable to regain control of his manitou—due in no small part to Stoker's bullet.

GRIMME'S CRUSADE

Reverend Grimme recently embarked on a "crusade" to further destabilize the Maze in the hopes of seizing even more for himself. His first target is the Union's Agency.

Working through agents back East, the Reverend obtained the actual bullet that felled Lincoln back in 1865. He had it recast and eventually passed into Stoker's hands, although the former Confederate had no idea of the bullet's most recent owner.

The round functioned exactly as Stoker hoped it would, weakening the Ghost's control over his own manitou. After the battle, the Ghost regained control, again as Stoker had hoped, but only for a short time.

REGINA COLEPORT

One of Grimme's fanatical cultists, Regina Coleport slipped into the Ghost's room and completed a short ritual to give his manitou complete power.

After putting a Texas-sized hurting on the remaining Agency field operatives in Gomorra—the Ghost managed to keep the manitou from actually killing any—the two headed to the East.

No one outside of Gomorra knows this, though, as the Ghost and Coleport have taken care to disable all telegraph lines leaving the boomtown. As the two travel east, Coleport is drawing on the Ghost's knowledge of Agency operatives to eliminate local offices.

Ghost Bustin'

If you're interested in exactly what the Ghost's manitou is up to at the end of its journey, pick up *Ghost Busters*, in stores soon.

Better yet, once your posse has finished the adventure, fill out the card at the end and mail it to us by the deadline to have a chance at shaping the official setting!

Cort Williams

Cort Williams worked for the Pinkerton Detectives long before the Agency became an official entity. The Ghost personally pulled him for duties in Gomorra, and over time, Cort became the Ghost's right hand man in the boomtown. Since the Ghost's disappearance, Cort has assumed the duties of coordinating and overseeing the Agency's affairs in and around Gomorra.

Cort is an experienced operative with a strong tendency for neatness. He always dons a pair of black leather gloves before entering an Agency operation.

In the aftermath of Knicknevin's defeat, Gomorra's condition is particularly unpleasant for Cort; the town is literally in shambles. He's set himself to seeing it cleaned up and Cort's not the sort to brook any argument about his mission!

Profile: Cort Williams

Corporeal: D:3d8, N:2d10, Q:4d6, S:1d10, V:2d6

Climbin' 1d10, dodge 3d10, fightin': brawlin' 4d10, horse ridin' 3d10, lockpickin' 2d8, quickdraw 2d6, shootin': automatics, pistol 5d8, sneak 3d10

Mental: C:2d12, K:2d8, M:3d10, Sm:3d8, Sp:2d6

Academia: occult 4d8, bluff 2d8, guts 4d6, overawe 4d10, persuasion 3d10, professional: law 3d10, search 5d12, scrutinize 4d12, streetwise 3d8

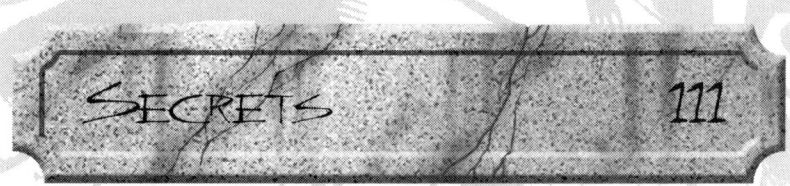

Edges: Belongins' 3 (Agency equipment), brave 2, rank (Agency) 2

Hindrances: Habit (neatness) -1, loyal (Agency), obligation (Agency) -3

Pace: 10

Size: 6

Wind: 12

Special Abilities:

Grit: 2

Gear: Black gloves, Agency duster, Gatling pistol.

Description: Cort is a square-jawed man just under 6' tall. He carries himself like a giant however, and few folks cross him. His clothes seem to be always clean and neatly pressed, even after a long trail ride.

Denver

In the Ghost's absence, one of Allan Pinkerton's most experienced field agents, Hattie Lawton has assumed administration of the Denver Regional office and day-to-day duties running the Bureau. While he was working in Gomorra, Hattie passed along all crucial decision-making to Lane, but now that he's gone missing, she's risen to the challenge—with the approval of the Agency Director himself.

Hattie spent time in Confederate custody in the early years of the War and still carries a grudge for the South's execution of Timothy Webster. Under her direction, the Bureau is taking a decidedly anti-South turn.

Hattie is very level-headed in her decisions and has a very solid understanding of the Agency's mission and authority. She won't jeopardize the goals of the organization or the lives of her operatives to revenge Webster's death, but it will take a *lot* of convincing to ever get her to work *with* Confederates.

And yes, it is still prestigious to pull off a Disputed Territories assignment! The next time the Agent is testing to advance a *rank*, he gets a +2 to all his rolls.

PROFILE: HATTIE LAWTON

Corporeal: D:3d6, N:2d6, Q:2d8, S:1d6, V:3d8

Climbin' 1d6, fightin': brawlin' 2d6, filchin' 3d6, lockpickin' 6d6, shootin': automatics, pistol 4d6, sleight o' hand 5d6, sneak 4d6

Mental: C:3d10, K:2d10, M:1d12, Sm:3d8, Sp:2d8

Academia: occult 5d10, disguise 5d10, guts 4d8 overawe 4d12, performin': actin' 6d12, persuasion 5d12, professional: administration 4d10, professional: law 4d10, scrutinize 8d10, search 6d10, streetwise 5d8

Edges: Belongins' 3 (Agency equipment), rank (Agency) 4

Hindrances: Intolerance (Confederate citizens) -2, obligation (Agency) -3

Pace: 6

Size: 6

Wind: 16

Special Abilities:
  Grit: 2

Gear: Gatling pistol (in field), lockpicks, ring derringer, impenetrable vest

Description: Like most successful spooks, Hattie cultivates a nondescript appearance. She looks to be anywhere from her late 30s to early 50s, with brown hair lightly streaked with gray. She usually wears nice dresses, only a year or so behind the latest fashion.

SEATTLE

The biggest part of the reason there are so few reports of trouble in the Seattle-Tacoma area is the spooks themselves are tied up in the worst of it!

PARTS IS PARTS

Years ago, civic leaders in Tacoma became caught up in a corrupted version of the Kwaikiutl Indian Cannibal Society. A British deserter brought the practices south and slowly drew more and more of the local populace into the cult.

Now, nearly one-quarter of all the influential leaders and merchants in the area—including the Agency operatives—have been converted. Although they restrain their horrific ceremonies to once a month, the group's actions have drawn two Wendigos into the area.

Worse yet, some of the members have begun to develop enhanced physical abilities and even black magic powers as well.

Any operative assigned to the area is either converted if possible, or quickly reassigned by the Regional chief (who is a member of the cult as well). Any spook getting too close to the truth is given a choice: join the feast, or join the stew.

For the average cult member see below. Use the typical Agent profile (or Spook, if you're feeling nasty) on page 106 of the *Marshal's Handbook* rulebook for the converted operatives, but add black magic as below.

PROFILE: CANNIBAL CULT MEMBER

Corporeal: D:2d6, N:2d8, Q:3d8, S:2d10, V:2d12

Climbin' 1d8, fightin': brawlin', knife 3d8, shootin': pistol, shotgun, or rifle 3d6, sneak 3d8

Mental: C:1d8, K:3d6, M:2d6, Sm:1d8, Sp:2d6

Faith: black magic 4d6, guts 3d6, overawe 2d6, professional: any or trade: any, scrutinize 2d8, search 3d8, trackin' 1d8

Edges: Sand 2, thick-skinned 3, tough as nails 3

Hindrances: Bloodthirsty -2, habit (cannibal) -3, outlaw -2

Pace: 8

Size: 6

Wind: *18*

Special Abilities:
  Black Magic: Some cultists have perfected a few spells. Those who have usually have one or more of the following: Forewarnin' 2, pact (Wendigos) 5, sendin' 3, stormcall 3
  Gear: Knife (STR+1d4), a pistol, rifle, or shotgun, and ammunition

DEADWOOD

Richard Speakman, head of the Deadwood Ward, has found himself in a moral dilemma. Normally, the Agency doesn't involve itself with non-supernatural events, but much of the current trouble in Deadwood is the action of purely human culprits. For the full story, see pages 150-155 in the *Marshal's Handbook* rulebook.

Speakman and his operatives have amassed enough information to deduce that the goings-on around Deadwood

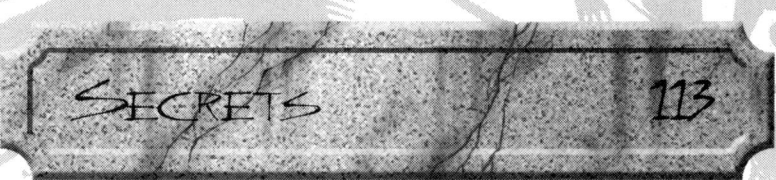

are not Event 070363 related, but are instead due to the meddling of the Deadwood Miner's Association, in an attempt to stir up trouble for the Sioux.

Through his deep cover operatives, he also knows that the leadership of the DMA is in contact with Custer. While he doesn't have the full details, he knows that something big is brewing.

Richard's quandary comes from knowing the DMA is committing crimes to incite the populace against the Sioux. Blowing his cover and that of his operatives to prevent a political event might harm the Agency's ability to prevent supernatural occurrences in the area. Like, say, the Cult of the Worm, Devil's Tower, or even the recent murders of Jack Call's jury.

Custer doesn't seem ready to move just yet—one of his operatives has infiltrated the General's mercenary band—which is good news for the Ward Chief. Speakman hasn't decided one way or the other yet, but he'd welcome an easy way out of the dilemma.

PROFILE: RICHARD SPEAKMAN

Corporeal: D:1d6, N:3d6, Q:3d6, S:1d6, V:3d8

Climbin' 2d6, fightin': brawlin' 2d6, shootin': automatics, shotgun 4d6, sneak 3d6, teamster 3d6

Mental: C:2d12, K:1d8, M:4d6, Sm:2d10, Sp:4d10

Academia: occult 4, disguise 3d8, guts 3d10, performin': actin' 3d6, persuasion 3d6, professional: law 4d8, scrutinize 4d12, search 4d12, streetwise 3d10

Edges: Belongins' 3 (Gatling pistol), big ears, rank (Agency) 3

Hindrances: Cautious -3, obligation (Agency) -3

Pace: 6

Size: 6

Wind: 18

Special Abilities:
  Grit: 1

Gear: Double-barreled shotgun, ammunition, homing slugs, ground stakes (2), hollow bolts (4), flash button (on vest), vial of invisible ink, Gatling pistol (stored in room), ammunition.

Description: Richard looks like the typical store owner on the frontier. He is in his early 40s, and has salt-and-pepper hair, slightly balding, with a neat moustache. Normally he wears a storekeeper's apron over his clothing while in the shop.

GOMORRA

If you've read the *Doomtown or Bust!* sourcebook, you know things in Gomorra were a short-fused powder keg with each of the factions holding a match. Well, somebody lit that fuse, touching off one Hell of a shootout.

We won't go too in-depth here—the situation there is so complex that we don't have the space to detail it all. We will give you a quick rundown of events as they affected the Agency in the town.

AGENTS CHECK IN, BUT THEY DON'T CHECK OUT!

The party got started when a team of agents raided the Golden Mare. They had reason to believe the brothel was hiding an abomination or two; what they didn't know was more than one, and the abominations—a group of vampires—knew they were coming.

The agents were quickly overwhelmed by the undead ambush, and Josef Rocescu, Mr. Slate, and Johnny Quaid fell to the monsters. Simultaneously, the Texas Rangers in the area made an attack on the Whateleys and also suffered heavy losses.

In the face of their defeat, both the Ghost and Captain Karl knew they faced dire straits indeed. The Agency and the Rangers agreed to put aside political conflicts and join forces—just in time

THE GATE OPENS

While the two government groups were mending fences, the opposition hadn't been sitting idle either. The prophet Ellijah's misguided group of cultists succeeded in opening a gate to the Hunting Grounds underneath Lord Grimley's Manor. While the coalition forces of North and South—as well as just about every other faction in town—fought the Whateleys and members of the Flock, the manitou Knicknevin emerged from the Gate.

Casualties were high all around, but with the aid of the wild-card Austin Stoker, the group finally succeeded in killing the now-corporeal manitou.

But the victory was not without a terrible cost. Three more Agency operatives lost their lives in the fighting.

"Boom-Boom" O'Bannon, the detachment's demolitions expert, was trapped in the basement of the Whateley manor when his explosives detonated. The Pennsylvania Kid was poisoned by the Flock cultist Envy's snakes. Perhaps most costly to the Agency, Melissa Hill, one of the few hucksters in the organization, was struck down by Elijah himself.

A number of operatives are still carrying injuries from the battle. And, of course, as we discussed earlier, the Ghost is AWOL, controlled by his manitou.

All's Well That Ends Well...Right?

Even though the Agency/Rangers coalition managed to halt Knicknevin's entry into our world, many issues remain unresolved in Gomorra. The Whateleys, though dealt a serious blow, are far from defeated. The Flock may be gone, but "missionaries" from the Church of Lost Angels have been seen on the streets of Gomorra.

And the events in Gomorra have finally attracted the attention of several of the more powerful groups in the Weird West.

Darious Hellstromme is eyeing the Collegium as a possible corporate ally against the bothersome Smith & Robards. Black River is courting a contract with Sweetrock, and whispers hint that a couple of folks with N'Awlin's accents have been seen in the company of the Whateleys.

What will settle out of the pan as a result of all this hubbub remains to be seen, however...

Salt Lake City

Nevada Smith, the most famous of all Agency operatives, is currently in charge of all Deseret missions. Smith is able to balance his notoriety and the directives of EO 347 by hiding behind the persona of his dime-novel alter ego. Now, most of what he writes about *is* real, but his readership takes it as

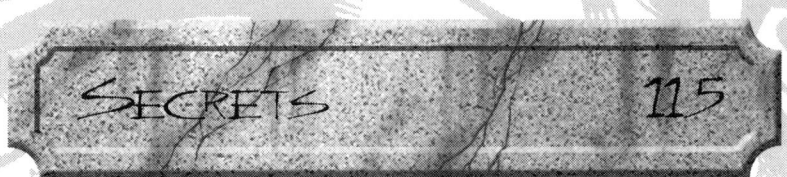
tongue-in-cheek exaggeration. He is also careful to mask most of his opponents as disguised Confederate spies or mad scientists gone insane with power.

The Wrench in the Steamworks

Nevada's original mission in Deseret had little to do with the Reckoning. He was ordered there by General Grant to gather evidence against Brigham Young. However, since then, he's found himself pitted against Hellstromme time and time again

Will the Real Nevada Please Step Forward?

Nevada Smith is known as the "Man of a 1000 Faces" and with good reason. He has a disguise for every occasion, and is so good he could probably convince the President himself that he was the real Commander-in-Chief and Grant was an imposter!

Nevada is sneakier than a rattlesnake wearing moccasins, to boot. He's so careful about maintaining his cover, he's hired a tinhorn, Michael Mullwood, to pretend he's Nevada. Or rather, that he's who Nevada isn't.

If that's confusing, here's how it works: Nevada writes his own dime novels under the pseudonym of I.M. Hymme. Most folks believe I.M. Hymme is really Nevada; after all, come on—"I Am Him?" How obvious, right?

So, to derail that train of thought, he hired Michael Mullwood to pretend he is actually I.M. Hymme, not Nevada. Talk about cautious—his cover story has a cover story!

Although Nevada is on permanent assignment there, the second operative in Salt Lake City varies according to availability. Right now it's Bo Buchanan, a strapping figure of a man—in physique at least, if not looks. Bo is a grand-fathered Pinkerton agent, so as you might guess, he's one tough hombre.

Bo usually runs cover for Nevada. Since his boss is so well-known, a whole battalion of other adventurers, gunslingers, reporters, and fans are always looking to catch a glimpse of the dime-novel hero. Normally, Nevada just avoids them, but Bo keeps an eye out for any who might be more than just publicity-seekers.

Profile: Nevada Smith

Corporeal: D:4d10, N:4d10, Q:4d8, S:3d8, V:3d8

Bow 1d10, climbin' 4d10, dodge 8d10, drivin': jetpack 2d10, drivin': ornithopter 2d10, drivin': steam wagons 5d10, fightin': brawlin' 6d10, filchin' 2d10, horse ridin' 5d10, lockpickin' 4d10, quick draw: pistol 6d8, shootin': automatics, pistol 6d10, sleight o' hand 2d10, sneak 6d10, swimmin' 3d10, teamster 3d10, throwin': balanced, unbalanced 3d10

Mental: C:4d10, K:3d8, M:2d8, Sm:3d10, Sp:4d8

Academia: occult 4d8, area knowledge: Deseret 4d8, artillery 4d10, arts 2d10, bluff 8d10, demolition 4d8, disguise 10d8, faith: Christianity 3d8, gamblin' 7d10, guts 6d8, language: French 4d8, language: Indian Sign 4d8, language: Mormon alphabet 3d8, language: Spanish 5d8, leadership 3d8, medicine 3d8, professional: law 4d8, overawe 3d8, performin' 6d8, persuasion 4d8, ridicule 5d10, science: chemistry 2d8, science: engineering 2d8, scroungin' 5d10, scrutinize 6d10, search 4d10, streetwise 8d10, survival: desert 4d10, tale tellin' 3d8, tinkerin' 3d10, trackin' 3d10, trade: blacksmith 1d8

Edges: Belongins' 3 (Gatling pistol), level-headed 5, luck o' the Irish 5, rank (Agency) 3, veteran o' the Weird West

Hindrances: Enemy (Hellstromme) -5, Heroic -5, Loyal -3, Obligation (Agency) -3

Pace: 10
Size: 6
Wind: 16

Special Abilities:
Grit: 2
Gear: Gatling pistol, disguise kit, wrist-spring derringer, rocket grapnel, hollow fountain pen filled with 2 oz.. of explosive putty.
Description: Yeah, right. "Man of 1000 faces," remember?

Profile: Bo Buchanan

Corporeal: D:3d6, N:3d8, Q:2d8, S:3d10, V:3d12

Climbin' 3d8, dodge 2d8, fightin': wrasslin' 3d8, lockpickin' 2d6, shootin': pistol, shotgun 5d6, sneak 4d8, swimmin' 2d8

Mental: C:3d8, K:3d6, M:4d8, Sm:2d8, Sp:3d8

Academia: occult 2d6, area knowledge: the Junkyard 4d6, bluff 2d8, gamblin' 2d8, guts 2d8, overawe 2d8, persuasion 3d8, scrutinize 3d8, search 3d8, streetwise 4d8, trackin' 2d8

Edges: Brawny 3, brave 2, tough as nails 1, rank (Agency) 1

Hindrances: Obligation (Agency) -3
Pace: 8
Size: 7
Wind: 20
Special Abilities:
Grit: 2
Gear: Agency credentials, Army pistol, scattergun.
Description: Bo's a big man, square at every angle, with a beard, mustache and all the fixings to look like a grizzly. He scowls at everything.

THE SRF

With the possible exception of the Salem Training Facility, the SRF is the single largest Agency installation. It occupies six warehouses on the edge of the Denver railyard. An extensive network of tunnels connect the buildings, and some of the SRF's more sensitive work is even conducted underground.

As noted in GM 28-52, these buildings are publicly marked as property of the Union Blue Railroad. Armed guards patrol the grounds under the guise of standard stock guards and railroad detectives, but all are Agency operatives—use the Cleaner archetype for these gunmen.

The warehouses hold the Technology Division—often called the "T" Section—responsible for exploitation and development of mad science gizmos. The SRF also serves as a warehouse/armory for the entire Agency, shipping out devices as requested by the Regional offices on secured Union Blue trains.

The grounds also hold an extensive arcane research facility that not only studies huckster-style magic, but also shamanism, blessed miracles, voodoo, and the like. Most of this research is conducted through theory and analysis of field reports and recovered texts; the Agency has had limited success in recruiting folks with the talent for actual magic.

A few mystics do serve in the Agency, but these are rare individuals indeed. As most practitioners of the arcane tend to be independent or ambitious sorts, the rather structured nature of the organization isn't particularly attractive to them.

On occasion, particularly unique abominations may be returned here for further study by Agency researchers. Of course, this is only after they've been killed—or killed *again*, as the case may be. Only with authorization from one of the Bureau Chiefs can an operative bring a carcass here. The SRF isn't a dumping ground for dead abominations!

Finally, the Agency's Star Chamber is also a part of the SRF. However, even most of the techs assigned to the SRF are unaware of the Chamber's existence. Only the Director, the Bureau Chiefs, the Ghost's Spooks and a few Senior Agents in either Bureau know about the Chamber. It's further detailed on page 107 of the *Marshal's Handbook* rulebook.

By the way, although Union Blue often works closely with the Agency, only Joshua Chamberlain, the railroad's owner, knows the real mission of the organization. In return for his service to the Agency, federal troops are often "in the right place" to step in and protect Union Blue from other rail barons' armed gangs.

However, the rest of the Union Blue employees believe the standard "spy" cover story—more or less, anyway.

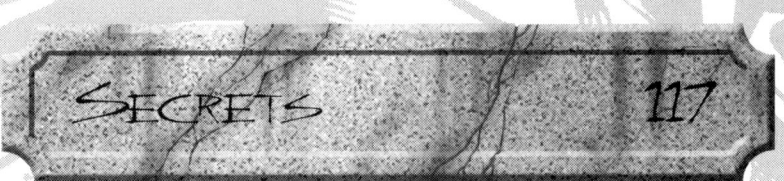

MT. KATAHDIN INSTITUTE

Okay, you just know this is bad news, don't you Marshal? Let's see—a group of people, all unbalanced by encounters with horrifying events, a remote location in the northern wood, a doctor who specializes in neurological problems. Almost sounds like the plot for a bad movie, doesn't it?

Dr. Geoffrey Kohms is truly as good as his reputation claims. The Institute itself is set in near idyllic isolation. The Agency honestly has the best intentions for the well-being of its operatives. So where does it all go wrong?

IN MAINE, NO ONE CAN HEAR YOU SCREAM...

The real problem is so obvious that the Agency completely missed it.

Putting a bunch of *really* scared people—who have a darn good reason for being scared in the first place—in an isolated area has one near-certain effect: It's going to put the Fear Level through the roof! The Mount Katahdin Institute and an area 10 miles in any direction has a constant Fear Level of 5, thanks to all the terrified patients there.

THE DOCTOR IS IN...SANE!

Dr. Kohms began his work under the assumption that his patients were suffering a form of mass delusion. In spite of his briefing, he didn't really believe what the Agency told him regarding the Event and EO 347.

Oh, sure, he believed that *something* was going on and that it was tied to national security, but not that the dead were spontaneously returning to life or any of the other claptrap he was being fed. At worst, he figured the Agency was experimenting with alchemy or some other weird science and had driven these poor souls batty.

Imagine his surprise when his patients' fears began to take form in the woods around Mount Katahdin!

Now, not unlike Darious Hellstromme, Dr. Kohms has begun experimenting with fear. However, Dr. Kohms has a couple of advantages even Hellstromme doesn't: government backing and a captive audience!

The Agency has no idea that Dr. Kohms is actually worsening the condition of the patients through his experiments. Any patient that claims otherwise is quickly dismissed by the staff as "delusional."

If word does get out, an operative or two may be sent in deep cover to get to the bottom of the cuckoo's nest.

The Staff

Currently there are 32 patients assigned to the Institute and a full-time staff of six orderlies, three nurses, and the good doctor. With the exception of one nurse and one orderly, the rest of the staff is not only aware of the doctor's experiments, they actually assist in their conduct.

The two other members will soon either agree to join the "research" or be eliminated. If that happens, Dr. Kohms plans to pin the blame on one of his "insane" patients—preferably one of the more troublesome ones!

Profile: Dr. Geoffrey Kohms

Corporeal: D:2d10, N:1d8, Q:2d6, S:2d4, V:2d8

Climbin' 1d8, dodge 2d8, fightin': knife 3d6, sneak 1d8

Mental: C:2d10, K:4d12, M:2d8, Sm:2d12, Sp:2d6

Academia: philosophy 4d12, Academia: occult 2d12, bluff 4d12, guts 5d6, language: English 4d12, language: German 3d12, language: Latin 3d12, medicine: general, surgery 7d12, overawe 5d8, persuasion 7d8, professional: law 2d12, ridicule 6d12, science: biology 4d12, science: chemistry 3d12, scrutinize 5d10, search 1d10

Edges: Keen 3, renown (medical field) 1, "the Voice:" grating 1, "the Voice" soothing 1, "the Voice" threatening 1

Hindrances: Curious -3, high-falutin' -2, loco (fear obsession; keep it hidden) -3, self-righteous -3

Pace: 8

Size: 6

Wind: 14

Special Abilities:

Gear: Notebook, pen, glasses, labcoat, scalpel (STR+1d4).

Description: A dark-haired, bookish doctor in his mid-40s. He wears reading glasses and often seems distracted by his studies.

Profile: Institute Orderly

Corporeal: D:2d6, N:3d8, Q:2d8, S:4d10, V:2d10

Climbin' 1d8, dodge 2d8, fightin': brawlin' 5d8, shootin': shotgun 3d6, sneak 2d8

Mental: C: 1d8, K:2d6, M:2d6, Sm:2d6, Sp:2d6

Area Knowledge: Katahdin Institue 2d6, general: medicine 2d6, overawe 3d6, scrutinize 2d8, search 4d8, trackin' 3d8

Edges: Brawny 3, sand 2, thick-skinned 3, tough as nails 2

Hindrances: Mean as a rattler -2, vengeful-3

Pace: 8

Size: 7

Wind: 20

Gear: Blackjack or club (STR+1d6), shotgun (if outside Institute grounds)

We Don't Need No Stinkin' Gadgets!

After reading through **Chapter 3: Tools o' the Trade**, no doubt you're wondering what to do about all those new toys Agency operatives are going to be trying out on your poor, helpless abominations. Well, never fear, Marshal, we're here to help!

In the **Posse Section** we explained the reason for this by saying the variety of the challenges faced made developing specific equipment too time-inefficient. That's certainly true, but there's another reason as well.

You've probably noticed that most of the new gizmos are more spy-oriented than abomination-stomping. That's because we wanted to add flavor to Agency characters without providing them with an overpowering advantage. An Agency character should be a cross between a spy, a detective, and a ghost hunter, not a manitou-manacle toting monster slayer.

It's not likely that false pocket watch will prove to be Grimme's undoing, but if you're afraid the equipment may overshadow the story, there are plenty of options available to help offset that danger.

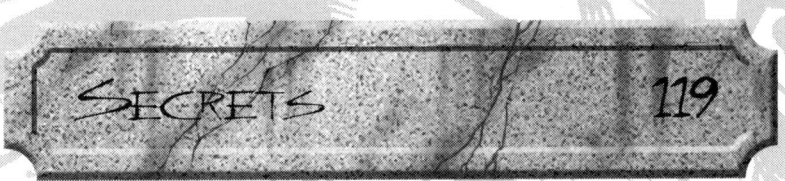
Request Denied

Unlike those confounded mad scientists, most Agency spooks don't really own all that nifty hardware—they only rent it. They've got to get approval from the boss to even take the gizmos out of the lockers in the first place.

The organization doesn't want to draw too much attention to its actions, and if the heroes have a penchant for charging in with guns a-blazing, it may want to cool their heels for a mission or two. Having to complete an assignment without automatic weapons might be just the ticket!

Uhm... That's on Back Order

You might well be concerned that ectoplasmic calcifier might short-circuit a really cool adventure centering around the investigation of a haunting. That's understandable—nothing's more frustrating than losing a cherished abomination to an unappreciative hero with a big gun.

Remember not *every* field office is going to have *every* piece of equipment an operative might request. The more exotic, the less likely it is to be available.

An alternative to this is to allow the operative to request the equipment ahead of time, not knowing when it will arrive. That way, she has to develop a backup plan or two, just in case the device doesn't come through.

It also gives a spook a reason to plan ahead somewhat—even though it may tie up some of her treasured Requisition Points!

Equipment Turn-In Time!

An operative may decide to get one or two really handy gadgets and keep them from mission to mission. That's fine; it may help develop the character and give him a "trademark" of sorts.

Unless the device is *so* handy it starts to overpower the posse and your campaign, that is!

In that case, his superiors can always recall the equipment. The Agency has a lot of operatives and someone else is bound to need that favorite gizmo at some point!

That Said...

Now that we've given you a few reasons to justifiably deny an operative's request, we'd like to add a word of advice: Don't overdo it.

Like we said a minute ago, the whole point of the game is to have fun. If the Agency character's requests are constantly denied or unavailable, he's likely to end up more frustrated with the game than enjoying it.

Few, if any, of the gadgets available should prove unbalancing to your campaign. It's much more fun to let the heroes play with the toys than put them away in a box.

Especially if they break them and have to explain it to the boss!

And with that happy note...

It's Not Supposed to Do That!

Here's the highlight of Marshaling a game with mad science gizmos—the Malfunction Tables! For convenience's sake, we've listed them alphabetically.

But before we get down to the brass tacks, here's a little inside information on one of the newest concepts in mad science in the Weird West.

The Identity Field Theory

This crackpot hypothesis actually works for one simple reason: Each chunk of ghost rock contains a tortured soul. The "connectivity" between the treated pieces is maintained as the soul is stretched.

It's not only the specially-treated nuggets that maintain the soul's connection to each piece once separated; every ghost rock chunk does this until its destroyed by burning. The treatment merely amplifies the connection, allowing the device containing the chunk to take advantage of it.

That should give you plenty of ideas of your own, Marshal, both for gadgets and for flaws in those gadgets.

Agency Black Duster

Minor: The attack hits a weak spot. The duster provides no protection for this attack.

Major: The duster's armor is weakened somehow by the damage. It works as light Armor -2 until it can be repaired at Agency facilities.

Catastrophe: The duster's protection is reduced to -2 for this attack and then its lining falls to pieces.

Agency Carbine

Minor: The barrels lock in place. Only one round is fired from the burst and the weapon jams.. An Onerous (7) *tinkerin'* roll fixes the weapon.

Major: The magazine springs fling it from the weapon, spraying ammunition everywhere. One round is fired from the burst and the gun is out of ammunition.

Catastrophe: The magazine breaks loose as above, but this time it pulls out part of the carbine's action spring as well. The spring lashes the firer across the face causing 4d6 damage (this includes the bonus dice for a noggin' hit).

Agency Shotgun

Minor: A cartridge jams in the action. A Fair (5) *tinkerin'* roll corrects the problem. No rounds are fired in the burst.

Major: The cartridge belt jams in the feed port causing the weapon to lock up and no rounds are fired. The belt breaks and must be replaced. A portion of the belt is also stuck in the action, requiring a Hard (9) *tinkerin'* roll to remove.

Catastrophe: The barrel doesn't align with the chamber, causing an explosive backfire. A 6d6 explosion with a Burst radius of 1 occurs. The weapon is destroyed.

Agency Walking Stick

Since this is a combination device, a number of results are possible depending on the particular gadget being used at the time of the malfunction. The following are merely presented as examples.

Minor: The handle falls apart, rendering the device unusable until replaced with a Fair (5) *tinkerin'* roll.

Major: The internal catch holding the handle to the cane locks into place. No device on the walking stick (except the listening cone and magnifying glass) can be used until the device is repaired with a Hard (9) *tinkerin'* roll..

Catastrophe: The pistol round is accidentally fired while the barrel is still blocked. It backfires, doing 3d6 to the wielder. Add +4 when rolling for the hit location.

Automatic Key

Minor: The key jams against a ward in the lock, causing a spring to disconnect. Until someone repairs it with a Hard (7) *tinkerin'* roll, the device is useless except as a paperweight.

Major: The key's springs over-torque the lock, jamming it. Even getting the gadget out of the lock takes a Hard (9) *Deftness* roll. The lock itself can be opened now only by a Hard (9) *professional: locksmith* roll. The key must be repaired as above.

Catastrophe: The probe breaks free and spins uncontrollably, lashing the user's hand with its prongs. The spook takes 2d6 damage to the hand he was using to work the key (most likely his gun hand!). The key is broken and completely useless.

Ecto-Plasmic Calcifier

Minor: The calcifier's charge bleeds off before the operative fires the liquid. It has no effect, and the hero must spend 2 rounds to rebuild it before he can fire again.

Major: The calcifier has a reverse effect, turning the operative incorporeal instead. For 1d6 rounds, treat the hero as if he had the Harrowed *ghost* power, but he has no control over or knowledge of when it ends.

Catastrophe: The calcifier's electricity is discharged into the wielder instead of the liquid, doing 3d8 directly to the poor sap's guts. This damage ignores any metal-based armor.

Explosive Putty

Minor: The wad of putty has a weak mix, causing only 1d4 for each ounce used. Shaping the charge still produces an Armor piercing effect, though.

Major: The operative might as well have used a batch of modeling clay. This batch of the putty is a complete dud; the fuse burns into the stuff and fizzles out with a sulfurous stench, but little more.

Catastrophe: This is an unstable batch of putty. The operative's body heat is enough to ignite it. The putty explodes immediately, doing normal damage (1d8 per ounce used).

False Pocket Watch

As with the Agency walking stick, this is a combination gizmo. Use these as examples for potential malfunctions, but don't feel bound by them.

Minor: The homing compass goes haywire, causing the watch hands to spin constantly. A Fair (5) *mad science* roll is all that can fix the device.

Major: The saw blade whips out, shredding the spook's pocket and dropping the watch to the ground. If the poor sap is holding it at the time, it causes 1d6 Wind and he has to make an Onerous (7) *Vigor* roll to avoid dropping it in surprise and pain.

Catastrophe: The watch stem breaks loose and ignites the explosive putty, causing an explosion doing 1d8 per remaining ounce to the wearer's guts (if in a pocket) or hand (if being held).

Fear Detector

The main reason little is understood about the workings of the detector is due to the source of one of the components. One of the Denver technicians is using steel "acquired" from one of Hellstromme's fear-channelling railroads. No one else knows where the material comes from and the techie claims to specially treat it with some alchemical compound.

Any attempt to reproduce the detector without the Hellstromme-created steel is doomed to failure (or at least a hand rank of Full House).

As yet, Hellstromme doesn't know about the Agency's little secret. What he'll do once he does learn of it is anyone's guess...

The rumors about the device reducing the surrounding fear levels are false—completely. Striking the tuning-fork device just temporarily screws up its functions. Each time someone hits the fork in this manner, secretly lower the Reliability of the gadget by 1!

The colors correspond directly to Fear Levels. Yellow is Fear Level 1, Green—Fear Level 2, and so on, up to Black which marks a Deadland!

This might be another Reliability roll you want to keep secret Marshal.

Minor: The detector reads the Fear Level as Yellow (1) regardless of its actual Level.

Major: The device sets off a high-pitched tone through the tuning fork that causes everyone in the area to become inexplicably nauseous unless they make an Onerous (7) *Vigor* roll. Those who fail lose 1d6 Wind—and their lunch.

Catastrophe: The gadget blows it big time. Somehow, the detector actually *raises* the Fear Level by one in an area 1 mile in diameter for 1d6 hours!

Field Boots

Again, this is a combination device, so feel free to have another of its component gadgets malfunction if it fits the situation better.

Minor: The air pump collapses, causing the left heel to sink nearly an inch in height. This leaves the spook with lop-sided boots, which

reduces his Pace by 1 and gives him a -2 to all *Nimbleness*-based Trait and Aptitude checks.

Major: The saw/spur blade spontaneously activates and buries itself in the ground or floor. The operative is stuck in place until she makes a Fair (5) *Strength* roll or removes her footgear.

Catastrophe: The boot knife comes off its track and shoots into the spook's foot, doing 2d6 damage to the right leg.

Flash Buttons

Minor: The button explodes weakly, causing a minor distraction at best. No *Vigor* rolls are necessary.

Major: The button fails to explode, instead rolling in a circle until finally rattling to a stop. The spook's only hope here is that the button wasn't holding up a vital piece of clothing as well!

Catastrophe: The button explodes in the operative's hand, doing 1d6 damage and forcing her to make a *Vigor* check to avoid being stunned from the button's normal blast as well.

Homing Slugs

Like a number of other gizmos, we recommend you make the Reliability roll on this one, Marshal.

Minor: The homing compass is jammed, unable to turn. Until some Mr. Fix-it makes a Hard (9) *tinkerin'* roll, the device doesn't work.

Major: The connection becomes susceptible to background "noise" and occasionally gives a false direction reading. The spook must make an Incredible (11) *Smarts* roll to realize when this happens.

Catastrophe: The connectivity between the slug and compass suddenly increases tremendously. If on a person or creature, the slug begins to tug slightly in the direction of the tailing operative. If at a fixed location, it begins slowly rolling at 1 yard a minute toward the homing compass.

Infrared Goggles

This is another good one to roll in secret.

Minor: The goggles fail altogether. A Hard (9) *tinkerin'* roll is necessary to get them working again.

Major: There is a one round delay between the goggles detecting a heat source and them transmitting it to the viewer. This means the user sees things where they *were* not where they *are*. Lots of fun in combat! A hero who makes Incredible (11) *tinkerin'* roll can fix this problem.

Catastrophe: The goggles over-magnify surrounding air temperatures, blinding the viewer for 2d6 minutes. The goggles are completely unrepairable.

INVISIBLE INK

Since the ink *is* invisible as soon as it dries, we suggest you make this Reliability roll in secret, Marshal. It keeps the heroes on their toes!

Minor: The ink completely evaporates leaving a blank page.

Major: The ink partially evaporates or smudges, altering the message in some way. Exactly what it now says is up to you, but it should be close to the original in structure—although the meaning can be completely different!

Catastrophe: The ink reacts with the paper to form a caustic acid. The paper burns, emitting toxic fumes. Any cowpoke breathing these must make a Hard (9) *Vigor* roll or take the difference in Wind. Going bust on this roll results in unconsciousness!

LETTER EXTRACTOR

Minor: The desealer has lost its potency and is little more than colored water. A cowpoke can reactivate it with a Hard (9) *alchemy* roll

Major: The desealer desolves the original enelope and/or seal, making it impossible to conceal the fact the letter was opened.

Catastrophe: The resealer reacts violently with the desealer, causing 2d6 damage to each of the user's hands as it burns away. The letter and envelope are consumed in the chemical fire as well.

PHOTO-CHEMICAL GOGGLES

Although most of the malfunctions on this one are obvious, Marshal, you may want to keep Reliability a secret due to the Major result for these goggles.

Minor: The goggles detect *everything* as photoreactive, making it impossible to determine one substance from the other. A spook can correct the filters by making an Onerous (7) *tinkerin'* roll.

Major: The goggles are slightly out of adjustment and read another compound as the one for which the operative is looking. A user making a Hard (9) *Smarts* roll notices this fact.

Catastrophe: The goggles temporarily burn out a color-receptive chemical in the user's retinas, making him blind to a particular color (Marshal's choice). This color blindness lasts 1d4 hours.

PISTOL CANE

Minor: The pistol misfires. The spook has to reload it before another attempt.

Major: The baffles give out without reducing the noise of this shot even a smidgen. They must be replaced before the cane will fire quietly again.

Catastrophe: The recoil knocks the head of the cane off and back into the user. The firer takes 3d6 damage to a random location and the explosion is likely to draw attention.

POCKET BLOWTORCH

Minor: The nozzle on the torch is badly adjusted. A tiny, flickering flame is all that comes out—absolutely useless for anything. A spook can adjust the nozzle with a Hard (9) *tinkerin'* roll.

Major: The device vents its entire tank in one action. On the downside, it's empty and useless afterward. On the upside, it does 4d8 damage to any one exposed to it during that time. Unfortunately, it burns far to quickly to cut anything, besides flesh, that is!

Catastrophe: The flame is sucked back into the gas tank, causing a 2d10 explosion with a Burst radius of 2.

Ring Derringer

Minor: The firearm misfires, jamming the round into the ring. The wearer must make an Onerous (7) *tinkerin'* roll to remove the useless cartridge.

Major: Recoil from the ring momentarily numbs the wearer's hand. Any *Deftness*-based rolls with that hand suffer a -4 for the next 1d8 rounds.

Catastrophe: The derringer explodes, doing 2d4 to the wearer's hand and numbing it as above.

Rocket Grapnel

Minor: The rocket misfires, jamming the gun until a Fair (5) *tinkerin'* roll is made.

Major: The rocket fires with too much force, breaking the cord. The spook must shoot another one to climb up.

Catastrophe: The rocket explodes in the barrel for 3d8 damage with a Burst Radius of 1.

Sleeve Dagger

Although this isn't a mad science device, having a spring-loaded dagger up your shirt is just asking for trouble! On a failure, the dagger either doesn't release at all. or it shoots out with more force than expected, causing the operative to miss her grasp on it. In either case the spook has to spend a round recovering or fixing the knife.

Sound Magnifier

As with many of the gizmos, the Reliability result on this one's going to be a lot more fun to keep to yourself.

Minor: The magnifier is slightly out of alignment. It picks up sounds from a location within 10' of the target spot instead. A spook making a Hard (9) *tinkerin'* roll brings it back on target.

Major: The device garbles the sound waves producing either unintelligible garbage or (at the Marshal's discretion) a completely new conversation/sound.

Catastrophe: The magnifier targets its own location, causing a feedback loop. The operator and anyone within 10' must make a *Vigor* roll against a Hard (9) TN (bonuses for *keen* and

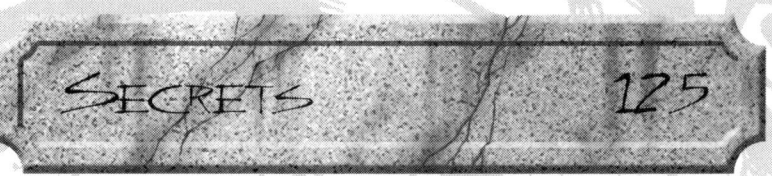

the like count as a *minus* here) or be deafened for 1d4 hours. The blaring noise can be heard up to 100 yards away, unless a wall or other object blocks it.

Suitcase Camera

Minor: The camera shutter jams closed. The camera can't take any more pictures until the user (or another helpful soul) makes a Hard (9) *tinkerin'* roll.

Major: Triggering the shutter also unfortunately triggers the case latch. The case opens, dumping any unused plates on the ground and exposing the camera, film, and embarrassed spook!

Catastrophe: The camera literally falls apart in the photographer's hands. It's completely ruined and the user is liable to have some explaining to do about the device.

Telegraph Tap

By all means, Marshal, keep the results on this beauty a secret! Not only does the operative have to worry about the device malfunctioning, there are those pesky gremlins to plague him as well (*Marshal's Handbook*, page 27).

Minor: The tap catches the message, but doesn't prevent it from going to the next relay station. If all the spook is doing is eavesdropping, this one isn't that bad. On the other hand, if he's trying to intercept or forge a response, he's got a problem.

Major: The tap doesn't even detect the original message. Hopefully, the operative figures this out quick, otherwise, he's in for a *long* wait.

Catastrophe: The telegraph impulses are magnified by the tap to the point of dangerousness. Since he was considerate enough to put the tubes into his ears, he takes 3d6 damage directly to the noggin (no bonus dice).

Trans-Mnemonic Olfactory Cataloger

The sniffer's Reliability check should be kept from the heroes.

Minor: The sniffer's filters are clogged, making it unable to detect any odor. A Fair (5) *tinkerin'* roll and about 20 minutes of time clears the filters.

Major: The sniffer misreads an odor classifying it as one of the Marshal's choice—most likely an exotic and unusual one!

Catastrophe: A violent chemical reaction occurs between the scent particles and some of the compounds in the sniffer. The user is sprayed with a caustic liquid that does 1d10 damage. Add +4 to the roll to determine the hit location affected.

Voice Projectors

This is another good gizmo for you to roll the Reliability on, Marshal. In fact, if you want to keep the players guessing, you can separate them and relay the message from one to the other yourself. That way, one operative never knows if she's *actually* hearing what the other spook is saying!

Minor: The projector only transmits every other word spoken into it.

Major: The projector transmits nonsense sentences. Maybe it rearranges the word order of the original message—and changes a few words to boot! Feel free to use your imagination here, Marshal, and do your devilish best to confound the posse! You'd be surprised what a little change in a sentence or two can do to a careful plan...

Catastrophe: The amplifier works *too* well. The speaker's voice is boosted to ear-splitting levels. The listener must make an Onerous (7) *Vigor* roll (bonuses for *keen*, *big ears*, and the like count as *negative* modifiers to this roll!). If she fails she suffers Wind equal to the difference in the roll and TN; going bust renders her *deaf* for 1d6 minutes. Needless to say, any secrecy is also blown by this screeching blast as well.

Wrist-Spring Derringer

Minor: The mechanism catches on the operative's clothing. The pistol is jammed in her sleeve and she must make an Onerous (7) *Deftness* roll to free it.

Major: The pistol flies out of her sleeve and off the spring holster, landing 1d6 yards in front of her.

Catastrophe: The derringer fires accidentally when she triggers the mechanism, striking her in a random hit location for 3d6 damage.

INDEX

Abercrombie & Sons 20
Agency Carbine 93, 120
Agency Duster 91, 120
Agency Shotgun 94, 120
Agecny Supernatural Research Facility *see SRF*
Agency Walking Stick 97, 121
Alaska Terrritory 25
Allen, Allen, & Roberts 20
Approaches 40-43, 66-67
Automatic Key 82, 121
Autopsy 65-66
Badges, Agency 18
Baker, Lafayette 12-13, 15, 108-109
Basic Training 67-68
Belongin's (Agency equipment) 68
Black River 115
Blackjack 92
Bleeding 103-104
Boot Knife 92
Bribery 41-42
Buchanan, Bo 115-116
Bureaus 18
   Eastern 19-21
   Western 21-24
Cameras 47-48
"Castle," the 21
Church of Lost Angels 22, 106, 110, 115
Classification of entities 53-56
Cleaners 56, 58, 69, 73
Codes 59-61, 72, 79-80
Code Wheel 79
Coleport, Regina 110
Cover Identities 36-38
Collegium
Constitution 7
Davies, Harry 10
Deadwood 113
Dead Drops 59, 84-85
Deadwood Ward 24
Demerits 70-71
Deseret 24
Disguise Kit 83
Ecto-Plasmic Calcifier 95, 121-122

Elijah 114-115
Envy, Flock Cultist 115
EO 347 *(see Executive Order 347)*
Event 070363 12, 14, 29-30
Event, The *(see Event 070363)*
Executive Order 259 14
Executive Order 347 6, 7, 17-18, 30-32, 46, 58
Expense accounts 72
Explosive Putty 85-86, 122
False Coins 80-81
False Playing Cards 81
False Watch 98, 122
Fear Detector 87, 122
Field Boots 98, 122-123
Flash Buttons 86-87, 123
Flock, the 114-115
Garrotte 92-93
Ghost, the *(see Lane, Andrew)*
Ghost Busters (adventure) 4, 110
Grant, Ulysseus S. 12-13, 107
Great Maze 22-24
Grim servant o' death 105
Ground Stakes 84
Gomorra 24, 111, 113-114
Hellstromme, Darious 24, 115
Hill, Melissa 115
Homing Slugs 88, 123
Hollow Bolts 84-85
Hollow Pen 81,
Hollow-Heels 82
Hollow Key 82
Identity Field Theory 80, 120
Impenetrable Vest 91-92
Informants 62
Infrared Goggles 88-89, 123-124
Interviews 40-45
Invisible Ink 79, 124
Iron Dragon Railroad 22, 24, 106
James, Conrad 63
Johnson, Andrew 15
Karl, Captain Katie 114
Knicknevin 110

Kohms, Dr. Geoffrey 26, 117-118
Lane, Andrew 22, 110, 115
Lawton, Hattie 12, 111
Letter Extractor 83-84, 124
"the Library" 26
Lincoln, Abraham 10 13-15
Listening Cone 89
Massive damage 104
McClellan, George 11-12
Men-in-Black, Baker's 108-109
Merits 70
Microdots 80
Mount Katahdin Institute 26, 117-119
National Detective Police 15
O'Bannon, "Boom-Boom" 115
Obligation, Agency 68
Pay scale 72
Pendulum Publishing 21
"Pennsylvania Kid," 115
Pinkerton, Allan 8-16
Pinkerton, Robert 16
Pinkerton Detectives 8, 9, 13-16, 18, 69, 109-110
Photochemical Goggles 80, 84, 89, 124
Pistol Cane 84, 124
Pocket Blowtorch 87, 124
Quaid, Johnny 114
Quitting 69
Rank, Agency 69-72
Regional Offices 18
   Boston 19-20
   Chicago 20
   Denver 22, 111
   Philadelphia 20-21
   Sacramento 22-23
   Seattle 23, 112-113
   Washington 21, 32
Recruiting 62
Reimbursement 72
Requisition Points 71, 77-78, 99-100
Rewards 71
Ring Derringer 95, 125
Rocescu, Joseph 114

Rocket Grapnel 84, 125
Ross, Martin 63
Salem Training Academy 26, 28, 67
Salt Lake City 24, 115
"Secret Services" 12, 15-16
Shotgun, Agency
Slate, Mr 114
Sleeve Dagger 93, 125
Smith & Robards 24, 46
Smith, Nevada 115-116
Sound Magnifier 89, 125
Speakman, Richard 24, 113
Special Action Teams *(see Cleaners)*
SRF 25, 30, 116-117
Stager Cipher 60
Sweetrock Mining Company 115
Suitcase camera 90, 125
Sword cane 93
"the Tank" *(see SRF)*
Telegraph Tap 90, 125
Texas Rangers 17, 22, 106, 114
Threat priorities 56
Tombstone Epitaph 24, 58
Trans-Mnemonic Olfactory Cataloger 91, 126
Treasury, U.S. Dept. of, 15, 16
Union Blue Railroad 26
Vigenère Code Table 60-61
Voice Projector 80, 126
Wards 19-24
Warne, Kate 10
Waterproof Bag 85
Weapons Table, Fightin' 100
Weapons Table Ranged 100
Webster, Timothy 12
Whateley Family Estate
Whateleys
Williams, Cort 111
Wrist-Spring Derringer 96, 126
Young, Brigham 24, 115

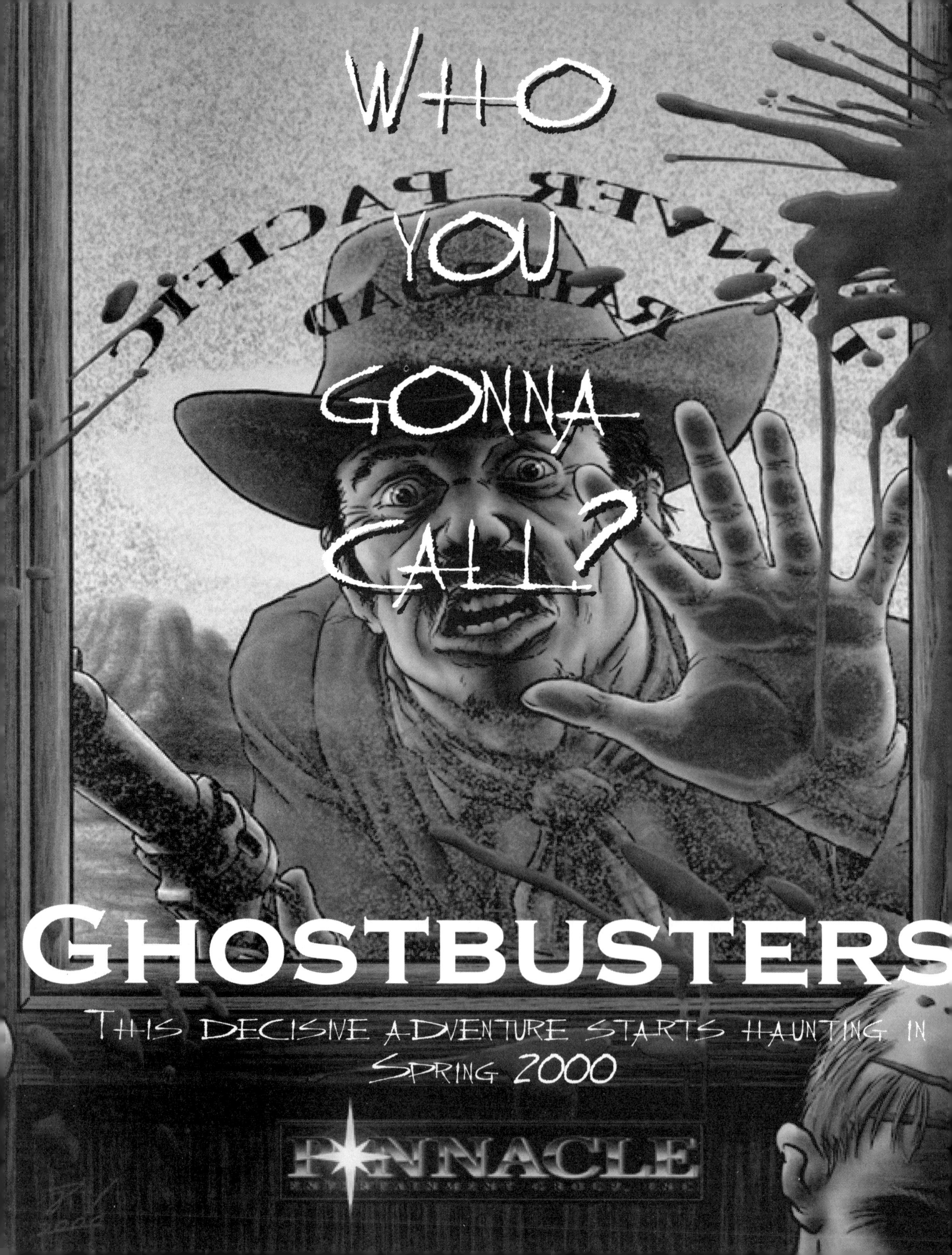

WHO
YOU
GONNA
CALL?
GHOSTBUSTERS
THIS DECISIVE ADVENTURE STARTS HAUNTING IN
SPRING 2000
PINNACLE